Gone
But Not
Furgotten

*St. Martin's Paperbacks titles
by Cate Conte*

Gone
But Not
Furgotten

CATE CONTE

St. Martin's Paperbacks

This is a work of fiction. All of the characters, organizations, and events portrayed in this novel are either products of the author's imagination or are used fictitiously.

First published in the United States by St. Martin's Paperbacks, an imprint of St. Martin's Publishing Group

GONE BUT NOT FURGOTTEN

Copyright © 2022 by Liz Mugavero.

For information, address St. Martin's Publishing Group, 120 Broadway, New York, NY 10271.

www.stmartins.com

ISBN: 978-1-250-76157-6

Our books may be purchased in bulk for promotional, educational, or business use. Please contact your local bookseller or the Macmillan Corporate and Premium Sales Department at 1-800-221-7945, ext. 5442, or by email at MacmillanSpecialMarkets@macmillan.com.

Printed in the United States of America

St. Martin's Paperbacks edition / July 2022

10 9 8 7 6 5 4 3 2 1

For Lori

Acknowledgments

There are so many facets of animal rescue that are difficult to deal with, but rescuers in hoarder cases are particular angels. While Maddie's hoarder case had a happy ending, many don't—and the animals suffer as well as the rescuers who wish it could have been different. The people who rush in to help in these situations deserve major kudos.

As for the book writing, my editor, Nettie Finn, and the team at St. Martin's did an amazing job helping get this book in shape—from the plot suggestions to the editing to the gorgeous cover. Thank you!

As always, thank you to my agent, John Talbot—can you believe we've been doing this for ten years? Here's to many more successful, productive years to come.

The fictional Cass exists because of the real Cass—the amazing sound healer who changed my life a decade ago. Thank you for bringing me peace and for letting me take such liberties with your name in this series.

My fellow Wicked author Jessie Crockett/Jessica Ellicott—my plot is SO much better because you were there to brainstorm with me, as usual! So many thanks.

Jason Allen-Forrest, thank you so much for being my

reader! I so appreciate your perspectives and your willingness to look at these books no matter what state they are in. So much gratitude.

For the rest of the Wickeds—Barbara Ross, Edith Maxwell/Maddie Day, J. A. Hennrikus/Julia Henry, Sherry Harris—you girls are such a safe place for me. Love you tons.

Chapter 1

"Maddie. You forgot to grasp the bird's tail."

Cass Hendricks' deep baritone voice cut through the Zen I'd finally sort-of achieved after maybe twenty times through the first set of tai chi movements. I'd gotten a little too confident, apparently—there was always one move I forgot. Although it usually wasn't this particular one.

With an exasperated sigh, I opened my eyes and dropped my arms from cloud hand position. We were outside in Cass's private Zen garden in the back of his downtown store, Jasper's Tall Tails, which also housed his second-floor apartment. The garden was amazing. It made me feel like I was in the middle of one of those fancy outdoor spas in California. I always marveled at how he had managed to create such a peaceful place in the middle of all the hustle and bustle that was Daybreak Island in the summertime, but peace was Cass's superpower. Although the peaceful environment wasn't helping me much at all. "I stink at this. I'm never going to remember the sequence."

JJ, my orange rescue cat and best bud, squeaked from where he sat on Cass's special chair, partly overseeing my efforts but really spending more time watching the koi fish in the little pond. I turned to glare at him. "I didn't ask you."

JJ flicked his tail at me and went back to watching the fish.

I dropped down to the yoga mat and pulled my hair up into a messy bun. It was getting hot out here. August on Daybreak Island definitely brought the dog days of summer.

Cass regarded me with that slightly amused look he reserved for his overly dramatic students. "You do not stink. And of course you will remember. You just need to focus. Just like I've been telling you since you were a teenager." He moved over to his tea table and poured some tea into a small cup. The giant silver rings he wore on each finger clinked against the teapot handle, a delightful accompaniment to the cello music playing softly in the background. "Here. Drinking this will help."

I would much rather sit here and listen to Cass teach than actually try to do something at which I was so inadequate. I loved listening to him talk. It didn't even matter really what he was saying. Despite his permanent residency on the island since, well, I could remember, Cass still sported a thick accent from his homeland of Haiti. He still wore his hair in long braids that reached his waist. And despite his six-foot-five, solid-muscle stature and slightly intimidating presence, he moved as gracefully as a ballet dancer.

Which, obviously, had not rubbed off on me.

He handed me the teacup, which I gratefully accepted, and I moved over to sit on one of the meditation pillows lining the side of the patio area where we practiced. He sat next to me, his braids spilling over his shoulders to nearly brush the floor. He looked exactly the same as when I met him, back when I was a kid. I estimated him somewhere between fifty and ageless, and fifty was only a guess based on how long I'd known him. When I said as much to him, he simply shrugged and said his meditative lifestyle was quite conducive to health and wellness. He'd never actually told me his age. Although I guess I'd never really asked, either.

Jasper's Tall Tails was a metaphysical bookstore that also served as the island's only tai chi studio, crystal healing center, and unofficial tea house. It really was the most Zen place on Daybreak Island, a place where people could come to escape the frenzy of the summer tourist season and simply be still. I also loved it because Cass had named it after his childhood dog, Jasper, back in Haiti. The one thing missing was a store cat, which I was working on changing by bringing JJ in every chance I got in hopes that he would decide to adopt one of my cafe cats.

"I just stink. I think the only thing that might work is hypnosis. They can rewire for coordination, right?" I sipped the tea, which did make me feel better almost immediately. Even though it was a hot summer day, the warmth of the tea felt good. I needed to spend more time here, something that had been on my to-do list since I moved home just over a year ago. Unfortunately, I always let other things get in the way. Although lately I'd been dropping by most Sunday afternoons like this for a private lesson, some tea, or just some peace. My boyfriend Lucas often went to his grooming salon on Sundays to clean and get ready for the week, so I'd been using the free time to work on my mindfulness.

Cass, on the other hand, never seemed to need to "work" on being mindful at all. He just was. I wished I could be like him.

"You underestimate yourself. You need to come to class at least once a week. And I know I don't need to remind you, but you should meditate every day. At least ten minutes." He acted as if he hadn't heard my poor attempt at a joke and nodded, as if agreeing with himself. "You will find much more peace in your life."

"Mmm." I sipped more tea as an excuse to not answer, since I didn't currently meditate every day. But it wasn't like he couldn't figure that out. He could read me like one of his favorite books, of which he had many. He knew me too well. "You know I would love to come to class more. I'm not always able to get away from the cafe, though. Besides, I kind of like the private lessons. That way no one else can see how much I stink."

He held up a giant ring-covered hand to ward off my excuses. "You have two co-owners and a full-time manager. You should be able to spare an hour a week on a regular basis."

It was true. I owned the cafe with my business partner Ethan Birdsong and my Grandpa Leo—we had turned part of Grandpa's large house into the cat portion of the cafe, and the stand-alone garage into the food portion, which was Ethan's happy place—and I had recently hired one of my longtime volunteers, Adele Barrows, as my shelter manager. Honestly, no one needed me around as much as last year, when we were in the frenzy of trying to open. I just liked to think they did. Plus, I enjoyed being in the hustle and bustle of the cafe, the cats, the guests, the smiles.

"I'm happy to continue with private lessons, but classes are also very helpful," Cass went on. "Besides, I cannot get you to commit to private lessons regularly either."

"I know, I know. Okay. I'll sign up." Giving in was easier than arguing with Cass. I'd never win.

"Excellent. My beginner class is every Tuesday at nine thirty. And," he added with a new gleam in his eye, as if whatever he was about to say had just dawned on him, "you will come to my meditation retreat."

I narrowed my eyes. "Your what now?"

"My meditation retreat. The theme is *Who Am I?*" He smiled and nodded. "We will all work on answering that question. It's in two weeks. I rented a house in Duck Cove, right on the water. Only ten students. I'm fully booked, but will make an exception for you."

I stared at him. A full weekend of meditating? "Um. I'm not sure—"

The hand went up again. "No arguments. It will be good for you. We'll meditate, do yoga, have tea, make healthy meals together. Discover who we are."

I frowned. "Can JJ come?"

"I think JJ already knows who he is. But if that will get you to agree, then of course."

"Do I have a choice?" I asked wryly.

"No."

I bit back a laugh. Cass was a man of few words, but those words packed a punch. I pulled my cell phone out to add it to my calendar. "Okay." Because arguing with him had never, in my twenty-plus years of knowing him, gotten me anywhere.

"We start on the Friday night, end on Sunday evening. You'll need to practice in the meantime. Ten minutes per day. To get you in the right headspace," he said with that incredibly effective *Cass* look when this time I did open my mouth to protest. "It's a prerequisite. And don't forget to add the Tuesday class to your calendar too."

I shut my mouth and added the Tuesday class dutifully to my calendar, complete with alerts to remind me to actually show up. "It's official. I will see you Tuesday."

He nodded, almost smugly. "Good. And skip the coffee before you come."

I stared at him. "You're serious."

"Of course I am. Caffeine—unless it's natural caffeine

like in my tea—will ruin your concentration. Monkey mind." He tapped a finger to his head. "You need calm."

"Hmmph," I said, because I knew better than to argue with him. "I thought your beginner classes were on Mondays, though? Did you change your schedule?"

"I did. I'm working in Fisherman's Cove on Mondays during the day now. And a couple of evenings."

"Fisherman's Cove? Really? Doing what?"

"The community there is lacking in wellness resources." He spread his hands to encompass his space. "The acting town administrator approached me earlier in the summer to ask if I could bring some of my practices to the people out there. They're also lacking in transportation, unfortunately, and many of the older residents don't leave the area much. I've been teaching there for about six weeks."

Fisherman's Cove was the smallest of the five towns on Daybreak Island. It sat at the westernmost point, known to us here on Daybreak Harbor as up-island, and most people who came to visit didn't even realize it existed. It was the "working town" of the island. There were no quaint downtown restaurants, fancy boutiques, or coffee bars like here in Daybreak Harbor or the other towns. It comprised mostly small, no-nonsense homes for fishermen who still made their living out on the sea and for others who had either some ties to the area or to working boats. It was pretty low-income for Daybreak, and some of the fishermen who lived here during the summer months had to leave for the winter with whatever earnings they'd made in the warm weather. Island life could be tough for anyone year-round, especially in the northeast, but I'd always felt like it was toughest out on Fisherman's Cove. With only about seven square miles total, it boasted less than three hundred year-round residents.

One silver lining to the lack of tourists, though, was that the great beaches and state parks remained largely unnoticed by those not in the know, which made them a prime place for islanders to escape to when the well-known beaches were overloaded. But other than the ability to access nature a lot more easily, I didn't think much about Fisherman's Cove and its residents, mostly because I felt like they kind of lived in a different universe than I did.

Still, it was good exposure for Cass. "That's great," I said. "What are you teaching?"

"I'm offering tai chi, qigong, and some tea events. Bringing some different teas for sampling, and educating them on the health benefits. It is a very diverse group of people, many of whom haven't had the exposure to this type of wellness care. I feel good about it. These people are very no-nonsense, so it's taken a bit of education to get them to see the value. There is one woman especially who wanted nothing to do with my classes, but over time she heard more and more about them and finally stopped by. I could see that she desperately needed something meaningful. Now she attends regularly. I can already see the difference it's made in her life after only a few weeks."

"Worked your charm, eh?" I grinned.

He smiled back. "I try."

I was teasing him, but this all sounded cool. Especially the tea event. "We'll do the tea thing on the retreat?"

"Absolutely."

"Cool. Where are your classes out there?"

"Sometimes outside in the big park. If the weather isn't good, I have access to the community room in a nearby church. That's where we hold the tea events."

"And it's all free?"

"It is."

"You're the best, Cass. It sounds awesome. Those people are lucky to have you."

He smiled at me. "Well, I do all that here too, you know."

I winced good-naturedly. "I know. And you're right. I need to get serious about scheduling more peace in my life." I drained my teacup and set it back on his little tea table, then stood to go. JJ hopped off his chair and trotted over to join me.

"Tuesday, then," Cass said.

"Tuesday," I affirmed. "Nine thirty. I'll see you then."

Chapter 2

"Of course, Mrs. Hennessy. I promise I'll call you as soon as some torties show up." I patted the older woman on the shoulder as I walked her to the door of JJ's House of Purrs, our cat cafe—yes, it was named after my JJ—on Monday morning. Angela Hennessy, a Daybreak Harbor resident, had been visiting the cafe every Monday since it had opened last year, and now that her ancient cat Ralphie had recently passed away at the ripe old age of twenty-two, she was in the market to adopt. But she staunchly refused to adopt anything other than a tortoiseshell cat. She'd had one as a child, and all her adult cats had been either orange or black. Now, she was determined to relive her childhood. I thought it was cute, if not a bit obsessive.

"Oh, good. Do you think it will be soon?" She peered at me with worried eyes. Mrs. Hennessy was one of those nervous women, always fretting about something. It seemed like an exhausting way to live.

"I really have no idea," I said. "I don't usually know what I'm getting until they show up." As if my words had summoned her, I saw my friend Katrina Denning's animal control van pull into the driveway. Another delivery. Katrina was the animal control officer for Daybreak Harbor, and my cat supplier. She was also an old, dear friend and my former babysitter when I was a kid. I wasn't sure how many cats she was bringing today. Apparently we'd all stopped counting, and my initial firm number of ten cats at a time in the cafe had long since gone out the window. I currently had somewhere around eighteen in here, but heck, that was a guess: I'd lost count too. I just thanked my lucky stars I had Adele and some good volunteers to help me manage them all. And my business partner Ethan, of course, although he spent more time in his new garage-turned-food-cafe than inside with the cats these days. He was the chef behind the operation, and the best coffee maker I knew. Which was also good because people were coming out for the goodies, not just the cats. And we in the household reaped the benefits as well—the freshly baked goods and new meals that he regularly tested out on us.

Katrina got out of the van, went around to the back, and pulled out a cat carrier. "Guess what I have!" she called out as she walked up. "Babies!" She looked like she'd been working for hours already. Her dark blond hair was pulled back in a headband, her go-to style since she'd started growing out her bangs and had no patience for her hair falling in her eyes all day, and there was a giant tear in one leg of her uniform pants.

"Oh, how delightful!" Mrs. Hennessy clapped. "Any torties?"

"Actually, yes," Katrina said. "How did you know?"

Mrs. Hennessy's eyes almost popped out of her head. "Really? I'll take one!"

I laughed. "Do you want to meet her first?" Torties were typically female, so I figured it was a safe assumption that it was a she.

"Well of course, but I'll still take her." For the first time, the worry cloud had lifted from her eyes.

Katrina raised an eyebrow at me, which I knew was code for *Is she a good adopter?*

I flashed a thumbs-up. Katrina handed her the carrier. "All yours, then."

I peered inside as Mrs. Hennessy reached for it, already cooing baby talk. There were five babies in there—not one but two torties, a ginger, a buff-colored, and a tiger. They tumbled over one another in that adorable kitten way, mewling the whole time. "There are two," I said to Mrs. Hennessy. "You know two is better than one, right?" I grinned at her delighted expression.

She squealed and hurried to one of the couches, clutching the carrier.

"Hopefully she'll take them both. Since otherwise this will put me well over twenty in here," I said pointedly to Katrina as Mrs. Hennessy walked away. When I got no response, I sighed. "What happened to you?" I indicated her pants.

"Huh?" She followed my eyes down to the tear, then grimaced. "Oh, that. Chasing Mrs. Montgomery's cat again. That annoying woman keeps letting her slip out, then calls me crying to help get her back. I swear next time I'm going to threaten to take her away."

"No you're not," I said, chuckling.

"You're right. I probably won't. But I want to. At the very least I'm going to send her a bill."

"Maddie! I'm taking them both," Mrs. Hennessy announced.

Katrina grinned. "Score. See you later."

I was just wrapping up the delighted new mom's paperwork when my cell phone rang. I hoped it was Lucas. I had missed him this morning—he was an early riser—and I hadn't heard from him yet, which meant his shop was probably hopping. Which was a good thing. He was the only year-round dog groomer on the island, so by default, he got all the business there was to get. I glanced at the screen. Not Lucas. Cass. Probably calling to remind me about class tomorrow. Or ask me if I'd done my daily meditation today, which I hadn't . . . yet. I'd call back. I hit DECLINE and handed Mrs. Hennessy her copy of the paperwork, along with a toy for each of the kittens and a small bag of food all packed neatly into a JJ's House of Purrs tote bag.

"Enjoy the babies. And send lots of pictures," I reminded her.

"Thank you, dear." She glanced at my phone as it began to ring again, insistently. Cass, again. "You may want to get that."

I waved as she left with her new charges, then answered. "I haven't forgotten about class tomorrow," I said by way of greeting.

"Good, but that's not why I am calling. I may have a problem."

"A problem?" Cass didn't usually have problems. He was so Zen that even if one occurred, it just rolled off his back. "What kind of problem?"

"I'm out on Fisherman's Cove. It's my teaching day. I stumbled across an incident. One of my students was having an argument with another resident. It involves cats."

"Cats?" I wasn't following.

"Yes." He took a deep breath. "I'm afraid my student may be having some trouble handling her cats."

I didn't like the sound of this. "What exactly does that mean?"

"She has some outdoor cats that are getting themselves in trouble with the neighbors," Cass said, almost reluctantly.

I sighed. Like Katrina, I didn't like when people let their cats outside. I was definitely one of those firm believers that unless a cat was feral, they belonged indoors. Ferals didn't know anything other than outdoor life and couldn't bear to be contained. They typically had no socialization and weren't used to humans, so an indoor life could be a miserable experience for them. That said, they often depended on humans to feed them and, in some cases, get them vet care when needed. There were a few feral colonies on the island that Katrina and I helped with. Only once had those efforts involved a murder investigation. But surely that wasn't the norm.

Rescuers had differing opinions on whether socialized cats should remain indoors. Some felt that adopting out to homes that let cats roam outside was preferable to them taking their chances in a shelter. While I understood that concept, I also worried about the possibility they'd be eaten by a wild animal or run over by a car. Here on the island was a bit different, though. There were no natural predators, given that we were in the middle of the ocean, and unless you were downtown, cars weren't a huge threat either. All things told, if a cat had to go outside, best to do it in this kind of environment.

"So are you worried that someone will hurt the cats?" I asked, mentally returning to Cass and his student's problem.

"Perhaps."

I waited for more, but all I heard was the crackle of the breeze from the other end of the line. Cass was typically quiet, but in this case I felt like there was something here he wasn't telling me. "Were the cats threatened?" I prompted. "Or the owner?"

"Not that I heard specifically, but . . ." He trailed off.

I bit back my impatience. And people wondered why I couldn't meditate. "Cass. What can I do to help?"

"Can you come speak to Laurel with me? I'm concerned she may be in over her head. There are a lot of cats, Maddie."

"What's a lot?"

"A lot. That's all I can tell you right now."

Oh, boy. "So she's a hoarder," I said, more of a statement than a question.

Long pause. "I don't want to make assumptions."

"Well, a lot of cats—which is relative, I know—could lean toward hoarding. And you're beating around the bush."

"You're right. I'm sorry. I went by her house. She lives right here, near the park. I stopped by to see if she was coming to class, and she was in the middle of this altercation. When it ended I went to see if she was okay, and when I went into the yard there were . . . many. I counted ten, hiding in various places. She also wouldn't answer the door, though I knew she was home. There were more cats in the window. With all that, and after hearing this conversation . . ." His voice again trailed off. "The neighbor was very angry and it sounds like a recurring problem."

I closed my eyes briefly. Hoarder cases were tough. I'd been involved in one back when I lived in San Francisco and worked with a rescue group. The person in that case had over one hundred dogs and cats living in a fifteen-hundred-square-foot home. The house was filthy and some of the animals were found dead, others extremely sick. Luckily, we had been able to save the majority of them, but it had been a brutal experience and not one I wished to repeat.

On the other hand, once I knew something, I couldn't un-know it. Which meant that even if I declined to get involved in whatever this was, it would keep me up at night knowing this was going on. In short, once someone told me something was wrong, I had to at least try to help.

"Is she . . . unstable?" I asked.

"I don't think so. She has a job and works on a town committee. She seems self-sufficient. Laurel's quirky, but who isn't?"

"How quirky?" I pressed.

"A bit of a loner. Cautious. Set in her ways. What you would expect from a woman who's a bit older, lower income, and living out here all year round. You'd really have to meet her and decide for yourself, although I would ask you not to be quick to pass judgment. She's not a bad person."

"How old?"

"Early sixties is my best guess."

So likely not a dementia case. I debated the situation: the best course of action would be to get Katrina to help, but technically she couldn't act in an official capacity in another town unless she got special permission from her chief. "Fisherman's Island isn't within Katrina's jurisdiction," I said. "It might be hard to step in officially if something really is going on."

"Does that mean you won't try?"

I sighed. "I guess I could do it in a rescue capacity. When do you want to go talk to her?"

"How about tomorrow? After class?"

I agreed, knowing I really didn't have a choice. After I hung up with Cass, I hesitated a second, then called Katrina.

"I might have a problem," I said when she answered.

"Great. I love a Monday with problems," Katrina replied. I could hear wind whipping around her, which meant she was still in the van. "What's up?"

"Cass just called me. He may have stumbled upon a hoarder situation in Fisherman's Cove."

Katrina muttered a curse under her breath. I heard dogs barking and assumed she'd made a pit stop after leaving the cafe and picked up some new charges. "How bad?"

"I don't know. I'm not even sure that's what it is, but he asked me to go out there tomorrow and talk to the woman. You think I should?"

"I think you have no choice," Katrina said. "There's no animal control out there. They use the other towns if they need something. Usually Turtle Point because he's the least busy which just means he's lazy. I don't trust him to do the right thing, but I can't go out there unless they call me. But a local rescue team can help . . . which would be you," she added, in case I hadn't caught on to that.

I grinned. "I had a feeling you'd say that. Good thing we have the Peyton Chandler financing, eh?" Peyton Chandler was a celebrity who had endorsed an event for us earlier in the summer and who, despite some unfortunate mishaps surrounding her involvement, had not only adopted one of our cats but set up a trust for island rescue efforts that ensured us ten thousand dollars a month. It was an insane windfall—one we were definitely putting to good use. In fact, it pretty much justified us taking in more cats at the cafe. And apparently this was our first major test case.

"Good thing," she replied. "Call me when you know what's going on. I'll start working my foster network. And hey, Maddie? You should prepare the house—and Leo—for some new arrivals. Can't let all that space go to waste."

Chapter 3

I showed up for tai chi class bright and early Tuesday morning as promised, but I had a hard time concentrating, thinking about Cass's and my upcoming adventure. I had used that same apprehension as my rationale for missing my meditation yesterday . . . and this morning. Our plans also meant I'd had to leave JJ home this morning, which he hadn't been happy about. He liked class, although his tai chi sequence needed more work than mine. And everyone liked having him there, evidenced by the fact that the other students didn't even bother saying hello to me—they just went straight to, "Where's JJ today?"

Cass, of course, seemed to have no problem staying in the present moment. He never did. But while I hid in the back of the class—although with only seven people aside from me, it admittedly didn't provide much opportunity to hide—I kept thinking of questions I wanted to ask about this alleged hoarding situation. Like, were the cats malnourished? Did they look sick? Were they fixed? Was the woman going to be resistant, which would mean we'd need to bring in reinforcements? And how could we do that if she wouldn't let us in?

I lifted my foot to do my heel kick, but unfortunately I had turned in the wrong direction and ended up kicking old Mr. Leonard's foot as he began his kick in the right direction, almost knocking him off-balance. Which wasn't so good for someone in their seventies.

"Crap! I'm so sorry," I burst out, as the woman behind him reached out to steady him.

Mr. Leonard laughed. "It's fine, young lady. No harm, no foul. I'm still pretty good with my balance, luckily."

"Yes. Lucky." I stole a glance at Cass, still leading the sequence at the front of the room, so deeply focused on the movements, he seemed not to notice. But I knew Cass noticed everything. He was clearly choosing not to see me, so with a sigh, I tried to slip back into the sequence with the rest of the group, but continued to be two steps behind until the class ended.

I waited impatiently as the rest of the class did their usual lingering thing, sipping Cass's tea and chatting amongst themselves. Cass brought a cup of tea over to where I sat against the wall.

But I wasn't in the mood for tea. I wanted to get moving. "We going soon?" I asked.

He smiled. "Patience. We'll leave shortly. This is a ritual," he said, waving his hand at the small crowd around his tea table. "It would do you good to slow down and enjoy the moment." He shot a pointed look at my phone, where I was checking the cafe's Insta account. One of our volunteers this summer was a college student majoring in marketing, and her skills were coming in handy. She had taken over managing our social accounts, and had proven herself a whiz at creating and posting adorable cat videos. As a result, our followers had grown nearly one hundred percent since she'd started a month ago, and our engagement was through the roof. "And maybe give yourself a break from electronics."

"Fine," I muttered, not wanting to admit he was right. I slid my phone in my pocket and blew on my tea, sipping it slowly as he'd taught me.

Nodding with satisfaction, he went back over to the group, poured another round of tea, then went out to the bookshop, where I presumed he was telling his store manager that he was leaving. A minute later, he came to the door and motioned for me to join him.

I drained the rest of my tea and went to the table to drop off my cup. Mr. Leonard grinned at me. "You've got one heck of a kick there, missy."

I felt my face turning red again. "Sorry about that."

He waved me off. "You keep it interestin' for sure. We'll see you next week? Bring JJ next time!"

I nodded and hurried out of the room, following Cass out back to his car. "I can't believe I kicked Mr. Leonard," I said, sliding into the passenger seat of his Prius.

Cass smiled. "Aside from that, you did well today."

I grunted and leaned back against the seat. What I really wanted was coffee, so I asked him to stop.

"You know coffee is not good for you, right?" Still, as he said it, he turned left—which meant he was going to stop.

"I do, but neither are hoarding cases." I turned and smiled at him.

"Touché."

Once outside of Daybreak, the drive to Fisherman's Cove took us about twenty minutes. Since the island itself is only about sixty square miles total, getting around is pretty quick in any season except summer. Summer always brought crowds of tourists, but even then, once you got out of the heavy traffic areas, things opened up. I rolled my window down and closed my eyes, breathing in the sea air. That was one of the things I'd missed about the island even when I was living in my dream locale of San Francisco—the constant smell of ocean air. It was just different here, being surrounded by water. Sometimes I thought I must have been a mermaid in a previous life: I could see myself disappearing under the waves and being perfectly happy, floating around in that watery bubble, the noise of the outside world blissfully blocked out.

As we drove past Rye Point Beach, distant memories filled my mind. When I was little, my grandma would take me and my middle sister, Val—our youngest sister, Samantha, hadn't even been around yet—to the beach at least twice each week, usually to a lesser-known beach far away from the mass of vacationers. Rye Point had been one of them, and my favorite. Grandma had made the whole day an adventure for us. I remembered spending hours in the sun and the water. Pure bliss. Summer made me miss my grandma even more than the rest of the year; it was still hard to believe it had been over a year since she'd died.

We crossed into Fisherman's Cove shortly after that. The houses out here were nothing like what you would see in Daybreak Harbor, never mind Turtle Point, our fanciest town. These places ranged from seaside shacks to small Cape Cod–style homes. We followed a few twisty streets until we got to the little downtown, which was really nothing more than a small town green, a town hall, and a library. Cass turned off the main road onto Berwick Street. Both sides were lined with small, run-down homes sitting uncomfortably close together. Some were tidy despite their tired appearance, while others were victims of less-caring owners. These were the houses with overgrown yards, trash piled up on porches, and in one case, a rusty car with no tires parked on what remained of some yellowing grass.

He turned into the fourth driveway on the right. The house seemed well kept, despite being in desperate need of a paint job. The probably once-sunny yellow facade had faded to a dingy, almost brownish color, but otherwise the place seemed inviting. There were small pots of flowers on the porch along with a small rocking chair. A cat sat in the chair, but when it saw the car pull in it scooted, jumping over the rail and vanishing around the side of the house.

"I take it we're here," I said.

Cass parked the car in the driveway and glanced over at me. "Now, Maddie. I know your first focus will be on the cats, but please be mindful of the person as well," he said.

"I know. I promise I'll be nice." Cass had reason to warn me. I, like a lot of animal rescuers, cared most about the well-being of our furry counterparts and as a result tended to behave like a bull in a china shop with any humans who appeared to be part of a problem.

"Good."

I went to open the car door and paused. "What's her name again?" If he'd told me, I couldn't remember. If he'd told me the cats' names, though, I'd have remembered those.

"Laurel McKenna."

"Laurel," I repeated. "Got it."

Cass opened the door and got out. I followed him up the rickety steps to the porch. A blue recycling bin sat on the top step. I stepped around it and stood behind Cass. He went to ring the bell, then paused, motioning to the door. "The door is open."

I peered around his giant shoulder and saw the door cracked. "Maybe she's getting some fresh air." I pushed the bell anyway.

No sounds from inside.

Cass pushed the door open another inch and leaned his head in. "Laurel? It's Cass. I've brought a friend I'd like you to meet."

No reply, but I caught a glimpse of something streaking away to a hiding place—a white or gray cat, I thought. I frowned. The island was safe for the most part, especially out here where the tourists didn't venture, but maybe it was just the city dweller—or the cop's granddaughter—in me that would never leave the doors unlocked, never mind blatantly open. "Does she do this often? Leave her house wide open?"

"I have no idea."

"Should we go in, or do you think she'll shoot us or something?"

Cass turned back to me. "You really do watch too much TV."

I grinned. "Maybe she's out back. I'll check."

"Yes, do that. I'll take a peek inside."

I went around the side of the house where the porch-dwelling cat had gone, entering a little backyard that again showed some level of effort. There was a small weather-beaten table and a couple of chairs, along with a tiny fire pit. Though small, the yard was well-maintained with a small flower garden and even some raised beds with vegetables off to the side and a couple of those creepy garden gnomes standing in various places.

And cats. I could see a bunch of them, lounging around the little garden decorations, watching me cautiously. I counted at least five. But no human.

I went back around to the front door and stepped inside a small kitchen, about to call for Cass, when I felt the strangest sensation that someone was watching me. I froze and looked around.

I was right. About twenty pairs of eyeballs stared back at me from the countertops, the top of the refrigerator, and from the space between the tops of the cabinets and the ceiling. Cats. Everywhere. On the kitchen chairs, on the windowsills. One was even curled up on top of the trash can.

Holy moly. Cass had been right.

Where *was* Cass, anyway?

"Cass?" I called. "No one out back." I moved into the next room, a living room, and almost bumped into Cass, who stood stock-still next to a battered couch that looked like it was consistently used as a scratching post. "What's wrong?"

Wordlessly, he stepped aside so I could see what he stared at. It took me a second to register the sight.

He'd found Laurel. At least I presumed it was Laurel. She wore jeans and a black T-shirt covered in cat hair. The shirt was twisted up under her body, which was sprawled at the bottom of a flight of stairs. And, from the angle of her neck, it was clear that she wasn't getting up again.

Chapter 4

I sucked in a breath and dropped down next to the woman, still hoping for a pulse even though I knew in my heart it was an exercise in futility. There was no way someone's head could be twisted that way and the person could still be . . . alive. Regardless, I put my fingers on her neck, reaching through the short, gray hair that barely brushed her shoulders. Her skin was unnaturally cold, her pulse silent, dull blue eyes staring off at something across the room.

My mind raced, trying to process the scene. I knew Cass had seen her yesterday morning, so whatever had happened—it looked like she'd fallen down the stairs—must've taken place somewhere between last night and shortly before we'd arrived. Which was probably why we hadn't been alerted by any super-foul smells upon entering the house. For some reason that made me feel better. I hated to think of anyone lying dead for days with no one to notice but cats. I think on some level I'd been afraid that could end up being me, given the crappy luck I'd had with relationships up until Lucas had come into my life. And then I felt guilty for thinking of how lucky I was to have a great guy when this poor woman was lying here dead.

I shook all these thoughts off and glanced back at Cass, whose serenity seemed to have completely vanished. He looked like he was about to cry, or throw up, or both. I jumped up, trying probably unsuccessfully to block the body from his view, but since he was so much bigger than me it was futile. Anyway, it seemed he'd been staring at it the whole time I was out back.

"Come on," I said, pulling out my phone. "We have to call an ambulance." As I turned him around, I caught sight of more sets of eyeballs staring at me from various locations around the room. This was bad. Laurel was dead, she certainly had a cat problem in desperate need of a solution—more desperate than ever now that they had no owner, not even a bad one. But I'd have to think about that later: 9–1–1 was the first priority. I gave Cass a gentle shove ahead of me to get him moving. He let me push him back out the front door, where he sat down unsteadily in the worn rocker on the porch. It creaked under his size.

With surprisingly steady hands I called 9–1–1 and told the operator that a woman was probably dead. I had to run over to the mailbox to look at the faded number—13—so I could tell her the address, then I sat down on the top porch step to wait. Cass just stared out at nothing, his eyes glassy. I wondered if he was in shock. The silence became way too loud, so I tried to get him talking.

"I take it she lived alone? Did she have any medical conditions?"

"Yes. She lived alone. I'm not sure about any conditions. She did not tell me about any. I always ask before my classes. Everyone has to fill out a form."

I thought about that. If Laurel really was in that pre-retirement range, it wasn't likely she would be unsteady on her feet and unable to navigate the stairs well, though of course medical conditions could apply at any age. She may have had some mild physical problems that didn't seem worth mentioning on Cass's form. Or she could have simply slipped. I cringed, thinking that maybe one of the cats had tripped her. The cafe cats—and heck, even JJ—were forever doing that to me, slinking around my legs, making me worry I was going to step on a tail and I would wind up tripping myself.

"I really didn't know her well, Maddie." Cass rubbed his big hands over his face. "She'd become a regular in class over the past few weeks. I mentioned her to you—she was resistant at first, but ended up finding value in the practice. At least I thought so because she kept coming back. She didn't talk much—at all, actually—about herself."

I didn't know what else to say, and I didn't know why the ambulance was taking so long. It had probably only been five minutes, but on the other hand I could throw a stone and hit the other side of town with it. I picked up my phone again and called Grandpa. He answered on the second ring. "Madalyn?"

"Grandpa. You busy?"

"I'm out for a walk. What's going on?"

"I came out with Cass to a woman's house in Fisherman's Cove to talk about her cats. But, she's . . . dead. Looks like she fell down the stairs."

I heard him suck in a breath. "That's terrible. Are you two alright?"

"We're fine," I said, glancing at Cass. I wasn't so sure about him, but I couldn't say that now. "I called nine-one-one. What's the procedure for this? Unattended death so the cops have to come regardless, right?"

"Right. They should proceed the same as any death that didn't result from natural causes." Grandpa was the former police chief of Daybreak Harbor until his retirement a couple years ago. He hadn't gone quietly, though, and kept his feet wet enough in local police business that he and the new chief had butted heads a few times. Now he had his own PI business. He'd started it last summer, once he realized that retirement wasn't really for him. This was the best way to keep his head in the game and stay in the know about island goings-on. He didn't always tell me the kinds of things he was investigating, but I got the sense it ran the gamut. Some days I was sorely tempted to join him, as I'd discovered I had a talent for investigation. The cat cafe kept me pretty busy but I still ended up helping out sometimes, whether Grandpa invited me to or not.

"How's the police force out here?"

"Small," Grandpa said after a moment. "I think they have five officers total. The chief is decent. She's fairly new. Came here after I retired, but I knew of her in previous roles."

A female chief. That was good. It struck me that there definitely weren't enough of those.

"I don't know about the officers, though," he said. "We didn't have much to do with them and frankly, they don't have a ton of crime out there. It's a small town and largely deserted for half the year. If you think it's quiet in Daybreak Harbor during the winter, that place is like a ghost town."

Pretty much what I expected. I could hear the sound of sirens in the distance and wondered who would arrive first, the cops or the paramedics. I hardly remember Grandpa mentioning Fisherman's Cove police at all during his tenure as Daybreak Harbor chief, he interacted with them so little. I guess I'd get a firsthand view now.

"We're going to have to get these cats out of here," I said.

"If the police give me a problem about that I might need your help."

"Ten-four," he said.

"I have to go," I said as the ambulance pulled up. "I'll keep you posted."

I stood up as the ambulance turned into the driveway. A petit woman with short black hair hopped out of the passenger side. "You have an injured person in here?"

"We do. There's a woman inside who seems to have had . . . an accident on the stairs," I said.

Without another word, she went around to the back of the van. Her driver, a skinny guy who looked like he should still be in high school instead of saving lives, joined her and the two of them hauled out a stretcher. They brought it past us up the steps and went inside. A cop car pulled up a minute later. I watched the cop inside fiddle with something in the car, check his phone, then get out a beat too slowly for the situation at hand. He looked like he was in his fifties, maybe—more late than early, though his receding hairline and protruding belly might have been making him appear older. He sported sunglasses he probably thought were cool, a shadow of a beard, and a bored look.

He plodded over and stopped at the foot of the stairs. "Morning," he said to us, crossing his arms over his chest. "Officer Jacobsen. Sounds like there's a problem here?"

I already didn't like the guy. "Inside," I said, jerking my thumb at the door.

"And you are . . ."

"Maddie James. This is Cass Hendricks."

My name didn't seem to mean anything to him, which didn't necessarily surprise me. Even if people knew my grandpa as the former chief, they didn't always automatically connect us if they didn't know him personally. Jacobsen gave Cass a long, curious look before he climbed the steps and sauntered inside, acting like he had all the time in the world. I glanced at Cass. "Not much fire there, eh?"

Cass didn't respond. He still stared blankly into the distance. I could see people now coming out of their houses to gawk at the commotion the ambulance and cop car had caused. I wondered if the woman Cass had seen fighting with Laurel was in this crowd somewhere and made a mental note to ask him when he had recovered a bit.

In the meantime, it looked like we had to wait. Which was not my strong suit. To pass the time, I called Katrina. "Remember that potential problem I told you about? In Fisherman's Cove?"

"Yeah. Let me guess. It's bad."

"And complicated." I filled her in on our discovery and what I'd seen so far. "I have no clue how many cats. And I have no idea if they're going to let me take them, or if this woman has any relatives. I need to talk to the cop once they're done inside."

Katrina was silent for so long I wondered if we'd been disconnected. "Oh, boy," she said finally. "That sounds like a circus."

"Tell me about it," I sighed.

"Let me know what happens. I've got some foster homes lined up already. Still working the rest. And I'll call Dr. Kelly." Dr. Kelly was the beloved island vet who had come out of retirement last year to fill a gap in quality care on the island. Since he didn't really need the money anymore, he did a lot of work for us in the rescue community at a huge discount, for which we were eternally grateful.

"Thanks, Katrina."

"No problem." She paused. "How do these things always happen to you, Mads?"

"I have no idea." I didn't need to be reminded about my track record with dead bodies. "I'll call you once I know more."

Chapter 5

I disconnected and went back to waiting. A few minutes later I heard the stretcher clanking across the kitchen floor and scurrying paws as skittish kitties who hadn't already hid rectified that situation. The paramedics emerged with Laurel's body covered with a sheet. Although I'd known she was dead, it still jolted me to see it.

They wheeled her past us, maneuvering carefully down the steps, and loaded her into the ambulance. Officer Jacobsen emerged a moment later, looking as unaffected by the scene as he had before he went inside. When he saw us still on the porch he paused and stopped in front of us. "Tell me again who you are?" he asked me.

I stood up. I was almost as tall as him. "Maddie James. My grandfather is the former Daybreak Harbor police chief."

That caught his attention, but he didn't react. "And you?" he asked, turning to Cass.

Cass focused on him. "Cass Hendricks."

Jacobsen waited. "Am I supposed to recognize that name too?" he asked, his tone slightly sarcastic and—was I imagining it?—a little suspicious.

"Not unless you've been taking my tai chi class," Cass said.

"Tai chi?" The cop looked at him like he was an alien who'd just hopped off his UFO in front of him.

"It's a martial art," Cass said. "But it's got a lot of health benefits. It's a form of moving meditation."

Jacobsen arched an eyebrow, but didn't ask. "So how did you come to find Ms. McKenna here?"

I held my breath. I didn't really want Cass to mention the cat problem, and I hoped I could telepathically convey that to him. If they called the wrong animal control, the poor cats wouldn't stand a chance.

"She's been taking my class," Cass said. "We stopped by because Maddie wanted to meet her."

Phew.

Jacobsen looked at me, but didn't ask anything else. "Well," he said. "Shame what happened to her. I bet one of those cats tripped her or something." He made a face. "Sure are a lot of them in there."

I worked hard to keep my face blank. "So what do you have to do next? Take photos, call in someone . . . from another department?"

He laughed. "Another department? Why would I do that? I took photos. This all looks pretty straightforward. A tragic accident."

"Sorry, I know a little about police work from my grandpa," I said. "Unattended deaths are usually treated a certain way."

I could tell he didn't like that I was telling him how to do his job. "Got it all under control, but thanks."

"Do you know of any relatives?" I asked.

"Got a boyfriend in town. I'm heading to him now."

This guy seemed completely uninterested in this whole event.

He pulled the front door shut behind him, then opened it again and made it a point to lock it. "You all can go now. Thanks for calling it in."

Cass and I walked slowly back to his car, taking our time, waiting for the cop to leave. He didn't stick around to make sure we were gone, though. He got in his car and drove away with one last, curious look at us.

We both watched his car disappear around the corner.

"What now?" Cass asked, leaning against his driver's-side door. "Do you think we should leave?"

"No. I have to get those cats," I said. "We probably need to wait for her next of kin to give permission, right? I wonder if that's the boyfriend or if she had anyone else."

Cass look pained at the thought of Laurel's loved ones having to deal with this.

"There's plenty of cats outside," I said, hoping to keep Cass's mind on the problem at hand and off of Laurel's death. "I can start with those. I don't know if I want to wait for permission. What if they try to just get rid of them?"

"They who?"

"I don't know. The cops? The neighbor you were telling me about? Did you see her today, by the way? Was she outside earlier? There was a crowd of people gawking."

"I didn't notice," Cass said.

I looked around, trying to figure out exactly what to do next. And saw the woman who had been standing in her tiny yard across the street walking toward us. She looked to be in her sixties, like Laurel had been. She had platinum-blond shoulder-length hair, an obvious attempt to cover up gray, and she was short and somewhat plump. She wore a black T-shirt boasting the Foxwoods Casino logo, a pair of stretched-out gray leggings, bright white sneakers, and a hot pink sun visor. Her oversized, turquoise-framed glasses didn't fit with the rest of the look, like she was trying to appear hip or something and it kind of missed the mark.

"That's not her, right?" I said in a low voice, inclining my head in her direction.

Cass focused on the woman and shook his head. "No. That's Beatrice. She's a qigong student."

"Well, let's see if she knows anything about Laurel or the cats," I said, doing my best ventriloquist act to try to not tip her off that we were talking about her.

Cass nodded. We both pasted on smiles as Beatrice approached.

"Hello there," she said, waving at us. "Cass! It's so lovely to see you. Are you teaching today?"

"I'm afraid not," Cass said.

Her smile faded as she looked from him to me. "What's going on over here? Where's Laurel?"

I glanced at Cass. "I'm afraid we have some bad news, Ms. . . ."

"Knightly. Beatrice Knightly. But please, call, me Bea." She had a pleasant face, slightly wrinkled and plump, like a grandma who spent a lot of time baking cookies. Her eyes were huge behind those glasses.

I nudged Cass. He knew her, so he should be the bearer of bad news.

He straightened, cleared his throat. "Bea, I'm sorry to tell you that Laurel had an accident."

"An accident? Oh, my goodness!" Bea exclaimed, her hands flying to her chest. "Is she okay?"

"She isn't. I'm so sorry."

Bea leaned against Cass's car unsteadily. Her face had

turned a bit pale. I truly hoped she didn't pass out on us. I couldn't handle another mishap today. "This is terrible. What on earth happened?"

"She appears to have fallen down the stairs," I said.

Bea looked at me blankly. Cass and I exchanged a look. "She . . . didn't survive," I said.

Bea's face contorted with horror, then she promptly burst into tears.

Panicked, I searched in my bag for a tissue. "Here you go," I said, handing one to her.

"Thank you." She sobbed, dabbing at her eyes. "I'm sorry. I just can't believe . . . I wasn't there . . . I didn't call . . ." She started sobbing again. "The cats killed her! I knew this was going to happen. I tried to tell her."

"What do you mean, 'the cats killed her'?" I figured she meant they'd tripped her or something like the cop had suggested, but in my mind I saw the evil reincarnated cat from *Pet Sematary* murdering people and shivered.

"She had too many of them!" Bea wailed. "I told her she couldn't take care of them all by herself like this. If I only hadn't gone to bingo last night! I might have known something was wrong."

She sounded so distraught it made me feel awkward, like I was intruding on her grief and had no right to be. But Cass and I had been the ones to find Laurel, and I couldn't quite let it go. I wanted to know what had led me to this small, dilapidated house and its occupants—for whom I now felt responsible. "You and Laurel were good friends?"

It took her a moment to regain her composure. When she looked up, I could still see tears shining in her eyes. She blinked rapidly to clear them. "We were. Dear friends. We grew up together. Been neighbors for a long time. I just can't imagine how . . ." She trailed off, hiccupping back a sob.

"I'm so sorry," I said awkwardly. I hesitated for a second, not wanting to be insensitive, but finally figured I had to ask. "Do you know anything about her cats? Is there . . . someone to care for them?"

"I doubt it," Bea said. "I don't even know if Billy knew the extent of it. Like, how many there were. That's her boyfriend. Oh my God! Does Billy know?"

"The police are heading to him now," I said. "But what do you mean he didn't know? How is that possible?"

She shrugged. "He didn't really come over."

Didn't come over? What kind of relationship was that? I shoved the thought away. Not my concern. "How many cats are there? Do you know?"

Bea thought about this, still dabbing her eyes with the tissue. "I stopped counting at fifty-five. I think a few more came after that. So probably sixtyish."

Sixty? I nearly groaned out loud. And honestly, why hadn't she reported this to anyone?

"Sadly, the cats are a . . . point of contention around here, I'm afraid," Bea said. "I tried to be supportive of Laurel but it was tough. And she never wanted to hear about it. Ultimately she ended up mad at me for trying to intervene." At this she looked sad.

"So, you did try to convince her to get help?" I asked.

Bea nodded. "I was hearing all the negative comments about her and I started to worry. So, I asked her to let me call someone. She got very angry at me. It was almost scary." Her eyes were far away for a moment, then she refocused on me. "Then she started avoiding me. I was only trying to help, both her and the cats. They run all over the neighborhood. Pooping and such." She half whispered the word *pooping*. "It made people very upset, especially the mothers who were so excited for the playground."

"Playground?"

"Yes, the playground at Murray Park, down the street. They just redid the whole thing." Bea adjusted her glasses and peered more closely at me. "Who are you again?"

"My name is Maddie. Cass and I are friends."

"Maddie. Well, you should go see the park. Jonathan really came through—he raised so much money to get it all done."

"Jonathan?" I looked at Cass.

"Jonathan Arquette," Cass said. "The acting town administrator, the one I mentioned who hired me."

"He's just wonderful," Bea said, almost swooning. "It's very exciting, how much progress we're making, thanks to him. New activities for us seniors, and of course the new playground. People were able to buy memorial bricks for the sidewalk in front of it. They arrive this week and we're going to have a party before they install them. Jonathan is very committed to making sure there are things for us to do now. We've even been going on trips off the island. That's where I got this." She stretched out her T-shirt proudly. "We just went this past weekend. It's so different from when Lucy was here." She wrinkled her nose.

"Who's Lucy?" Poor Bea was all over the place. Probably her way of not falling apart in front of us.

"Lucy Leone. She was our town administrator. Jonathan was her assistant. She died a few months ago. . . . Cancer," she added in a stage whisper, as if she couldn't say it out loud for fear of attracting it to herself. "Terrible, but good to have a new perspective. Jonathan actually cares about bringing new life to the town. That's why he applied formally for the job. The selectmen have to go through the whole *external search* though." She used air quotes around the words. "I have no idea why. He's perfect for it and he's already been doing it."

"Well. I'm sure it will all work out," I said, not really sure what to say.

She sighed. "I certainly hope so. But some people want things to stay the same. It's difficult to drive real change in an environment like this. Jonathan really believes in shaking things up. We've seen such a difference at the senior center too! That's where I work. Office manager," she said proudly. "Been there fifteen years."

"Did Laurel work?" I wondered how these poor cats were eating.

As if I'd flipped a switch, Bea's entire mood shifted at her name. Her eyes filled with tears again. "Laurel was an assistant town clerk here in town. It was only part-time. I told her a city job somewhere else on the island would pay more and give her more hours, but she was hell bent on staying close to home. She also spent a lot of time on her budget committee work, but that was volunteer." She sighed heavily. "She had a big heart, but she didn't always go about things in a way that made sense."

"What did you suggest Laurel do to get help for the cats?" I asked, trying to get poor Bea back on track.

"I asked her why she kept taking them in. She always said she just wanted to help whenever she found a stray, but I could tell it was finally starting to stress her out. Especially after the ones she had kept having babies. I told her she should call a rescue, but she told me to mind my own business."

Great. So most of them weren't fixed. I was about to

ask her more, but our attention was snatched away by a car coming around the corner so fast it appeared to be on two wheels, followed closely by a police car—no doubt Jacobsen's. The first car, a ratty Toyota sedan, skidded to a stop in front of Laurel's house. I caught only a quick glimpse of the guy—tall, balding, dressed in chinos and a button-down shirt. He left his car door gaping open and the engine on as he raced to the door, shouting Laurel's name.

Chapter 6

Officer Jacobsen pulled up behind the Toyota and got out at a much more leisurely pace, which didn't surprise me at all given his lackadaisical attitude from earlier. He glanced at us, his displeasure at our remaining presence obvious, then followed the Toyota driver, who I assumed was Bill the boyfriend, to the door. Jacobsen placed a hand on his shoulder and spoke to probably-Bill, who paused with his hand on the doorknob. Bill listened to the cop, then instead of opening the door, he seemed to change his mind and instead leaned against the side of the house, resting his head against the doorframe.

Bea frowned. "There's Billy. Oh, I feel terrible for him. Do you think I should go comfort him?"

"Um. I don't know," I said. "Do you know him well?"

"Yes of course. Billy and I go way back too. All of us— we've been here in this town since we were kids. But I'm the only one who can get away with calling him Billy," she added. "Laurel doesn't even—didn't. Everyone else has to call him Bill. Bill Cavanaugh, the resident boating expert." She assumed a bit of a haughty tone, making me think Bill's status was largely overblown in his own mind and his friends found it amusing. "I should go talk to him." She started across the lawn to Bill.

I let her go, hanging back. I had every intention of asking Bill about the cats now that he was here, since he seemed the closest thing to a next of kin that Laurel had. If anyone would be able to tell me if there were any contingency plans for the cats, it should be him. Or at least he should know if there was someone else, like a family member.

I watched Bea approach Bill and the cop. She reached out and squeezed Bill's hand. The three of them spoke for a minute or two, then she turned and hurried back past me, waving her tissue at me. She looked like she was crying again. Bill said something to the cop, then they both started back to their cars.

I took that as my cue. I had to ask Bill about the cats while I had the chance, and from what I'd experienced of Jacobsen so far, he wouldn't put himself out by calling animal control anyway. "Excuse me," I said, hurrying over to them.

They both turned and looked at me.

"I'm Maddie James. I'm so sorry for your loss," I said to Bill, holding out my hand.

He took it hesitantly, still staring at me like he was confused about who I was or why I was even there. Understandable. Bill was a decent-looking guy, probably mid-sixties, same as Laurel and Bea. Large build, but not fat, except for maybe a few extra pounds around the middle. He had a neat, gray beard. His arms and face had the color and texture of someone who spent a lot of time outside.

We shook hands awkwardly. His hand was large and calloused. Given what Bea had said about his boating expertise, it made sense that he worked with them on the daily. "I'm sorry to bother you during this difficult time, but I work in animal rescue in Daybreak Harbor and I was wondering about Laurel's cats. Do you . . . will you be taking care of them, or is there someone else who will be?"

"Her cats?" Bill repeated, but I could hear what he really wanted to ask underneath those words: *Are you seriously asking me about cats right now?*

"This probably isn't the best time to discuss cats," Officer Jacobsen interrupted, stepping in front of Bill as if he were protecting him from some violent criminal.

"I understand you've just had a terrible shock," I said. "But it appears there are a lot of cats here and they need to be taken care of. I'm offering to do that if you're unable to."

Bill gave me another long look, then shook his head. "I don't know much about her cats. I knew she had some. I don't much care for cats. Allergies. So we didn't . . . spend time here," he said, indicating her house with a tilt of his head. "All I've ever done is pick her up here. I don't think she had any . . . she never asked me to do anything with the cats if anything . . ." He seemed unable to finish a sentence. After a moment he turned to walk away but I called him back.

"Does she have any other family?" I asked when he turned around.

"A sister. But they don't like each other much. She doesn't seem like a cat-lady type, so I'm guessing she won't take them. She lives in Turtle Point. Margery Haberle. "Take them if you want," he said finally. With one last glance behind him at the house, he went back to his car, got in, and peeled away from the curb.

I watched him go, trying not to be offended about the "cat-lady type" comment. Laurel had a sister. I filed the information away for later in case I needed permission to come back here.

Jacobsen still stood there glaring at me. When I didn't acknowledge him, he moved into my field of vision. "Listen, Miss, you really need to—"

"It's Maddie," I interrupted. "And I'm trying to help out. I know the cats aren't everyone's top of mind right now, but they need to be looked after."

"Noted. Now I think you should leave."

I stood my ground. "He just told me I could get the cats. You heard him."

"Well, then, have at it. Otherwise we'd probably have to round 'em up and gas them anyway."

I wanted to punch him. This was the kind of cop who gave law enforcement a bad name. And now I was going to be paranoid about them doing just that until we got every last one out.

"I'm assuming you're going to notify her sister?" I asked instead.

Jacobsen shook his head. "Don't get out to Turtle Point much."

I stared at him, sure I'd heard wrong. "Surely you have to let her next of kin know she's . . . passed away," I said.

"Bill's her next of kin, far as I'm concerned." Jacobsen coughed, then spat on the ground, barely missing my shoe.

I didn't give him the satisfaction of seeing me recoil. What a piece of work. I tried not to grit my teeth. "So, I can go in the house?"

"Sure. If you've got a key, you can go in." He tipped his hat then sauntered back to his car, got in, and drove away.

I wished he would come back so I could throw one of Laurel's garden gnomes at him. What was I supposed to do now? He'd locked the door. I could get the cats outside, but there were a ton inside and they needed food. And water. And vet care. Bill might have a key, but probably not if he didn't ever go inside. Maybe the sister could help, but first I needed to track her down, and it really wasn't my place to tell this Margery her sister was dead. I could feel my blood pressure rising as I thought about that horrible cop, and I knew I was about to do something rash like drive to the police station and cause a scene. Which would probably end in Grandpa having to bail me out—maybe even literally—and that would not go over well. Maybe I could get Grandpa to call the chief. At this point I wasn't above tattling on Officer Jackass—I mean Jacobsen.

I paced around the driveway, trying to focus on one of Cass's breathing exercises to keep my anger in check. Inhale for four counts, exhale for eight. Something about a longer exhale breaking stress patterns. As I breathed, I walked in a slow circle. A recycling truck pulled up, across the street. I breathed and watched the man jump off the back and begin methodically collecting the blue recycling bins and dumping their contents into a big bin on his truck. He worked his way down the opposite side of the street. When he got to Bea's, I watched him take a few soda bottles and newspapers out, mostly papers, and toss them in the large bin, then empty the rest into a second bin in the truck. He continued down the street while his buddy drove the truck slowly behind him.

I watched them work, feeling my breathing even out with the repetitive tasks. When I finally got myself in check, I went over to Cass.

"You okay?" he asked, still looking a bit rattled himself. "That was some good breathing."

"Yeah. Great. I needed to breathe so I didn't beat the crap out of that cop."

"He's not so friendly, huh," Cass said.

"That would be an understatement. Do you know if

she kept an extra key around somewhere? He locked the door." I hurried up the steps and tried it just to be sure. Yep, locked.

"I don't," Cass said. "She wouldn't have told me if she did, Maddie. We weren't that friendly. But I don't think we need it."

I stared at him. "What do you mean?"

Cass shrugged, but his eyes twinkled a bit and he seemed more like himself than he had since we'd found Laurel. "Good thing the cop isn't very bright. There's a back door right off the kitchen. It was open earlier, just a bit. I just went around back to check, and it's still open. He must not have noticed, which is good news for us: it means we can get inside and help the cats."

Chapter 7

I wanted to throw my arms around Cass and kiss him. I settled for a high five instead. "Good detective work. I'll go check it out. Want to wait here and call me if someone shows up?"

Cass nodded, looking happier with this small win but still slightly unsteady.

I walked around the side of the house and approached the dilapidated back porch, stepping gingerly on the middle step—which looked like it might collapse if I put any weight on it—and opened the screen door. Cass was indeed correct. The inside door was slightly open, enough that Jacobsen wouldn't have noticed unless he'd been really paying attention. Which clearly he wasn't.

It struck me as odd, though. Why would both the front and back doors be open? Maybe Laurel had left them unlocked and they had blown open? Although that didn't make much sense as the weather was calm and still and had been for the past few days. Or maybe it was typical for her, and she left the doors open for the cats? Bea had said they were a neighborhood nuisance, so that meant they had outdoor access, at least some of them. I wondered if all sixty-something were all free to come and go and cringed at the thought.

Still, I wasn't about to look a gift horse in the mouth, as they said. I had to take advantage of the situation at the moment while I figured out a long-term solution to get access to her house. Now that I'd confirmed the back door was still open, I stepped down to the safer ground of the backyard and called Katrina again.

"I'm guessing this is going to become the focal point of my week," she said when she answered.

"I need people and carriers over here now," I said, and recited Laurel's address. "We should probably try to get as many cats today as we can. Her boyfriend said I could take the cats, but the cop wasn't so friendly and wouldn't help me get in. The back door is unlocked so I'm taking advantage of that, but not sure how long that will last."

"How many are there?" Katrina asked.

"The neighbor said she lost count at fifty-five. And it's probably over that now." I waited for the curse I knew was coming.

Katrina obliged with a particularly spirited choice of words.

"I know. I'm about to go back in and take a better look around."

"Okay. We'll need to get creative." She paused. "I was serious before, though. I'm counting on you to take some cats."

I groaned. "I know, I know. You're killing me."

"Sorry. The shelter is full and you know my place isn't as big as yours. I can take a few, though."

"I have a guest room and Grandpa's area downstairs he'll have to share," I said. "But let's get as many fosters as we can. I'll see if I can find some too. And I'll have Clarissa focus on a marketing plan to get as many cats moved as possible." Clarissa was my college student volunteer and marketing expert. "Maybe we'll do an adoption event." My mind was already racing through marketing campaign ideas.

"Great. Stand by, I'll send reinforcements." She hung up.

I stuck my phone back in my pocket. Normally she'd be first on the scene, so I assumed she was trying to keep a low profile because she wasn't authorized to work in other towns on the island and her chief could be a pain in the butt.

I turned back to the house and started debating next steps. I wished I had Grandma's car with me. I kept a carrier in the trunk just in case, along with emergency food, but since we'd come in Cass's car, I had none of my supplies. With nothing better to do until help arrived, I figured I'd check inside. Maybe Laurel had some carriers.

I glanced around to see if anyone was watching. None of the porches facing her backyard had any people on them, and I didn't see anyone outside, so I slipped inside quietly, trying to shake off the feeling that I was trespassing. I took a moment to look around. I was standing in the kitchen, which I'd had a glance into when I'd been in here earlier. The air was still, as if the energy from this morning's activity had settled. The house had taken on an empty, sad feeling.

Or maybe I was imagining it. Because it certainly wasn't empty. Some of the cats I'd seen earlier lounging throughout the room were still there, but the others seemed to have scattered. I felt certain they were hiding nearby observing me. Perhaps wondering if I had food, which I would definitely take care of before I left. We'd also have to get people on a schedule to come out here and feed every day until we got them all.

The little house itself was orderly, though. One would expect that with as many cats as I suspected were here it would be a giant, smelly mess. I've certainly seen that before. But this . . . it was different. The kitchen counter, aside from cats climbing on it, was uncluttered and clean. There were a lot of food bowls on the floor, placed on mats ostensibly to try to avoid food splatter. The cats had thwarted that plan. The bowls were empty, with remnants of wet food dried and crusted to the sides. The dry food bowl was empty as well. Escaped pieces of kibble were scattered around the floor, but few enough that Laurel must have been sweeping up pretty regularly. The water bowls were mostly dry too. I filled those up from the kitchen sink. I could smell the faint hint of kitty litter, but given the circumstances, it could have been much worse.

Same in the living room. While the room was sparse, Laurel had taken some pains to make the place homey. She had a couple of pictures on the wall that looked like they'd come from Bed, Bath & Beyond, a floor lamp next to the worn, scratched-up couch, and a coffee table that had probably once been stylish but now looked tired, the wooden legs scratched up likely by cat claws. A lone wooden coaster and a *Woman's World* magazine sat on top of it. I peered into the bathroom. Same. Neat, orderly, sparse but clean, with the exception of the corner where a litter box sat. Litter was scattered across the floor mat in front of it and around the floor, but heck, that happened in houses with just one cat.

I wondered about this. Where were all the other litter boxes? Or did she truly let all the cats outside to use the yard and neighborhood as their potty, thereby earning the wrath of neighbors who did not share her love of felines?

I turned around and went back toward the front door, peering outside. Cass was in the car, probably not wanting to call attention to himself by standing on the street. Hoping he was doing okay, I continued to investigate. Next to the front door was a hall closet. I pulled it open and checked for cat carriers, but there was nothing in there but a few coats and some winter boots, all lined up neatly. The coats too, I noticed, were in order, with the winter coats pushed farthest against the back of the closet and the lighter jackets hanging within easier reach.

I shut the door and looked around. The house was small enough that I could see the rest of the downstairs from where I stood—kitchen, living room, bathroom, the stairs leading to a second floor—at the foot of which was where Laurel's body had rested. I shivered and turned away. When I did, I noticed another door off of the kitchen. This one had a cat door in the bottom of it. I crossed the room and tapped on the cat door. Locked. I gingerly pulled the big door open. A dark stairwell confronted me, likely leading to the basement. From the cobweb that greeted me, it didn't look like a nice, finished one, and from the smell of it, this was where the cat hoarding would be obvious. I was certain I'd found my answer to where the litter boxes were hidden. I guessed she kept certain cats upstairs, whom she let outside, while the remainder stayed down there.

I grimaced and flicked the light switch at the top of the stairs. A bare, dim bulb came on. Bracing myself, I started down.

I used my phone flashlight for some extra visibility and crept down the steps, praying no spiders were jumping into my hair. I hated basements like this—the dirty, unfinished, serial-killer-hiding-place basements. And I heard noises coming from below, which were creeping me out. I assumed it was just cats, but then realized that all too many horror-movie stars had comforted themselves in similar ways before meeting hideous demises.

I paused and shined the light around before I hit the bottom of the stairs. In the wake of my flashlight's swath of illumination, I could see what looked like vomit stains along the walls and stairs, as if the cats had gotten sick and no one had cleaned up. My stomach lurched a bit and I tried to breathe through my mouth instead of my nose as I got to the bottom of the steps.

My heart sank as I looked around, my eyes finally adjusting to the gloomy light. Cats filled the entire basement. Cats in makeshift cages made out of extra pieces of fencing; cats hiding in missing ceiling panels above me, with only the twitching tip of a tail giving away their presence; cats scrambling for cover wherever they could find it at the sight of me. If I'd felt the presence of multiple cats upstairs, that was nothing. It definitely looked like there were more than sixty cats just down here alone. And not only were there cats, but a plethora of litter boxes and food bowls. Litter boxes were lined up against the length of one whole wall. Litter was scattered around the floor, and I could tell the boxes hadn't been scooped in a while. Or maybe just since last night, but because there were so many, they'd filled up again pretty quickly.

"Crap," I muttered. Clearly, she'd tried to keep her problem hidden. I was getting the sense that the outdoor cats were a group in and of itself, and that these cats were part of a whole different population.

My phone rang, making me jump. I glanced at the caller ID. My mother. I'd call her back. I declined the call and went back to surveying the room.

This was already promising to be a way bigger venture than I'd thought. Where the heck were we going to put all these cats? And how was I going to get them all vetted? Dr. Kelly was only one person. Well, two, if you counted the new vet he'd brought on recently when he came out of retirement to reopen his practice. But still—the island was small enough that there wasn't a plethora of veterinary practices. And the one or two in the fancy towns were certainly not going to do this kind of work at the discounted price Dr. Kelly offered. Even with the stipend the cafe was getting, this was a lot for us to take on. And it was doubtful Katrina's chain of command was going to want to help much if it meant more cost to the department. I mulled over my options. Maybe I could get the newspaper involved: a public outcry would get the chief's attention, and luckily, I had an in. My best friend Becky Walsh was the editor of the *Daybreak Island Chronicle*.

I wondered how many of these cats had real health problems versus just some simple hairballs. I heard sneezing, and from the looks of things, there were some, er, bathroom issues that had to be addressed. The more I thought about all these cats needed, the more I realized just how bad this was.

I'd been feeling sorry for Laurel—especially since she was dead—but now I was getting angry at her. Hoarders were the worst. I understood it was usually an illness, but that didn't make it any better for the animals that were being hoarded. Usually, hoarders convinced themselves they were "rescuers" who were taking good care of the animals they were keeping, although it was actually the complete opposite. In extreme cases, animals died in hoarder homes. I truly hoped that wasn't the case here.

But I couldn't fixate on that now. Laurel was gone where I couldn't reach her, and I had to focus on the work ahead of us. And the fact that I couldn't take all of these cats today. So, I had to make sure there was enough food and water for those left behind, and then make sure I had a way to get back in here to rescue them when I could.

First things first, I found some bags of food stacked up

in the corner and refilled their bowls, then went up to wash out and refill the water bowls. I still hadn't found any carriers in all my travels.

Once I was done with food and water, I did one more sweep of the first floor. An orange cat who was clearly well adjusted sunned himself in one of the living room windows, oblivious to my presence. I went over and scooped him up, testing the waters to see how friendly he was. He purred and nuzzled his head against my chin. I had a fondness for orange cats, especially since JJ. My heart melted a little.

"Well, I guess we'll start with you," I said. "Want to get rescued?"

He purred again and snuggled up. Guess that was a yes.

Chapter 8

I carried the sweet orange cat outside to Cass's car and put him in the back seat. "Can you turn the air conditioner on for him?" I asked.

Cass got in and turned the car on, cranking up the air-conditioning, then stepped out again. "You found more cats, then."

I grimaced. "It's a mess in there. The whole basement is full of cats. This is bad, Cass."

He nodded solemnly. "I was afraid of that."

"Katrina is sending some people now to rescue those we can, but I feel weird leaving the door unlocked, especially given what that nasty cop said about rounding them up and gassing them." My blood pressure went up just thinking about it. "We're going to have to figure out how to get back in here."

"I checked for a spare key in all the normal places," Cass said. "You know, under the mat, inside a potted plant. Nothing that I could find. We may have to leave the back open, Maddie."

I shaded my eyes and glanced down the street. Most of

the neighbors had gone back inside, though Beatrice still puttered around her front yard, obviously pretending to be working but clearly watching us. And I could see another woman two houses down on her front stoop, keeping a closer eye on us than she was on her kid, who was playing on an old swingset in the yard. I turned back to Cass. "Let me ask Bea. She said they were friends—maybe they swapped keys. Otherwise, I'm going to have to ask Grandpa to step in, or we'll need to call the sister. But I don't really want to be the one to break the news, and it doesn't sound like anyone else plans to."

"I'll wait here."

I started across the street.

Bea saw me coming and waved. "Still here?"

"Yes. Bea, do you happen to have a key to Laurel's house?"

"A key? No, honey. I'm afraid not. Laurel wasn't . . . that type of neighbor."

"What type is that?" I asked.

"You know. One comfortable with others having access to her space."

"I thought you were friends?"

"Yes, but she was still extremely private." Bea shrugged. "To each her own, right? Personally, I like my friends to feel like my home is their home."

"Right. Well, what about her sister?"

"Oh." Bea cleared her throat, looked away. "Margery."

"Yes. You said you all grew up together. You must know her, right?"

"Technically," Bea said.

I bit back an impatient sigh. "What does that mean?"

"I knew her when we were children. She left the island

and was gone for a long while. Returned a different person. She didn't spend much time with Laurel."

"Still, it should be easy to contact her, yes? Maybe she can help with the cats? And she needs to know what happened. I don't think the police plan on telling her."

"I don't think so, dear. I'm afraid Laurel and Margery weren't on good terms. I'm sorry I can't help you."

I wanted to ask her more, but she clearly didn't want to talk about Laurel's sister. I thanked her and headed back across the street. Cass looked at me questioningly. I shook my head, pulling out my phone to call Grandpa again.

Then I had a thought so obvious I couldn't believe I hadn't thought of it earlier. I smacked my palm against my head. "Her purse!" I exclaimed. "She has to have keys in her purse, right? I didn't see any sitting around, like on the counter, but that would be the next logical place to look."

"You're going to go through her purse?" Cass called after me, but I ignored him.

I hurried back into the house and rechecked the kitchen and living room for Laurel's purse or a set of keys. Nothing. No cell phone anywhere, either. I went back to the hall closet and searched through the coat pockets, even though it was too warm for a coat—maybe she was one of those people who liked to keep her stuff out of plain sight—but there was nothing there either. The next obvious place would be her bedroom. I hadn't gone to the second floor yet, and I wasn't really looking forward to it. Alas, it had to be done.

I gritted my teeth and climbed the stairs, averting my eyes from the spot where we'd found her. The stairs were a bit steep and there was no runner on them. I could see how easy it might be to slip and fall, especially if she was moving quickly, or wearing socks. I paused at the top and observed my surroundings. The bigger room to the left of the stairs was likely the bedroom. I could see another small room to the right, and a second bathroom.

I stepped into the bedroom first, sending a flash of black fur scrambling under the bed. I wondered how many cats we would find up here once we'd cleared out the rest of the place. I looked around. Not much furniture aside from a cat tree. There was a bed, an old dresser, a chair that, like the rest of her furniture, looked like it had seen many kitty claws over the years and could use a good reupholstering. There were a few items of clothing strewn on the chair. The bed was haphazardly made. A *People* magazine and a pair of glasses sat on top of a rickety table being used as a nightstand. Otherwise, there wasn't much in there. No desk, no filing cabinet. No drawer in the nightstand. No purse. I checked the closet. Laurel definitely wasn't a fashionista. Practical items only. Three pairs of shoes, a pair of winter boots. Most importantly, no purse.

I checked the rest of the upstairs. The other room held a small desk, chair, and bookcase. I checked the desk drawers. No purse. No keys. Some files, which I needed to come back to later because we'd need to see if any of the cats had vet records. A cursory search of the bathroom just because, and I was still empty handed.

I pondered this. If Laurel had been home, why wouldn't her bag be here? Unless she was one of those women who didn't carry a purse, but then where were her wallet and keys?

Something about this didn't feel right to me. The house was wide open, and no typical personal belongings were anywhere in sight. Weird.

I went back downstairs and outside to where Cass waited. He opened his mouth, likely to lecture me about staying out of other women's purses, but I shook my head before he could speak. "No keys," I said, not ready to go into detail yet about the lack of personal items. "What are we going to do about this? I need to make sure I can get back in here."

As if the Universe had heard me, a white van careened around the corner and screeched to a halt in front of Cass's car. Adele hopped out of the passenger side, brandishing a carrier in each hand. Another woman I didn't know got out of the driver's side.

"Let Operation Catfish commence!" Adele shouted in that unmistakable raspy, pack-a-day voice.

"'Operation Catfish'?" I repeated. "And keep your voice down. We don't want to let the whole neighborhood know what we're doing."

"Operation Catfish," she repeated. "It's what we named the op."

The op. I had to laugh. But Adele was serious.

She frowned at me. "Don't laugh. This is Dinah. She's a dabbler." Adele tipped her head at her friend, a short, pudgy woman with curly gray hair peeking out from under a black bucket hat with daisies. She wore cropped jeans, a bright yellow T-shirt with lettering so faded I couldn't read it, and pair of neon pink Crocs. She waved at me.

"Nice to meet you," I said, reluctant to ask what a dabbler was. "Okay then. There's a guy in Cass's back seat that needs a carrier. He's super friendly."

"Got it," Dinah said, grabbing a carrier and heading over.

I took one of the carriers from Adele. "You're not going to be happy with this situation. Just a forewarning."

"Great. Any dead ones?" Adele was nothing if not to the point.

I winced. "Not that I've seen, but here's the thing. I don't really have permission to be in the house right now. I kind of have permission to take the cats, but the cop wouldn't help me with the logistics of that. We found an open door."

"So let's get 'em and go," Adele said.

"I wish it was that easy. There are a lot. Like, *a lot*," I said, trying to emphasize it.

Adele sighed. "Yeah, Katrina warned me. Looks like we're all gonna be taking cats home. I'll fit some more in. And I'll make Harry take a few. Dinah can take some. She's only got four." She rolled her eyes. "Like I said, a dabbler."

This time, I covered my laugh with a cough because Adele was dead serious. To a non-rescuer, four cats was a lot. To some rescue people, four meant you were establishing boundaries. To others, four meant you were squandering space and could take in many more, or worse, just pretending to want to help but not ready to really commit. Adele was clearly part of the latter camp—she had no boundaries when it came to cats. People were another story.

"How many carriers do you have? Why don't we first just aim to fill what you've got," I said. "Is Katrina all set with Dr. Kelly, do you know? The basement gang looks rough."

"I don't know what she lined up. She just told me to come out here with carriers and some help, so off I went."

"Who's working the cafe?"

"Harry and your grandfather. Those two. They look like a couple retirees who should be sitting on a park bench, but then they get to talking and you gotta wonder."

I knew what she meant. Grandpa Leo would always be the de facto Daybreak Harbor police chief, retired or not. While I knew he loved his new gig as co-owner of the cat cafe and resident private eye, if he could go back to his lifelong career tomorrow he'd do it without a second thought. And Harry, Adele's beau (although she hadn't really admitted it yet) had a much more colorful past than

I'd been aware of. While I knew him as a retired widower, turns out he'd had a lively career as a cop also, which gave him and Grandpa a lot to talk about related to the good old days of policing. He'd retired early from the gang unit of a big Massachusetts city after a shooting had sent him out on disability. He'd returned to Daybreak Island and opened a small market with his wife until he'd decided to sell it and retire when she passed. Now he volunteered at the cat cafe, and seemed to be making my friend happy.

"Our cats are in good hands," Adele said. "Now. Let's get this show on the road before someone realizes we're not supposed to be here."

Chapter 9

Adele had put traps in the van, so I set those up in the yard. Then I led Adele into the house, figuring we'd get a sampling of the friendliest and the sickest cats out of there first. The street had turned eerily quiet. When most of the activity had ceased, the neighbors who had been watching seemed to lose interest and return to their preplanned summer day. Even Bea had gone inside.

Better for us.

Adele followed me through the back door into the kitchen and set the carriers down, taking in the scene the same way I had. "Not a 'stuff' hoarder then? Only cats?"

I shrugged. "This floor looks pretty normal, right?"

"It does, aside from all that." She pointed up above the kitchen cabinets, where multiple cats still huddled, watching us suspiciously. She checked out the living room too. "Upstairs?" she asked.

"Pretty much the same as here. They're mostly hiding. Down in the basement, though . . ." I shook my head. "That's where the big problem is. Brace yourself," I warned as she opened the door.

Figuring I'd let her have some alone time down there to

assess the situation, I turned to the counter where a tiger cat lounged between two canisters, one holding coffee and the other pasta. He—or she—looked fairly healthy, which cheered me. "What do you think, bud? Ready to go find a better life than this?" I asked.

The cat swished its tail. In one deft move I scooped him or her up by the scruff and deposited it in one of the carriers. I received no protest, maybe just a small sigh of relief, unless I was imagining it. I continued my sweep of the friendlier cats who had started to venture out, curious now about me. I put an open carrier on the floor. A small gray cat made a beeline for the inside of it and curled up. Apparently, these guys wanted out.

By the time Adele came upstairs with one cat who looked like he had some kind of respiratory infection, I had carriers lined up at the door. Dinah was transferring them and the ones she had already picked up to the van.

Adele's mouth was turned down at the corners and two deep lines furrowed in between her brows—a sure sign that she was not happy. "I'm glad she's dead," she said. "Saves me from punching her in the nose. That basement is vile."

"Adele!" I shook my head. "I know what you mean, but some tact, please."

"Oh, give me a break. This is unconscionable. This one needs a vet right now." She held the cat out for my inspection. Up closer, I could see my assessment about the upper respiratory issue was spot on. The poor cat's eyes were crusted with gunk, nose running like crazy. He—or she—looked pathetically thin, all skin and bones. I hated to see it too.

"I get it. But look. We never got to talk to her and see what was going on here. Maybe she truly did think she was helping. You know some of them do."

But Adele was completely unforgiving. "What's going on here is that she was hoarding cats. And we all know hoarders don't take care of anything. They just try to convince themselves they do."

She was right. The official definition of an animal hoarder, according to a million veterinary journals, was basically someone who has accumulated a large number of animals and fails to provide "minimal standards of nutrition, sanitation, and veterinary care"; fails to take action when animals are sick, deteriorating, or even dead; allows an unsafe environment (severe overcrowding, extremely unsanitary conditions); and usually is unaware of the negative effects the situation has on their own or their family's health and well-being. Laurel fit the bill in spades.

Adele put the cat in a carrier and tucked a blanket she'd found around it. "There's a couple more like this. but they're hiding and I can't get to them. I mean, they're hiding in walls down there." She shook her head in disgust. "You know how dangerous that is."

"I do." I couldn't argue with her. I didn't like what I'd seen either. But the woman was dead, and there was nothing we could do except try to save the cats. "Want me to call Katrina and give her an update?"

"Yeah. Tell her to give the doc a heads-up." She grabbed two more carriers and disappeared back downstairs.

I sighed and pulled out my phone to call Katrina for what seemed like the hundredth time already that day.

"How bad?" she asked by way of greeting.

"Adele's not happy."

"Adele's hardly ever happy," she reminded me.

"True story. She's really mad," I amended.

"So it's bad. Great. How many vet appointments do we need today?"

"I would say at least ten right off the bat. And I don't think any of them are fixed."

"I figured."

"Hopefully he'll be able to keep them overnight, unless someone has a place where they can be isolated." That was another thing that was hard as a rescuer. Usually you had your own cats, so it was hard to take in some of the sick or contagious cases unless you had enough space for an isolation room. Which wasn't often the case, because rescuers usually didn't have a ton of money to spend on big houses. I could already tell that all of Grandpa's spare space would be claimed. Good thing there was a lot of it.

Grandpa's house had been in our family for generations. Built by his great-great-grandfather and enhanced by a number of the generations following, we'd had room to create a cat cafe and still have plenty of living space left over for five people. It was one of the most admired houses on the island for sure, to the point where someone had tried—using extreme amounts of money and power—to take it away from Grandpa. I'd had to help him save it last summer—it was one of the reasons I'd ended up staying on the island.

"What's the plan? How are we going to stagger this?" Katrina asked.

"How many can Dr. Kelly hold? We can work backwards from there."

"I'll ask, I'm just worried about leaving them here too long," she said.

"Same." I filled her in on the lack of keys, the boyfriend's verbal consent about taking the cats, and the cop being downright nasty about the cats. "I already know the neighbors don't like the cats. I'm afraid if I don't lock the door something could happen; but if I do, I can't get back in."

"You really think someone will do something? Is it a bad neighborhood?"

"No, it's just—it sounds like there was a lot of friction about the cats. I don't want to put them in any unnecessary danger. You know better than anyone how awful people can be."

"That I do. No relatives?" Katrina asked.

"She has a sister, but doesn't sound like they're close. I may need to ask Grandpa for help if we run into any problems. He knows the chief a little."

"Okay. Well, you should get on that," Katrina suggested, then hung up.

"Thanks for the input," I muttered to the dead phone, and shoved it back in my pocket. Then on second thought I pulled it back out and called Grandpa again.

"What's up, Doll?" he asked when he answered.

"I can't find keys to this woman's house," I said.

He paused. "Okay." He let the question of what that meant hang in the air between us.

"That's not good because I need to be able to get back in here tomorrow and I don't want to leave it unlocked. But also . . ." I hesitated.

"What?" he prompted.

"Do you think it's odd that there are no keys anywhere? No purse? I mean, she lived here, she was home. Where would her stuff be?"

I could literally hear Grandpa thinking about this, sifting through what he knew about women and their purses—which was a lot, because, well, he'd been surrounded by women his whole life. My grandma had been a huge purse lover. She had a different purse for nearly every outfit—all of them the size of a small suitcase—and basically carried her life in them. As a result, she was prepared for anything. My mother was a little more whimsical in her purse habits, often forfeiting size for style if something struck her fancy. Still, she always had one with her for the essentials.

"Did you do a full search?" he asked.

I had to smile at his terminology. "I looked in all the places where it would make sense. I mean, most people I know come home and toss their keys on the kitchen or hall table, or if you're a woman, you stick them in your purse so you don't lose them. There's no purse, no cell phone. No keys anywhere."

"Were they with her? Like in a pocket when she died?"

I hadn't even considered that. I tried to think of the outfit Laurel had been wearing. Jeans and a T-shirt. It was possible there was stuff in her pockets, but if there was it was long gone with her body. Although if Bill was her next of kin, they'd have to give anything they found to him. "You're right. Maybe. I can ask the boyfriend, but he probably wouldn't get the stuff for a couple days, right?"

"Probably right. Can you leave the back door unlocked?" Grandpa asked.

"I can. I wasn't sure that was the best idea because of the cats, but I guess I have to. Unless I pick the lock tomorrow." I was only half kidding.

"No," Grandpa said immediately. "Leave it unlocked for now and we'll figure out if we need an alternate solution tomorrow. Okay?"

I really had no other choice but to agree.

Chapter 10

Adele, as usual, ran a tight ship and had more cats in carriers within an hour than I would've thought possible. I counted twenty, not including my friendly few. I'd told her I'd asked for ten appointments, but she didn't care. She didn't mess around when it came to this kind of thing. It was one of the things I admired most about her. She might bypass an injured person on the side of the road—especially if she'd once seen that person had done something to harm an animal—but she'd risk her life to save a cat. Or any animal, bird, or other nonhuman species.

Personally, I thought it took a lot of guts to admit humans weren't your favorite thing and stop trying to pretend otherwise. There were days I too preferred animals over people, but given my line of work it wasn't always possible to act on those feelings. I had to charm the people to get them to take the animals, or else my house would start looking like Laurel's.

"What are we going to do with the ones Dr. Kelly can't see today?" I asked, although I had a sinking feeling I already knew the answer.

But Adele gave me that look, the one that said I hadn't

been paying attention. "They're going to have to come back to your place," she said.

"My place?" I looked doubtfully at the stack of carriers. If Dr. Kelly could see ten of them, that still left about twelve that needed shelter. Unless he had secret space somewhere that he would give up. "I'd planned for some, but . . ."

"Yep. One of those upstairs rooms your grandpa has as a guest room. These can be the guests."

"Let's bring the whole lot to Dr. Kelly and see what he says first. Maybe he'll take pity on us." I turned to Cass, who had been helping Dinah load cages into the van. "Why don't you go home? Do some meditation or tai chi? I'm going to go with them to the vet."

"You're sure?" he asked. "I'm happy to accompany you."

"No, it's fine. Really. You should go do something to feel better." I patted him on the back and led him over to his car.

"And you?" he asked, pausing before he climbed in.

"What about me?"

"What are you going to do to feel better?"

I thought about that. "I'm going to help the cats."

He smiled. "That's lovely. And later?"

"Meditate?" I suggested with a smile.

"Yes. Don't forget, ten minutes a day. Especially after all this. No excuses," he warned when I opened my mouth, ready to remind him that we had a big rescue operation to conduct here, and what if the cats weren't all safe by then? "You need to take care of yourself, Maddie."

"I know," I said, properly chastised. "I'll figure it out. And I promise I'll do my daily meditations."

"Good. I will email you some of my favorite guided meditations to help you along." He walked toward his car, his shoulders slightly hunched with the stress of the day.

That, out of everything, threw me off-balance. Cass always had a way of looking at everything that made it not seem as bad as it could have.

This time, he had nothing.

I hopped in the van with Adele and Dinah and held on for dear life while Adele drove to Dr. Kelly's office like she was a finalist in the Daytona 500. His office was in Duck Cove, and he'd been the vet here since, well, since I could remember, except for a brief stint the year I returned when he'd retired. A new vet had opened up shop, but extenuating circumstances had made that a short-lived endeavor and Dr. Kelly had graciously come out of retirement. Having him back was not only comforting because he was a great vet, but because he was generous—he did a ton to support our rescue efforts, including emergencies like this.

Dr. Kelly's assistant, Nora Slattery, was waiting when we arrived. Nora had been a fixture here at the office too. I couldn't really tell how old she was, but assumed she had to be in her late fifties, although she was in great shape, possibly with some help here and there.

Adele and I left Dinah in the van with most of the cats while we each brought two carriers to the door.

"Hello, hello," Nora said, opening the door for us and holding it wide. Her blond hair looked freshly colored, with some highlights added for good measure, and her long red nails made me wonder how she performed any work here other than answering the phone. "Good to see you, Maddie. Dr. Kelly is seeing his last patient of the day, and then he cleared his calendar for you. Katrina said there were some potentially hard cases coming in? Poor little things." She peered into the carriers, cooing at them.

I nodded, holding up the carrier I held. "We have twenty-three with us, but there are plenty more where they come from. A lot of them are sick. We have a couple that looked worse than others. It would be helpful to know if it's just regular upper respiratory stuff, or something worse." I sincerely hoped it was nothing worse.

"Twenty-three? My Lord. You can bring them into this room. He'll look at a few at a time," Nora said, leading us down the hall. She paused in front of an exam room and opened the door for us, clucking with sympathy at the snottiest kitty as we passed her. "Crystal will be in to get started soon." She closed the door behind us.

I set my two on the floor. Adele put one carrier next to them and hefted the other onto the table. Her sick kitty cowered in the back of the crate. His nose was caked with snot, his eyes were runny, and he looked petrified. Poor thing.

The other three were faring slightly better. They had the same snotty nose and had each sneezed a few times, but definitely looked better than the other cat.

A young woman came in from the door facing the vet quarters, smiling at us as she pulled the door closed behind her. She wore her hair in braids as long as Cass's. "Hi there. I'm Crystal," she said.

"Maddie. And this is Adele," I said. I'd never met Crystal before, but I knew Dr. Kelly had hired a few new techs for this summer. Maybe he'd been anticipating a ramp-up in rescue efforts. It seemed that had been a safe bet.

"Nice to meet you. Who do we have here?" She deftly flipped the crate open and reached in to scoop out the kitty in one graceful move.

Adele and I looked at each other, realizing we had no idea if these cats had names or anything. "Henry," Adele said, never wanting to look like she'd forgotten anything when it came to a cat.

I hid a smile. "I hope it's a boy," I murmured to her. She gave me a dirty look.

"They don't officially have names yet," I confessed to Crystal. "Or at least none that we know of. We're pulling them out of a hoarder situation. These were the first ones we were able to get out."

"Oh my gosh. That's terrible." She shook her head as she placed Henry on the baby scale and got a weight, then wiped his eyes with a damp cloth as Dr. Kelly came in.

"Hello, ladies," he said. "I heard you have some cats in need?"

"Sure do. You may be working around the clock," Adele informed him wryly.

"I can always count on you to keep me busy, Adele." Dr. Kelly smiled at her. They went way back, and while this was true for most people on the island who had lived here for most of their lives, it was especially true with some of the old timers. Dr. Kelly was definitely older than Adele, but given their line of work, they'd been friends for many years.

"Seven pounds," Crystal informed the doc, handing Henry over to him while she repeated the steps with my charge. "And definitely a boy. So Henry works." She winked at me.

Dr. Kelly examined both cats then sent them back with Crystal for some blood work. "Looks like a simple URI," he said. "But we'll make sure. Poor Henry is pretty skinny. We'll have to make sure nothing else is going on. You have others here, yes?"

"Yeah. Lots. I'll get Dinah to bring them in." Adele went out front, leaving me alone with the doc.

I eyed Dr. Kelly. "How much space do you have for rent?"

He smiled. "I don't have any overnighters right now, so it's all yours. I can even use the dog spaces. I'll need to keep a couple free in case of emergency, but I can fit"—he did some quick math in his head—"fifteen or so. More if a couple can be roommates in a bigger cage."

"Bless you," I said.

"So how many are there in total?" he said, leaning against the table.

I repeated the information for what seemed like the hundredth time that day.

Dr. Kelly shook his head. "These are Fisherman's Cove cats?"

"They are." I saw Nora hovering near the door. When she saw me looking, she averted her gaze and hurried back to her desk. "Any of your peers may want to help out?"

Dr. Kelly thought, tapping his finger against his nose. "Aside from my partner? Probably not," he said. "Dr. Andreas in Turtle Point might, but she's not really one for discounting visits. And Dr. Solomon in Duck Cove isn't inclined to work very hard most days. I think he sees three or four animals a day at most and spends the rest of the time on the golf course."

I resisted the urge to roll my eyes. I hated people like that, especially out here where options were limited. It made me extra grateful for Dr. Kelly, but I also worried about his stamina. He was getting older too, although he still looked as spry as I remembered him from before I left the island a decade ago—although he definitely had less hair.

"There is a small clinic in Fisherman's Cove. I'll call over there, see if they knew any of these cats."

"Great. I'm looking for any vet records at her place too. I'll bring what I find."

"Sounds good. You'll have to meet Katherine—Dr. Vance—soon. She'll be helping me. She's here Monday, Wednesday, and Saturday, and she'll do some extra shifts if needed. You'll meet her tomorrow if you come by."

"I'll definitely try to stop by. I'd love to meet her. Listen, we need to move fast on getting them out of there. We're going to have to bring another batch tomorrow."

"Let me see what we're dealing with today and we can figure out our plan. I assume they all need surgeries too."

"Most of them, yes," I said.

Adele and Dinah came in with another load of cats. Since the room was getting pretty crowded, I slipped out and went to sit in the waiting area. Nora was wrapping up a phone call. When she hung up, she glanced around, then leaned forward.

"Maddie. Do you know the person's name? Who had these cats?"

I nodded. "Laurel McKenna."

To my surprise, Nora sighed. "I was afraid of that."

I frowned at her, not sure I understood. "Sorry?"

Nora glanced behind her again, as if she was afraid someone was going to come out of the office and hear her.

"Unfortunately, I'd heard about this situation. I didn't know details," she added hurriedly when my eyes widened. "My dad and stepmother moved to Fisherman's Cove years ago, after they got married. He passed away a few years back, but my stepmother is still out there. It's a tiny town, as you know." At my nod, she went on. "She lives near Laurel. The street behind her, actually. There have been issues with her and her cats for years now."

I tried to not sound judgmental or disappointed when I responded. But how many people had known about this and had done nothing? To me, that was almost as bad as being the hoarder. "How come no one stepped in to help?"

Nora hung her head and studied an imaginary chip on her perfectly painted thumbnail. "Patty—that's my stepmother— was asking me what could be done. She's . . . a bit of a spit- fire," she added, looking back up at me. "Knows everything that goes on in that town. And not just knows, she's *involved* in most things. I mean, if you can join it, she is part of it. Quilter's club, Senior Center volunteer group, garden- ing club, travel club. I'm sure there were others. Thinks that once she quits being active, she'll die. She's got a more ac- tive social life than I do. Anyway, she was keeping an eye on the situation and she got wind that there were a lot of issues. She told me we needed to help. Meaning Dr. Kelly. But I put her off." Nora sighed and dropped her gaze again. "I didn't think we had the bandwidth and I wasn't sure what to do about it, so I kept postponing talking to Dr. Kelly."

I was really glad Adele wasn't here to hear this conver- sation. She would blast Nora into next week without think- ing twice about it. But we couldn't do anything like that now—we needed their help.

But then to my horror, Nora's eyes filled with tears. "Oh, I hope those poor cats are okay. I'll never forgive myself if any of them are really sick."

Chapter 11

Adele and I were both quiet on the drive back to my place. I felt like I'd been up for days, and I'm sure she did too. The adrenaline rush since the moment we'd discovered Laurel's body and gone into action mode was starting to fade, and I wanted to curl up in bed and go to sleep. That would have to wait though, since I was taking home six cats and had to get them settled. Plus, I knew that the chances of being left alone in my house, especially after a day like this, were pretty much slim to none. I still hadn't called my mother back—she'd called twice more—and honestly, I just didn't have the energy.

But that didn't mean my brain wasn't still churning, trying to plot out our next moves, but also thinking a lot about Laurel and what had happened. I still didn't think it was normal that her doors were open and there were no personal effects to be found, and I needed to talk to Grandpa Leo more about this.

Lucas waited for me on the front porch. I'd called him on the way to tell him I needed a place to put six new cats in quarantine, and he'd promised to help. I kind of just took it for granted that he'd be staying at my place. Lucas still had his own place, but most days I kind of forgot about it. He was never there anymore, after all. I felt bad that he was still paying for it. Now that I thought about it, it would make sense for me to suggest that we remedy that. I was kind of nervous to do it—things were going so well for us—but maybe he was waiting for me to suggest it since it was, after all, Grandpa Leo's house. Guess I had to screw up my courage and just go for it.

But that wasn't a problem for tonight. I had six cats to get settled. *At least it wasn't all twenty-three,* I consoled myself. And I was definitely grateful that all of them were still alive. The rest, we'd figure out.

I was happy to see him. He looked like he'd just showered, and his damp hair was pulled back in a ponytail. Just as sexy as always. Oliver, his twice-rescued black and white pit bull mix, bounded down the porch steps when he saw Adele and me get out of the van. Ollie loved me best, but I didn't like to rub that in Lucas's face. He'd rescued him once from a shelter, and for the second time last year from a complicated situation involving his ex-girlfriend, one that had been fraught with miscommunication and had caused a lot of heartache between us. But all was well now and we had Ollie, who was so worth it.

Adele went around to open the back while I crouched down to rub Ollie's ears. He promptly dropped to the ground and rolled over so I could rub his belly. Lucas joined us. "He got no attention all day," he said solemnly.

"I bet. Poor, neglected puppy." I patted Ollie's belly and stood.

Lucas went over to help Adele. "I already started getting the basement set up."

"You did? How'd that go?" I asked. Grandpa sometimes got territorial about his man cave.

"About as expected," he said wryly.

Adele snorted.

"Don't worry. You'll be taking some soon enough," I said sweetly.

"Promises, promises." We each took two carriers to the porch. Adele set hers down, promised to see me tomorrow, and went back to the van.

Lucas and I watched her go. "You'll give me a proper thank-you later, right?" he said, putting his arm around my shoulders and squeezing.

"Absolutely." I gave him a kiss. "Let's do this."

Grandpa Leo looked up from the book he was reading on the couch when we came in. "Need any help?"

I nodded. "If you want to grab a carrier, that would be great."

He grabbed two to match the two each Lucas and I carried, and we all trooped downstairs. When I stepped into the basement, my mouth dropped open in amazement. Lucas had done an amazing job. He'd set up litter boxes, food, water, beds, and a couple of dog crates that I had no idea where he'd found piled with comfy-looking blankets.

"Just in case they want some privacy," Lucas explained when he caught my surprised look. "We had them in the shop."

"Aww. You are so sweet."

Grandpa humphed a bit, but I could tell he really didn't mind sharing his space with the cats. He just had a reputation to uphold.

I smiled. "Thanks, Grandpa. You can leave them. I do need to talk to you before you go to bed."

"I'll be upstairs."

When he'd gone, I went over and hugged Lucas. "This is lovely. Really. Thank you." Being so close to him, smelling that scent that was just so *Lucas*—soap and salt, oddly enough, nothing related to wet dogs, despite the amount of time he spent around them—it hit me all at once what a long day it had been and that I needed to process what had happened. I'd found a dead woman. I was now involved in a hoarder situation. There were cats in desperate need. Cass was shaken up. A community was in shock. Maybe some more than others, but still.

And suddenly there was the weight of the world on my shoulders, and I realized I was crying.

Lucas realized it the same time I did and hugged me tighter. "I know. It's a lot," he said, tucking my head under his chin. "But we'll figure it out."

Which made me cry harder. Aside from Ethan, who had been putting up with my business-related meltdowns for years, and my family, who *had* to put up with me, I'd never had this kind of support system. And I didn't know what to do about it or even how to receive it gracefully. "I'm sorry," I said finally, pulling back and wiping at his wet shirt in dismay. "I have no idea what's wrong with me."

"Babe. You just found a dead woman and inherited like, sixty cats. I think that's probably what's wrong," Lucas said. "And now, you're going to let these guys get used to their new digs, and you're going to bed with a cup of tea that I'm going to make you. Okay?"

"Okay," I said, swiping at my eyes. "But first I have to talk to Grandpa real quick. And I have to meditate. I promised Cass."

Lucas raised an eyebrow at that, but to his credit said nothing, just slung an arm around my shoulder and led me upstairs. He went into the kitchen to make tea and I joined Grandpa in the living room.

"Where are Val and Ethan?" I asked. I hadn't even heard from either of them all day.

"They went out," Grandpa said. "Ethan didn't feel like cooking."

I raised my eyebrows at that. "He feeling okay?"

Grandpa laughed. "I'm sure even *he* needs a break. And we all know Val's kitchen capacity."

My sister wasn't the best cook in the world and usually chose to let others do that particular chore.

"So what's on your mind?" Grandpa asked.

"Remember how I told you that Laurel's keys and phone were missing?"

He nodded.

"Well, I think it's weird. Both her doors were open, and no personal items at all? Not to mention the people in the neighborhood were not happy with her about the cats. And the cop didn't seem to care." I made a face, remembering Jacobsen's complete lack of empathy to the whole situation. "He wouldn't even get in touch with her sister to tell her she's dead because she lives in another town. I mean, how lazy is that?"

Grandpa's complete look of disdain told me the guy wouldn't have lasted a day under his watch. "Unacceptable," he agreed. "But I'm guessing you've got something else on your mind besides his incompetence."

"I do." I knew if I could tell anyone about the paranoid thoughts I was having, it would be him. Grandpa Leo's default brain activity was permanently tuned to a police frequency. It was one of the reasons why he had been so successful in all of his roles. He never dismissed an idea out of hand and always had a way of looking at it from every angle. This had made the difference in many difficult cases.

My mom and grandma had regaled me with tales of Grandpa's successes over the years, including when I was away in San Fran. Grandpa was never one to toot his own horn. I took a deep breath. "Do you think that maybe it wasn't an accident? It all just . . . feels kind of weird, even if it doesn't necessarily all fit together. And how hard is it to shove a small, older lady down the stairs and pass it off as an accident?" I watched his face closely to see if I could get a clue to what he was thinking.

He was silent for a full minute. I could see he was sorting the information, trying it on in different parts of his mind to see if something fit together.

I lifted one shoulder in a half shrug. "I know it sounds paranoid, but figured I could tell you." I smiled a little. "At least you'll tell me straight up if I sound unhinged."

But he didn't smile. Instead he said, "Why?"

"Why what? Why am I so paranoid?"

"No. Why would someone kill her?"

"Well, I just listed a whole bunch of scenarios—"

But he was shaking his head. "There's usually a bigger reason than what's on the surface."

I held my breath, not really sure where he was going with this.

"One thing I learned during all my years as a cop is that if something feels wrong, that means it probably is wrong," he said. "And you've got good instincts. It's really not that hard to shove someone down a flight of stairs. If no one saw you go in or out . . ." He trailed off. "Of course, someone always sees something. If there's something to see."

I let my breath out in a whoosh. "Does that mean you think it's worth looking into?"

"I think it's worth asking the question," he said. "Maybe

one of those things alone, I would say you're reaching. But thinking about all of it together . . ." Again he trailed off.

"Do you think you could talk to the sister?" I asked hopefully. "Someone at least needs to tell her Laurel is dead."

Grandpa hesitated. "I'm not sure that's my place."

"Can you at least see if you can find out anything about her?" I asked. "Her name is Margery Haberle. She lives in Turtle Point." If nothing else, I'd love to know why they had such a bad relationship, as Bea had suggested.

"Let me see what I can do," he said.

"Thank you."

Lucas came out with my tea then. I said good night to Grandpa and we went upstairs, JJ and Ollie on our heels. Lucas tucked me in, then went to go find his phone downstairs. I took a few sips, then leaned back against my pillows and closed my eyes, trying to quiet my mind. Unfortunately, all I could think of was the rest of the cats stranded at Laurel's house, roaming the street and possibly getting into trouble. I thought of her unlocked doors, and the odd relationship she had with her boyfriend, and the sister who she didn't get along with, and felt incredibly sad imagining her on the ground at the foot of those stairs for so many hours.

Feeling sad made me even more exhausted, and despite my desire to stay awake to finish my tea and meditate, by the time Lucas returned I was sound asleep.

Chapter 12

The day after our grisly discovery at Laurel's house I joined six other people—including Adele, Dinah, and Cass—in Laurel McKenna's small front yard. Katrina held court over the group, all business, waiting impatiently as we gathered. She was there unofficially, as she had not yet spoken to her chief about stepping in to help in an official capacity. She wanted to assess the situation for herself first.

Together, we were the group behind Operation Catfish— and our mission was to get every last cat out. Out of Laurel's house, her yard, and the surrounding area. Given the number of shy cats that were hiding from us, the job could prove difficult. Then, there were the health issues to contend with. Dr. Kelly had his work cut out for him. We were waiting to hear if he'd had any luck with getting his veterinary counterparts on the island to help, but I wasn't holding my breath. Nevertheless, we were committed to pulling at least another twenty cats out today.

I was also having real doubts about Bea's math skills, because even after the twenty-three from yesterday, there were still way more than forty cats awaiting rescue. Admittedly, I couldn't get a good handle on the basement because so many were going into hiding. Nor could I determine how many were actually outside—after our arrival I thought they had gone into hiding or left the premises. I was hopeful with more volunteers we could get a better assessment and make a better plan.

There were a few pieces of happier news: the back door had remained unlocked as I'd left it, and no one was waiting on the property with handcuffs to arrest us for trespassing. Gotta take the small wins, I guess.

Cass was a slightly unusual addition to our group. Grabbing cats wasn't exactly his forte, but he'd insisted on coming along to do what he could, mostly because he seemed to feel bad about bringing this problem to us. I'd tried to explain to him how that was silly, that of course we'd want to help the cats, but he clearly felt responsible. So, we'd named him the designated driver to help transport the next load to Dr. Kelly.

We planned to get the healthy ones up for adoption as soon as possible once they'd been spayed or neutered and cleared by the vet. Clarissa was taking the lead on putting together a marketing plan, with my sister Valerie and Grandpa assisting. Lucas had also offered to help, as he did all his own marketing for the grooming salon. Truly a man of many talents. So lots of work going on in the background as well.

"Okay," Katrina called, clapping her hands to get everyone's attention. "We don't have a lot of time, so let's be organized about this. We have to set up traps outside and possibly even in the basement, depending on how timid the cats are down there. Maddie will show you where the traps should go. Adele, you and Jen can do that. The rest of you, inside with me. We need to grab as many from the basement as we can." Katrina headed inside to assess the rest of the house followed by the other volunteers.

I took Adele out back to show her where to set up the traps. As I looked around to determine the best place, I saw a little old lady in the house behind Laurel's walking around her yard, peering over our way and jotting things down in a notebook. I wondered if she was going to call the cops on us. I waved, to show her I was friendly and nice and not a robber. She waved back. Hopefully that was a good sign.

Once the traps were set, I joined Katrina in the kitchen.

"We've got to look for vet records," she said. "You haven't found any yet, have you?"

"No," I said. "But I didn't really spend a ton of time looking. I was overwhelmed by cats and trying to find keys."

"It would make Dr. Kelly's job a lot easier, and we definitely don't want to over-vaccinate anyone. Although I suppose it might be wishful thinking to hope that any of these cats were vetted. Still, we should check."

I agreed. I followed her inside and through the living room, where one of the volunteers was trying to coax a cat out from under the couch with some treats. "It looks like she was using one of the rooms upstairs as an office," I said. "That's probably the sensible place to look."

"Let's go."

I motioned Katrina to follow me, stepping gingerly around the space where Laurel's body had come to rest at the bottom of the stairs. I led her into the little office, where I'd done a cursory search yesterday for the nonexistent purse.

She eyed the small room and tiny desk with skepticism. "Hardly a two-person job. Anywhere else?"

"I can do this. You could check the bedroom? Or the kitchen?" I suggested. "Sometimes people keep paperwork in junk drawers."

"Good idea. I'm on it." She left the room. I heard her heading into the bedroom first.

I sat down in the old kitchen chair Laurel had been using as a desk chair and looked around. Like the rest of the house, contents were sparse. The only thing Laurel McKenna seemed to have in spades was cats.

There were only two drawers in the tiny desk. I pulled open the one on the right. It held a jumble of pens, pencils, elastics, old Post-its that didn't seem to stick anymore, paper clips. I riffled through, but nothing of any interest. I pulled open the bottom drawer, which was bigger and looked like it had more potential to hold files. This one looked a little more promising—it had a stack of papers jammed inside, some of them folded up and caught in the drawer itself. I untangled everything and pulled the stack out.

Most of it appeared to be shoved in there in no particular order. There were pharmacy receipts for medications, bank statements, cards for holidays and occasions long past, and a bunch of brochures from neighboring New England attractions—Salem, Massachusetts; Foxwoods Casino; Boston's Museum of Fine Arts; Block Island. After some digging, I did find a few vet receipts from a clinic out here called All Paws Veterinary Services. Must be the one Dr. Kelly had mentioned. The visits were recent—May—but they didn't even have names for the cats. "Tiger One" and "Tiger Two" had apparently been tested for FIV (feline immunodeficiency virus) and feline leukemia and luckily came back negative. I still had no idea who they were, but assumed kittens. I hadn't seen any kittens in the mess of cats so far, but they could be hiding. Or they could be a lot bigger now. I placed the receipts to the side and kept digging.

She had old bills in here from a decade ago. Coupons, long expired. Yellowed newspaper articles about the island and the town. I recognized Becky's byline on an article about a traffic accident that had resulted in a man running naked through the streets, and had to laugh. As the editor of the *Daybreak Island Chronicle,* Becky didn't get as many bylines these days. Unless it was a huge piece of news or an opinion piece, editors didn't typically write. I put that in the pile to share with Becky. She'd be nostalgic about it.

I was heartened when I opened a few manila folders and found some actual histories on some of the cats. Unfortunately, there were no pictures so I wasn't sure how helpful it would be, but at least it was something.

I wasn't even halfway through this mess of papers when Katrina stuck her head back in the room, impatience vibrating around her like a force field. "You done? Find anything?"

"I'm not done. Found a couple things. Even a few seemingly complete histories, although we still have to figure out which cat is which. You?"

"Nada. And we need to get the next load over to the doc's. Dr. Vance is working with Dr. Kelly today and has time to squeeze ours in between her regular appointments, so we need to get moving. Can you go with Cass? Just take that with you. We can go through it all later."

I hesitated.

Katrina blew out a breath. "You can bring it back," she pointed out. "I hardly think there's anything in there worth stealing, from the looks of it."

"Fine. Coming. Hey, you didn't happen to see a purse or any keys in your search?" I asked Katrina.

"No. The lack of stuff—aside from cats—still boggles my mind." She shook her head. "I'll meet you downstairs."

Leaving all the unrelated papers I'd already picked through, I got up to go. And kicked something over under the desk. Glancing down, I saw a small paper shredder that I hadn't noticed before tucked against the back leg of the desk.

It had tipped when I kicked it, and spilled out a bunch of its contents. It still looked pretty full. I dropped to my knees and swept the loose shreds out with my hands. I righted the shredder bucket and peered inside, wondering if it was lazy of me to just stuff the papers back in.

But inside there were a bunch of papers that hadn't been shredded. I pulled them out. The blank sides were covered in scribbles with dates, names, and a couple of heavily underlined words: *supervisor* and *fraud hotline*. I flipped the pages over. Credit card statements.

Interesting. Laurel's financial issues were none of my business, so I put the papers back in the shredder. Then I thought maybe there were some vet charges on here that I could track back to specific cats. I hesitated, then when Katrina yelled for me again, I grabbed the papers, added them to my pile, and headed out of the room.

Chapter 13

I hurried downstairs and out the front door, shoving the papers into my bag as I pushed the screen door open and stepped outside.

And almost walked right into a man bent over on the porch, riffling through the recycling.

We both jumped. His knee upended the bin. Cans and papers went flying everywhere.

"I'm so sorry!" I said, bending to retrieve some of the debris.

"No problem," he said. "Leave that. I'll get it. Are you okay?"

"Fine. Yes." I readjusted my bag on my shoulder and assessed him. A family member no one had mentioned, perhaps? Did Laurel have a nephew? Why was he in the recycling bin?

"Sorry. I just . . . it's recycling day and since I oversee that department, I figured I'd grab this for the guys. If it's not out on the curb, they don't come in the yard. I'm Jon. Jonathan Arquette." He went to shake my hand, then realized he held a Coke can in it and awkwardly dropped it back in the bin. "I heard about Laurel and just needed to come by and . . . be here."

The town administrator. The one who had brought Cass into this whole mess. "Oh yeah," I said. "Cass told me all about you. "I'm Maddie James."

At Cass's name, though, he brightened. "Nice to meet you, Maddie. Cass is one of my favorite people. How do you know him?"

"I've known him since I was little, when he came to the island," I said. "He told me how you asked him to do programming here."

"Yes. I'm a huge proponent of tai chi. It helped my mother quite a bit when she was recovering from an illness. I thought it would be something our residents could use. And of course I know Cass has a lot more to offer than tai chi. His type of healing is holistic, as you're well aware. I was very excited about him bringing his expertise to town. And he was already helping people. Like . . . Laurel." His tone faltered and he trailed off into silence.

When the silence threatened to drag on, I jumped in. "I run a cat cafe in Daybreak Harbor. Cass brought me here to help with the cat situation." I tilted my head and studied him. "Did you know about the cats?" I was trying to decide if I needed to ream him out for letting it get to this point. A part of me was determined to find someone to blame, since Laurel wasn't around to hold accountable.

Although perhaps she had already paid the ultimate price.

Jonathan hesitated. "I'd heard rumblings of complaints. Especially once the playground was redone. There's no animal control out here, so the residents come directly to the town officials. Bea let me know the neighbors were upset and Laurel might need help, but warned me that Laurel was very defensive. I was trying to get a better sense of the situation before I tried to help her. She was . . . private."

"She was a hoarder," I said bluntly.

He winced. "I was afraid of that. But I honestly didn't know what to do about it. I wanted to get her help, not get her in trouble. And I wanted to make sure the cats were okay."

I was surprised at the answer. Unless he was putting me on, it seemed like he actually cared.

"How many cats in total?" he asked.

"Upwards of sixty."

By the look on his face, I guessed he really hadn't known the extent. Before he could say anything, Katrina shouted from the driveway.

"Maddie! We're getting behind schedule!"

I gritted my teeth and turned to tell her to hold her horses, when Cass hopped gracefully out of the back of Adele's old van, where he'd been arranging cat carriers. When he saw who stood with me, he said something to Katrina and hurried over.

"Jon," he said warmly, climbing the porch steps.

Jonathan Arquette's eyes got big at the sight of Cass, but then he shook it off and smiled. "Well. Speak of the devil," he said, shaking Cass's hand and clapping him on the back with the other. "What are you doing here?"

"I am helping with the cats," Cass said. "I feel responsible for all the work that is now happening to solve this."

"You're the last one to feel responsible," I said, once again. "You're the only one who raised the alarm bells."

Jonathan Arquette sighed. "I wish Laurel had let more people in. This could all have been avoided. It's unfortunate and tragic. Whatever you thought of her, she was dedicated to this town."

"What did *you* think of her?" I couldn't help it. I was curious now.

Jonathan looked around again, as if searching for the answer in one of Laurel's neighbors' yards. "Opinionated. Old-school. Quirky. Set in her ways." He paused. "Honestly, she wasn't very fond of me."

"Why?" I asked.

Cass put his hand on my shoulder. "Maddie often speaks before she thinks," he said apologetically.

I frowned at him. "He brought it up."

"It's fine," Jonathan said, trying to smile but only succeeding in looking constipated. "It would've been public knowledge soon enough. I believe she was successful in submitting her op-ed to the paper. As soon as it runs, everyone will know why she didn't think I was fit for the job of town administrator."

"Op-ed?" I had to ask Becky about this.

He spread his hands ruefully. "What can I say. She was very opinionated and didn't think I was the best person for the job."

"Yikes. She wrote a whole op-ed about *you*? Why did she think that?" I asked.

"Her reasoning was that all the things I was trying to 'push people into doing' were taking away funding from important town upgrades."

"Things like Cass's classes?"

"Not so much that, because they were free. And I know for a fact she found value in the classes. Cass here has a way of getting people engaged," he said, with a nod at Cass. "No, there were other activities I've been organizing for our seniors. Trips off the island and the like. But her claims were simply not true. It was even more disturbing since she was on the budget committee and could see the numbers for herself. Many things were free, but she took a lot of offense at things like the bus trips. She thought they were frivolous, expensive, and that if people wanted to take a vacation, they should do it on their own dime. Which they basically were, if you think about it—we were negotiating a discounted rate for the bus, so the town was paying only a small portion of that fee. Residents were still paying a share, and if there was a hotel stay involved, they paid seventy-five percent of that negotiated rate. All in all, the cost to the town was very small. We did spend a bit more on the overall programming. For instance, if a famous author was coming to Daybreak for an event, we'd book them here too. We actually have Glennon Doyle on the schedule for August." He beamed with pride at this. I was kind of impressed myself. "That kind of thing brings others to town, and helps breathe life back into a place that has, unfortunately, gone a bit stale. Those kinds of events, yes, we're paying for. But why not? Life is here to enjoy, in my opinion. And if people need help along the way remembering how to enjoy it, well, then I'm happy to be of service."

"Laurel was very conservative," Cass said. "But it all came from a good place. I am just sorry I couldn't do more for her while she was still . . . with us."

Jonathan nodded solemnly. "It's a tragic loss, whatever our differences. Sure, we disagreed on the direction the town was going in, but I wasn't doing all this for personal gain. I want to make people happier. I want to bring in new things, give people opportunities. This community"—he gestured around him—"is beaten down. They do the same thing, every single day. They mostly don't have a lot of money. They work hard. They're purists. They don't expect good things to happen." He sighed. "I was hoping to bring a little life here. The rest of the island is so different, you know? I wanted the people here to get a taste of something better. So, when our town administrator passed away and they asked me to serve as interim, I saw a chance to not only prove myself for the official job, but really make a positive change for these people."

I studied him. He was young, probably around my age or maybe a few years older, and definitely seemed passionate about living life to the fullest and certainly for this town. "How did you end up here?" I asked, now genuinely curious about Jonathan himself.

"My dad was a lobsterman," he said. "We lived out here for a while when I was a kid. I always loved it. And look around. It's beautiful." He waved at the street around me. I studied it, trying to see past the run-down houses and the small, cookie-cutter yards, the tired-but-determined people. The smell of salt air wafted toward me, a gentle reminder of how special this entire island was, whatever the limitations of each community's specific situations.

"After he passed away, I felt the calling to come back. See what I could do to honor his love for the place. Some people only see a dead-end town that they can't wait to leave. I see a place with amazing potential, and I knew I could make a difference." He spread his hands wide. "So here I am. I learned a lot of this stuff from Cass," he added with a wink.

Katrina, who had been standing in the driveway with her hands on her hips, marched over to us. "Are you going?" she said through gritted teeth. "The vets are on a schedule, so whoever they don't get to is going home with you."

"Coming," I said, waving her off. "We better go, Cass."

"I have to get to back to the office myself," Jonathan said, falling into step beside us as we headed toward the van. "Today's a big day for the town. We're getting our engraved bricks for the playground sidewalk. I'm unveiling them at our town meeting tonight."

"The playground fundraiser," I said, remembering that Bea had mentioned it.

"Yes," he said admiringly. "How did you know?"

I shrugged. "I get around."

"It's a great way to bring the town together for a common goal, and tonight will be a nice sneak peek for the two or three citizens who actually care enough to come to our town meetings." He said the last part with a wry smile.

I nodded and headed down the steps, pulling my phone out of my pocket as it began to ring. My mother. I felt a stab of guilt, realizing I still hadn't returned her calls from the day before, but I couldn't talk to her right now. I texted her that I'd call her back soon and stuck the phone back in my pocket. Then I realized Cass wasn't beside me. I turned to see Jonathan holding Cass's arm, keeping him back a few steps.

"We're still on for later, yes?" I heard him ask, his voice somewhat urgent.

"Yes. I'll see you after the meeting."

Jonathan waved at us both and hurried off to his car, a beat-up Nissan Sentra parked haphazardly at the curb while Cass rejoined me. As the car drove away, I started to ask Cass what that was about but then I heard someone shouting, "Hey!"

I turned to see a woman rushing over to us from a house across the street. And she didn't sound happy.

Chapter 14

Wednesday, 11:15 a.m.

I felt Cass stiffen next to me and turned to him. "Who is that?"

Katrina, who had finally stopped staring daggers at me and gotten in her van, pulled up in front of us. "I have to go. I just got a call. Someone has a raccoon trapped in their shed." She rolled her eyes. "I told him to just let the poor thing out, but he insists it may be sick. Adele and the rest of them will stay here and keep rounding up as many as they can so they can just load up the new ones when you get back. Go. Now. Capisce?"

"Yes, now, capisce," I agreed, waving. I sighed in relief as her van roared away, then turned back to Cass. "So?"

"That is Delaney. She came to a couple of my classes." He sighed. "She's also the woman I told you about. Who was fighting with Laurel."

"You're kidding." I turned back and observed the woman who had paused at Laurel's mailbox like she was afraid to come any closer, tapping her foot impatiently waiting for me to acknowledge her. "What does she want?"

"I'm afraid I don't know," Cass said. "But we should go, yes? The cats may get restless. Katrina certainly has."

"In a minute." Now I was curious. Without waiting for Cass, I started toward the woman. "Can I help you?"

She reached up to shade her eyes from the sun. She was pretty, super young, with freckled skin and long red hair that didn't look like she had to put a lot of effort in to make it look good. It was pulled back into a loose braid that hung over one shoulder. She wore a black maxi dress and a string of purple mala beads around her neck. Earrings made out of feathers brushed her shoulders. "What's going on over here? I heard Laurel died?"

Jeez. Blunt, if nothing else. "Unfortunately, yes."

"And you're taking the cats?" She pointed at Dinah, who hurried down the porch steps holding two more carriers. Cass went over to help her stash them in the van.

"We are," I said. "I run a cat cafe in Daybreak Harbor—"

"Well, finally!" She cut me off without a second thought, a triumphant grin spreading across her face. "I mean, too bad she had to die to get to this solution, but at least it's happening."

I was so taken aback, I didn't know what to say. My mouth opened, then closed again.

"I'm Delaney Mathews. I live over there." She pointed to a little red house two doors down on the opposite side of the street. "I don't mean to sound like a jerk, but I'm tired of these cats. You're definitely taking them away?"

"We're rescuing them," I said, aware that my voice dripped icicles.

"So, like, taking them away," she confirmed.

"That's what rescuing is, yes."

"That's a relief," she said, not even registering my snarky tone. When my eyes narrowed, she must've realized how it sounded because she quickly added, "What are you doing with them?"

"We're taking care of them," I said. "Getting them medical care and finding them real homes."

Delaney studied me for a minute, then sighed. "I don't mean to sound nasty," she said again, and I could see how young she really was, maybe mid-twenties. "She just let them run all over the place. They were destroying the playground that we finally got money to put in, and they tripped all the motion lights on the street running around all the time. I swear, it was like a nightclub around here, lights going on and off all night long."

"You knew about them for a while, then?"

"Well, yeah," she said in a tone that suggested it was a really dumb question.

"You could've tried to find someone to help," I said.

"I tried that. I called animal control. We don't have one in town because it's too small, but the Duck Cove ACO is supposed to cover us. They wouldn't come."

Oof. Katrina would flip her lid at that one. "Still, it's not the cats' fault," I said.

"I know. It was her. Believe me, I didn't love her either." She flushed, seemingly realizing how that sounded. "I mean, I'm sorry about . . . what happened and all. But she wasn't exactly the best neighbor. When anyone tried to talk to her about it she bit our heads off."

"You spoke to her about the cats?" I asked.

"I tried. She always either ignored me or just got really mad and told me to mind my own business."

"Did others on the street talk to her about it too?" I asked.

"A few people tried. Mostly other parents who came to talk to me about it. I've never, like, taken a poll or anything on the street. But she was pretty antisocial, so I'm sure she didn't have a lot of allies." She paused. "Did it have anything to do with the break-ins? Like, how she died?"

"The break-ins?" I asked, not following.

Delaney nodded. "There have been a ton of break-ins in the area lately. It's actually really unnerving."

My heart started to speed up, just a bit. Was that why her purse and cell phone were missing? Had someone broken in and stolen them? "Has anyone gotten hurt?"

"Not that I know of. I've just seen this rash of burglaries on the news lately. All houses in, like, this neighborhood and the next one. Scary. I moved here from Burlington, Vermont, last year. My husband got a job." She didn't look thrilled about that. "He said it was safe, but all these people coming and going on the island . . ." She trailed off, then refocused. "How did she, um . . ."

"Looks like she fell," I said.

"Yikes. That's sad," Delaney said. "How many cats did she have, anyway?"

"I'm not sure yet," I said evasively. No use fanning the flames at this point. I tried to soften my demeanor. I wanted to make sure there were no issues for the outdoor ones until we were able to grab them. "Look. I'm sorry that the cats were a nuisance, but it really isn't their fault. Let me just make sure I have them all, okay? I need a little time. Is someone planning to hurt them?"

To her credit, she looked mortified at that. "No. I mean, *I'm* certainly not. We just wanted her to be more considerate about everyone else. It was like they were community cats, you know? And this whole street was their playground. And litter box. Like I said, we just finally got funding through the town for the soft-turf stuff for the playground. The nice stuff, you know?"

I nodded like I knew what she was talking about. Playgrounds weren't my thing. I had no idea what soft turf was, and to be honest, I didn't actually care.

"And the cats have kind of destroyed it already," she went on. "We don't have money to keep fixing it, and I don't want my kid playing in cat poop, personally."

That, I agreed with. "I'm sorry," I repeated. "I'm doing my best to get them all as fast as I can. Can you spread the word please, so no one decides they need to take matters into their own hands?"

Delaney's eyes were bright with curiosity now. "Who are you again?" she said, instead of answering. "I mean, like, how do you know Laurel?"

"I'm Maddie. And I don't, really. A friend of mine became . . . acquainted with her situation and asked me to help. Before she passed away," I added. "That was just an unfortunate complication."

Delaney nodded. "It probably worked out better that way." Then she reddened. "That didn't come out right. I just meant, if she was alive and you'd tried to talk to her she would've shut you down. At least this way she couldn't fight you."

I was starting to get a picture of Laurel in my head that wasn't very complimentary. I mean, Delaney was no prize, but I could see her point. If you didn't really like animals—which I'd never understand, but still—then having them running around allegedly wrecking things in the neighborhood would just make you mad. It was, sadly, human nature to direct that anger onto the innocent animals if they couldn't make any headway with their supposed caretaker. "She was a fighter, then?"

"Oh, you have no idea," Delaney said. "When she got mad, forget it. It got worse when people called the cops on her."

"You called the cops on her? About the cats?"

"I didn't, personally. Someone did, though. Twice. I have

no idea if it was the same person. And man, was she mad when they actually came out." She shook her head at the memory.

"When was this?" I asked.

"Probably a month, three weeks ago? There were two separate occasions. They came out both times. Laurel bit their heads off from what I could hear."

"Did anything happen? Did she get fined or something?"

Another shrug. "No idea. She tried to keep them in for a couple days after each incident, but after that, they were right back at it."

Super. "Do you know how long she's had the cats?"

Delaney shrugged. "She had a lot when I moved in. I have no idea. I wasn't friendly with her or anything. I didn't go to her house. I just saw them coming and going."

"Any idea where she got them?"

"Like I said. My interactions with her were limited to 'Please keep your cats out of the playground.' She would get very upset about it whenever anyone tried to tell her this, so there wasn't a lot of dialogue."

"You had words with her about them," I said. Not a question, but so far she hadn't specifically mentioned the fight Cass had told me about.

Delaney looked for a moment like she might not answer me, but then she shrugged. "I got kind of upset with her over the weekend. My son tried to pet one of her cats and it scratched him."

"When was this?" I asked.

"It happened Sunday. I saw her Monday morning and said something to her. She freaked out on me." Delaney made a face. "Not cool."

"Freaked out how?" I asked. "Did she threaten you or something?"

Delaney gave me a strange look. "No. She just, you know, started yelling at me about how I needed a hobby and to leave her alone. Then she went inside and slammed the door and pulled all the shades." She shook her head at the memory. "Anyway, I'll spread the word about the cats as much as I can. Good luck getting them." She turned and headed back to her house, her dress swirling around her ankles.

Chapter 15

I returned to where Cass waited. "I guess you weren't kidding," I said, sliding into the passenger seat of the van. "She's really fixated on the cats."

"That's what I was afraid of," Cass said, fastening his seat belt. "It's why I wanted to get you involved."

"Yeah. Well, I'm involved," I said with a wry smile. I watched Delaney walk up the front steps and into her house. "Did you know people had called the cops on her?"

"I did not." He glanced at me. "Delaney did that?"

"She said it wasn't her who called the cops, but she could be lying. According to Delaney, someone called in Laurel twice. And she said that her fight with Laurel Monday was because one of the cats had scratched her kid." I couldn't help rolling my eyes a bit during this part of the story. "I'm sure the kid was bugging the cat."

Cass hid a smile as he turned the van around and we drove away in the opposite direction. "I have no doubt," he said wryly. When he stopped at the stop sign on the end of the street, he glanced at me. "Are you okay?"

I sighed, keeping my gaze out the window. "I just feel bad. There was a lot of bad blood out here about these poor cats. And about Laurel." I turned to him. "Was she nasty? I keep hearing she wasn't very nice. Got really upset at people."

Cass frowned. "People act certain ways based on things that have happened to them. If they don't have a good understanding of themselves and ways to cope, sometimes that makes them . . . act a certain way. If she was always feeling attacked, maybe she felt backed into a corner."

I wasn't really in the mood for philosophy. "People tried to get her to pay attention to the problems they saw with the cats and she lashed out. According to them. Although, like Grandpa says, there are three sides to every story, right? Yours, mine, and what really happened." I loved Grandpa's vast library of sayings, but that one especially had helped me in many sticky situations in the past.

"That is very true," Cass said. "I really don't have any idea what kinds of conversations took place between her and the neighbors. I do think it's a shame they are vilifying her now."

"Sounds like they just want the cats gone. And now that she's gone, they'll feel like they don't have to put up with them. I won't rest easy until we have them all." We had grabbed another ten so far today in our van, and Katrina had five with her that she'd been on her way to drop off before she tackled her raccoon rescue. Adele and Dinah were gathering the rest for the next run this afternoon.

I felt another flare of anger at Laurel. It was hard for me to understand why she didn't feel like she could reach out for help if she was in over her head. I knew hoarders often had some level of mental illness that made that difficult, but looking at it from the cats' point of view, I was unforgiving. And people like Bea and Nora, who had known about the situation, were just as culpable, in my mind. I knew Nora felt bad about it and didn't want me to say anything to Dr. Kelly, but she had been remiss in her decision to not alert anyone to this situation. As had Bea in trying to be loyal to her friend. But possibly this could have all been prevented, or at least stopped before it got any worse. I got that people had made an effort, however minimal, but just waiting around for someone else to do something infuriated me.

I had a good mind to make Nora foster a bunch of them.

We were almost at Dr. Kelly's before I remembered what I'd wanted to ask Cass before Delaney had interrupted. "What's going on tonight?"

"Tonight?" He glanced over at me.

"With Jonathan. He asked if you're still on for tonight."

"Oh. Yes." Cass kept his eyes on the road. "We're meeting after the town meeting to talk about the next round of programming."

"At night?"

Cass shrugged. "He's busy. He didn't really say what he wants to talk about specifically, but I assume that's it."

"Why did he come over to her house?" I asked.

"I suspect because he's a good man and he cares about the people of the town," he said.

Even if they didn't like each other? That seemed doubtful to me. Unless he'd done it as a political move? I didn't have time to ask Cass what he thought, because the next moment we were turning in to Dr. Kelly's parking lot. Katrina pulled up next to us on her way out. She paused and rolled her window down.

I braced myself for the lecture, but it didn't come.

"Dr. Kelly will let me know later who's staying and who will need to be picked up. Can you bring the ladies pizza when you go back?"

"Sure thing," I said.

"Thanks. Off to save the raccoon!" She waved and took off, careening around the corner on two wheels. I had to smile. Katrina could totally be a new superhero—Animal Avenger. I needed to get her a cape. Then I sat up straight, the idea taking hold. Maybe we could make our own JJ's House of Purrs children's book, with Katrina as the superhero. I pulled out my phone and made a note in my Notes app. That would totally sell.

Cass parked and we each brought in two carriers. Cass stacked his in the doorway and went out for more while I waited for Nora to get off the phone and check us in. When she hung up, she glanced up at me. I could tell she was still embarrassed because she didn't quite meet my eyes.

"Hey there. How many more?"

"Ten," I said.

"You're certainly keeping us on our toes," a voice from my right said.

I turned to find Dr. Katherine Vance—at least I assumed so, given the white doctor's coat she wore—standing in the doorway of an exam room. I wasn't sure what I was expecting in Dr. Kelly's new partner, but it definitely wasn't the tall, model-like woman who smiled at me. I could see her on my father's board of directors at the hospital, or an attendee at one of Lilah Gilmore's society parties, not cutting cat testicles for a living.

"Hi," I said. "Um, sorry about that." I held up my hands in a *What can you do* gesture.

She smiled and stepped forward, holding out a hand. "Kate Vance. Pleased to meet you. And don't be sorry. It's why we're here."

"Maddie James," I said, returning the smile and handshake. Up close I could see she was older than I'd first thought, with little lines around her eyes and mouth, but still quite pretty. "And that's so sweet of you. We're very grateful you're helping these poor cats."

Kate Vance waved that off as if she were swatting away a fly. "Dr. Kelly tells me you are the famous cat cafe owner. I need to get over there soon. I can't wait. I haven't had a chance to do much since I got here—I've been pretty busy between this job and some volunteer work I'm doing—but it's at the top of my list."

"You're not from the island?" I asked.

"Oh my, no." She laughed and the sound reminded me of Tinkerbell. "I wasn't lucky enough to grow up here. I'm afraid I'm from the plain old suburbs of Boston. I came over because a friend of mine needed help with some volunteer work she's doing. Jade Bennett. You may know her?"

"Jade! Yes, of course," I said. Jade Bennett was a non-local who had come to the island probably about five years ago, according to my sources (i.e., Becky) and had opened a cool bar, Jade Moon. She was funky and fun and she was now dating my ex, Craig Tomlin, who was a cop in Daybreak Harbor. I wondered what kind of volunteer work she was doing. Whiskey tasting? If that was it, I'd certainly volunteer. "You two are friends?"

"Yes. She's doing amazing work helping domestic-violence victims on the island who don't have access to support because they're, well, out here. She's connecting them to resources off-island. Since I also have a psychology degree, she convinced me to come over and help out. She also helped me find this job so I would have an easier time saying yes." She grinned. "So here I am."

"Wow, that's impressive," I said. I hadn't known that about Jade. I wondered why Craig had never told me. Maybe she didn't want it getting around. It could ruin her tough-girl reputation. "Well, it's a great place. You'll love it," I said.

Cass came in with the other carriers just as my phone rang. I held up an apologetic finger and pulled it out of my pocket. Adele.

"What's up?" I asked.

"You gotta get back here."

"What's wrong?" I turned and walked away from the curious ears around me.

"The cops just showed up at Laurel's. And they're not too happy about finding us here."

Chapter 16

This was one time when Cass's calm, slow personality didn't work for me. He drove the speed limit, taking his time (not really, he just wasn't speeding like a maniac like I would have been) while I fidgeted around in my seat, pressing my foot down on an imaginary gas pedal to make him go faster. I tried to take my mind off it by calling Grandpa to tell him we needed his help, poor guy. Although I knew he loved being part of the action. Retirement wasn't really his jam, so I capitalized on that when I needed to. I did try to walk the line, though, understanding that he needed to balance helping out with retaining his reputation.

"I'll make some calls," he promised when I filled him in on the situation.

"Thank you," I said, breathing a sigh of relief. "Adele sounded pretty mad and I don't want her to get arrested for punching a cop in the face when he gets between her and a cat in need."

Grandpa snorted with laughter. "My powers don't reach *that* far. Try to keep her from assaulting an officer, please."

By the time we pulled onto Laurel's street, though, it was clear that Grandpa's call hadn't gone through yet. There were two cop cars outside her house and a whole gaggle of neighbors gawking at Adele and Dinah, whom the cops had standing against one of the cars. I spotted both Bea and Delaney in the mix. Delaney held a squirming toddler.

I could see even from down the street that Adele was about to take the cops' heads off. Her face was red and she was shuffling from foot to foot, a sure sign of barely controlled rage. Her lips moved furiously and she gestured wildly at them. It was pretty clear she was yelling. Dinah, by contrast, looked like she'd been crying.

At least the cops hadn't cuffed them. Yet.

Cass had barely stopped the van before I jumped out. "Wait here," I told him, then hurried over to them. "Hey. Excuse me!"

The two patrol guys turned and looked at me, eyebrows raised. Neither of them was Officer Jacobsen. They were both much younger than him. Which could be bad. Younger usually meant more eager. And more likely to drag the two culprits down to the station to make examples of them.

"Hold it!" the shorter one barked, stepping forward with his hand up. He was bald and bearded and stocky and looked like one of those guys who really had to work to keep the muscle from turning into extra pounds. "Who are you?"

"I'm Maddie James. I'm in charge of this rescue operation," I said, trying to pull myself up so I surpassed his height. I was short myself, but it still wasn't difficult to do.

"Rescue operation?" He looked confused.

"Yes. We're rescuing all the cats from this hoarder situation. And you are?" I made a point of leaning in to peer at his badge.

He puffed out his chest. "Officer Ward. These people are trespassing. And if you're traipsing in and out of this woman's house, you are too. You know, there have been some burglaries reported around here lately." He looked at me pointedly. "Random people trying to get into people's homes look pretty suspicious to me anyway, but now . . ." He nodded with satisfaction, ostensibly at this genius theory that concluded we must be the robbers.

"We're not trespassing, you moron!" Adele shouted. "Do you know who her grandfather is?"

"Settle down," the other cop said matter-of-factly. "Let us get this straightened out." He looked more amused by the situation than his friend Ward, who seemed to want us to know how tough he was.

I sent Adele my best *Keep quiet* face then turned back to Ward just as their radios crackled and a man's voice came in over the static. "Ward! Blondin! Report your location."

Ward turned back to his cohort with a questioning look, then reached for the radio button on his shoulder. "Ward here. We're at thirteen Berwick Street. Holding trespassers."

"Well, stand down," the dispatcher said. "Per Sergeant Mills. Those people have permission to round up the cats."

"See?" Adele just couldn't help herself. She pointed her finger at Ward. "Stand down!"

The two cops ignored her and looked at each other again, then Blondin shrugged. "Guess they're cleared."

Ward spoke into the mic again, his tone clipped. "Copy." Once he was off the radio, he walked back to his partner. "We still have to wait for Bill. I can do that, if you want to head out."

"Fine with me," Blondin said. "I'm taking my dinner break." And with that, he walked to his car and drove away.

He'd barely turned the corner when a pickup truck with the words Cavanaugh's Boat Repair and a picture of a sailboat on the side door pulled onto the street. The driver

stopped at the curb in front of Laurel's and got out. It was
Bill the boyfriend. This must be his business—Bea had
mentioned he owned a business and had called him the
resident boat expert.

Bill paused and let his gaze roam over the scene, then
shook his head. "What is this?" he demanded, coming over
to where I still stood in a semi face-off with Ward.

Ward stepped forward. "Bill. We were told to stand
down. They okay to be here?"

"I told them already, they can take the cats," Bill said,
sounding exasperated. "Do I need to sign something so you
stop calling me? And how long does it take to get some
cats?"

This last question was clearly directed at me, and I'd
had enough. "Longer than you would think when there are
over sixty cats at last count and half of them are hiding in
the walls," I said, adding a pleasant smile to my face to
mask the annoyance I knew seeped into my words.

At that, Bill turned his full attention on me. Unless he
was a superb actor, the shock on his face was real. "I'm
sorry? Did you say sixty?"

I nodded. "At least."

Bill thought about that for a moment, then said to Ward,
"You can go. All good. Tell your supervisors to leave them
alone."

"You got it," Ward said. "Sorry to disturb you." No apol-
ogies to Adele or Dinah, though. He nodded at me, then
headed to his own car and drove away. The neighbors started
to disperse now that they realized the drama had ended
mostly amicably.

Bill still stood there watching me. I saw Adele marching toward me, but I waved her back. "Bill, listen," I said.
"I really am sorry you keep getting dragged back here, and

for everything . . . else, but we're just trying to make sure we help the cats."

"No, I get it. It's fine." He turned and gazed at the house a moment, like he couldn't believe the secrets it had kept from him all this time, then turned back to me. "I had no idea. I mean, I'd heard people talking. Whispering about her around town. That she was one of those, you know, cat ladies. I never listened. Figured they didn't know what they were talking about. I mean, she never acted like one, you know?"

I wondered how exactly a cat lady acted, but resisted asking.

"And I really didn't know what the cat-lady thing even meant. I knew she had more than most people do but . . ." He trailed off. "I guess I should have paid more attention. But she was more than happy to come to my house or go out, so I never thought much about it."

"Did you ever hear anyone threaten to do something to the cats?" I asked.

He looked at me, surprised. "Never. Although maybe they wouldn't have in front of me. Everyone in town knew we were together. I don't listen to the gossip anyway. Around here . . ." he shook his head. "It's constant. I know she struggled with it too. People can be, well, mean."

They could at that. I felt a flare of sympathy, then I remembered the situation. Laurel had certainly been a complicated woman. I hesitated for a second, then figured I needed to seize this opportunity, like any good investigator. "Did Laurel use a purse?" I asked.

He frowned, trying to connect the change in subject. "Sure. Don't all women?"

I forgave the stereotyping because I'd done the same thing myself when I questioned the lack of a purse at Laurel's house. "I thought perhaps I could find a set of keys so we could lock the house up. I didn't want to leave it open at night. But I can't find anything, not even a cell phone. She did have a phone, right?"

"Absolutely," he said with certainty. "I mean, she was definitely practical with her clothes and her stuff, but she did use a small purse and she had a cell phone. She didn't want a landline, so the cell was all she used."

"You don't know where she might've kept it?"

Bill sighed. He suddenly looked very tired. "Like I said, I didn't go inside her house. Probably because of . . ." he trailed off and waved at the scene around him. "I didn't know. We had . . . a good arrangement. Not a lot of pressure, you know? I liked my space, she liked hers. We went out three times a week, and we went to all the town meetings together because we were both so invested in the town. It was our thing." His gaze dropped to the pavement. "I'm gonna miss her."

"I'm sorry," I said quietly.

"Yeah. Well." He straightened, back to business. "Why are you so concerned with her purse and cell phone?"

"I just thought it was odd that they weren't here."

"You think someone . . . broke in and stole them? Like, after she died?" He looked distraught at that thought. "We have been having a lot of burglaries in the area. What can I do to help?"

I had no idea what he could do. "I guess just make sure they leave us alone so we can get the cats. And make sure they leave the cats alone."

"I'll do my best," he said. "Where are you taking them?"

"To get vet care, first. Then back to Daybreak Harbor. I'm working with the animal control officer there. We'll get them adopted either through her facility or my cat cafe."

"Cat cafe?" He shook his head, bewildered. "I never knew people put this much thought into cats. Well, good luck." He turned to go.

"Hey," I said. "Do you know if the police contacted her sister?"

Bill's lips thinned, almost disappearing in the process. "No idea."

"It seems she should know her sister died, yes? I mean . . . wouldn't she want to organize the funeral? Or are you doing that?"

Bill's face had completely closed off. "I'm doing the funeral. She had me as her next of kin. As to whether Margery should know, or not, well, some would say she doesn't deserve to know."

With that, he turned and walked back to his car.

Chapter 17

I was starting to get really curious about Laurel's sister. Probably it was none of my business and I should just stick to the cats and my traumatized volunteers, but I hoped Grandpa was making headway on his search for her.

After Bill left, I headed over to where Adele was ranting and raving and threatening to sue the police department. Dinah, in the meantime, was still crying. I talked them both off their respective ledges until they'd calmed down, then finally sent them on their way to Dr. Kelly's with thirteen more cats. I realized I hadn't been able to bring them their pizza, and I was sure the lack of food was adding to their distress. As their van pulled away, I called Katrina.

"Everything okay?" she asked.

"The cops just left Laurel's house. They were giving Adele and Dinah a hard time."

She cursed. "Do I need to get McAuliffe involved?" McAuliffe was her chief. "He's gonna love this one. I still haven't told him yet that we're helping."

"I don't think so. Grandpa made a call. They were told to stand down. After Adele almost assaulted a cop and

Dinah couldn't stop crying." I narrowed my eyes when I heard a barely concealed snicker of laughter. "You think it's funny?"

"I don't. I really don't," she said, her voice changing back to serious. Then she burst out laughing. "I kind of do. I can picture Adele's face. She must've cursed them out. I mean, it's funny unless they got arrested. Can you imagine if they got arrested?"

The thought of short, stout Dinah in a striped uniform— did they still make prisoners dress in those?—struck me as funny too and before I knew it, we were both cracking up. Cass watched from a distance, perplexed.

"We shouldn't be laughing about this," I said when I caught my breath.

"You're right. We shouldn't, but I needed that," Katrina said, still giggling, then pulled herself together. "Okay then. All is well."

"Yeah. Grandpa saved the day. I wonder if the chief out here will tell your chief, though. On second thought, you may want to preemptively strike and let him know. Make it sound good for the department."

"Probably." Katrina sighed. "I'm sure I'll be on the bad list again. Oh well. What can you do? I'll just say I was helping in my spare time."

"The neighbor told me that the Duck Cove ACO refused to go out and help."

Katrina snorted. "Doesn't surprise me. Gary's a lazy piece of work. Probably for the best. They would've just put them all to sleep probably." Katrina was definitely an out-lier in her profession. She'd told me once that a lot of her counterparts really didn't like animals and didn't make a ton of effort to do the right thing. She was convinced there were only a few—herself being one of them—who cared so much it kept them up at night and who went to extremes to help. I wasn't entirely convinced there were as many bad eggs as she thought, but I did agree with her about Gary. "Hey, by the way. Dr. Kelly got one of the other island vets to help."

"Nice. Which one?"

"The Turtle Point clinic. But we're going to probably need to bring some more to your place tonight."

"No problem. The basement's all set up. Last night's gang is doing fine, so they'll join them. We're also going to have to set some traps tonight. I'd like to catch some of the outside cats before the angry neighbors get any angrier." I told her about my conversation with Delaney.

"Not okay. You're right, we should trap tonight. I'm not sure who I can get to go out on short notice, but we can start putting together shifts."

"I'll do it tonight," I said. "We can see what happens from there. I'll see if Lucas wants to keep me company. Quality time sitting in a car and all that."

"If only people knew how romantic our lives were," Katrina said wryly. "Oh. On a more somber note. One of the ones from yesterday tested positive for FIV."

FIV—feline immunodeficiency virus—certainly wasn't a death sentence, but it did mean that we needed to be extra careful where the cat was placed. It was transmitted through blood, so usually somewhere a cat could potentially fight was the biggest risk. We needed to make sure that the cat wasn't put in a situation where it could infect another cat. I also hoped there hadn't been a lot of infecting going on here already.

"That stinks," I said.

"It's okay. We have a potential foster already for the FIV cats."

"We do?"

"Yup. Told you I'm a miracle worker. I gotta go. Let me know if you trap anything later. And I'll be by at some point with the cats."

"Roger that. I'll tell Grandpa you're coming." I hung up and turned to Cass. "We can go now."

He studied me. "What were you saying? About coming back tonight?"

"I was just telling Katrina we're going to have to come back tonight and set traps. Just in case."

"Would you like me to help you trap?"

I had to smile at that. "No. But thanks. It's not as glamorous as it sounds. It's actually a lot of sitting and waiting."

"I didn't think it would be glamorous. But I would like to help."

"Cass. You *have* helped. You let us know about the cats so we could help them. Do you know how huge that is? Some people would've just ignored the whole thing. Some people *did* ignore the whole thing," I said. "And if you hadn't told us about the cats, that poor woman might've been lying there for days." I shuddered at the thought. "Besides, you have to meet Jonathan later."

"Yes, well. I'm still happy to help if I'm needed. I am very sad about her death," Cass admitted. "She needed help. And she seemed to be coming around to learning how to take better care of herself. This whole thing is very unfortunate."

"I'll say," I muttered. I knew this was where I could be off-putting to some people. While I felt terrible Laurel had died, I was still angry about the way she'd lived. I knew my animal peeps understood that. My other peeps, who actually liked humans too, sometimes had a hard time with that approach.

"Come on," he said. "I'll take you home."

Chapter 18

It was late afternoon when we got back to Daybreak Harbor, and that meant the streets were packed. Tourists poured off the ferry in droves, joining the crowds who were out looking for appetizers or drinks before making dinner plans. It was so different here than Fisherman's Cove—alive, thriving, full of smiling faces and people with money to spare.

Cass pulled up in front of my house. "Keep me posted," he said as I got out.

I waved and watched him drive off, headed back to his store and his little apartment. I figured he'd light some candles, have some tea, and maybe do some tai chi. I wished I had time to join him. I was better at meditating if someone was sitting in front of me forcing me. But I had things to do, and I needed to check in with Lucas. If I was lucky, he'd come trapping with me and we could at least spend some time together tonight.

I popped inside to check things out in the cafe. Harry was there, hovering over the three people who were visiting with the cats. When he saw me, he abandoned his post and rushed over.

"Is Adele okay?" he asked anxiously.

"She's fine. Why?"

"She called me and said she almost got arrested!"

I sighed. Adele did have a flair for the dramatic some-times. "She didn't almost get arrested." I didn't think so, anyway. "She's fine, the cops just wanted to talk. She's taking some cats to the vet, but she should be back soon." I patted Harry on the shoulder.

One of our customers came up to ask him a question, so I used the opportunity to slip away. I went out the side door and I stuck my head into the garage-turned-cafe, where Ethan manned the counter. He had a line, which was good for business, but hard on Ethan because he clearly needed help. I knew he was actively looking to hire, but hadn't found anyone quite yet. I went back inside and asked Clarissa, who was hunkered down with her phone doing social media posts about the cats, to go help him. I'd have gone, but I needed a break before I figured out the rest of my day. And maybe a nap if I was going trapping tonight. I checked my watch. I had to get my daily meditation in, then I'd reward myself with a nap. Then I'd call my mother back. She'd left me another voice mail while I'd been dealing with the police and Adele. I felt like I hadn't talked to my family in days outside of Grandpa Leo.

I went up to the third floor to find JJ, whom I'd been worried I was neglecting terribly. He was in my bed, snug-gled in a ball with his tail wrapped around his eyes. He didn't even shift in his sleep as I walked in, so I guessed he wasn't too worried about it. I grabbed my phone and my earbuds, and settled onto the window seat in my book nook. The view of the sea from here was breathtaking, and I spent a couple minutes looking outside before I refocused on the matter at hand. Meditation. Right. Couldn't looking at the water be meditation? It totally could.

But Cass had given me specific meditations and now I felt obliged to do them. I sat cross-legged, popped in my earbuds and scrolled through my phone for one. I picked one with the title "Witnessing your thoughts and observing awareness." And apparently while I listened, I had to breathe in a very specific, very strange way. I practiced it for a minute or two before I started, just to make sure I had the hang of it. It felt funny, basically panting like a dog, but maybe that was good.

I closed my eyes and pressed PLAY. It took all of my concentration to keep doing the breathing thing while listening to the sappy-sweet woman—whose name was Ish, apparently—telling me to work with my thoughts rather than push them away.

I'd just gotten to a place where I felt myself relaxing and falling into the rhythm without too much effort when I heard the faint sound of my name being called. I tried to tune it out—"observe only," as Ish would say—but the voice got louder and then the pounding of feet accompanied it. Then I heard the unmistakable sound of someone knocking on the wall over my head.

"For God sakes!" I opened my eyes and glared at Val, who stood in front of me. She looked concerned.

"What the heck are you doing?" she asked.

"Meditating! But jeez, you make it hard." I pulled out my earbuds and jabbed at the PAUSE button on my phone. "What do you want?" I felt kind of guilty when I said it. A few minutes ago I'd been thinking about how I'd barely seen anyone in my family. But her timing had always stunk.

"Meditating? You sounded like you were hyperventilating."

I glared at her.

"You should meditate more. You're cranky." She ignored

the sound of frustration I made. "I wanted to share the good news! I'm doing your event." My sister had started her own business as an event planner when she'd divorced her obnoxious husband last summer. She was amazing at it, and a recent fundraising event we'd done for the cafe had thrown her business even more into the spotlight. So much so that she'd had to hire actual staff. I was proud of her, not that I felt like admitting it at the moment.

"My event? What event? Did Clarissa already put an adoption event together?" Darn, the girl was fast.

But Val shook her head. "Your retreat. Well, technically it's Cass's event, but I know you're going. He said you were really involved in it? And Sam wants to go too."

That didn't surprise me. Our younger sister was very woo-woo. She was everything Cass wanted me to be. But right now, I was focused on the development that Val was going to be running this shindig. "It's a meditation retreat. Which Cass said was already full. I didn't know it needed an event planner. I thought it was supposed to be minimal-ist," I said. Then my eyes narrowed. "He's doing this to make sure I go, isn't he? You're supposed to be my chaper-one. Both you and Sam."

"You are *so* paranoid," Val said, rolling her eyes. But I wasn't completely convinced I was wrong. Cass might be Zen, but he could also be sneaky.

"And what do you mean I'm really involved?" I asked. "I'm just going. A last-minute addition, at that."

Val held her hands up in mock defense. "That's what he told me. I just wanted to tell you. See if there were any tips or preferences. I know you're all cooking together at least one night, and for the rest I'm supposed to do all healthy food, so I'm working on that today."

"Cooking together?" I repeated.

She nodded. "Yes, for the tea ceremony meal."

I wondered who else was going to this thing, and exactly what I'd signed up for. Not that I'd so much signed up as been told to show up, but still. "Goody," I muttered. "Can I go back to what I was doing now?"

"If you're gonna be this much fun at the retreat, maybe you shouldn't go after all," she said, and flounced back to the stairs.

"You're not supposed to talk at those things anyway," I called after her. I wasn't sure if that was true or not, but hopefully it was. I didn't think I'd really be up for being friendly and fun when I couldn't even have coffee.

Chapter 19

I tried to get back into the meditation, but my brain had kicked back up again. No matter how much I tried to simply observe my thoughts, they kept knocking even harder at my consciousness to get me to pay attention. And then all the things I had to do rushed in full force, and the guilt I felt sitting around got the better of me.

I could still tell Cass I'd done something, right? I was pretty sure I could. I checked to see how long I'd meditated, and stared at my phone in dismay. Three minutes? That's all I'd managed? The whole meditation was twelve minutes. One quarter successful. That's it. I was a failure.

I heard a thud as JJ hopped off the bed and came out to the hall, squeaking when he saw me. "Hey, bud," I said, bending down to scoop him up. "Have you heard? Momma's a failure at meditating. And I'm having cat problems."

He squeaked his sympathies. After all, he'd been a stray in need of rescue once too.

"Let's go find a snack. And Lucas." I ruffled his fur and set him down. He led the way downstairs, his tail high and regal. I followed, calling Lucas as I walked.

He didn't pick up right away and when he did, he sounded

breathless. "I'm sorry I haven't called," he said. "Got kind of busy today. You can blame Katrina. She dropped off a dog that needs a lot of help."

"A dog?" This was news to me. "Seriously? I talked to her a little while ago! She didn't mention that." Lucas was kind enough to offer his services to the town's strays at no fee. I felt bad sometimes—I didn't want him to think I was taking advantage of our relationship—but he insisted he was happy to do it, and Katrina was more than happy to use him.

"I think it just came up. Anyway, it's fine. I'll meet you at the house in an hour, hour and a half?"

"That sounds great, but I do have to go trapping tonight at that house in Fisherman's Cove. Want to come with? We can make out in the car like we're sixteen."

He laughed. "I'm in. I'll be there as soon as I can."

I loved that about him. No questions asked and no protests even though he'd had a long day too. "Thank you," I said. "Can't wait to see you."

"Me too, babe."

I hung up and headed into the kitchen to make something to eat. I was suddenly starving. I hadn't eaten lunch. With the police interference, we hadn't had a chance to get pizza. I needed a snack to tide me over until dinner.

JJ did too, apparently, from the way he was sitting there squeaking at me. I reached for his treats in the cabinet, but then decided instead to run down the street to my friend Damian's Lobstah Shack. Damian Shaw had bought the restaurant a couple years back from a family who had lived on the island forever. At first, we'd all been a little skeptical at a Midwesterner in his mid-thirties attempting to successfully run a demanding business out here, never mind move to an island where the winters were challenging, but he had exceeded all—admittedly low—expectations. His place was thriving, and he'd recently even expanded to include a fish market. Best of all, Damian loved JJ and saved him all kinds of scraps. He was also fond of me, which meant I could probably get some French fries.

I put JJ's harness on and loaded him into the car—I was too hungry to walk the half mile. Damian's place was right next to the ferry dock, which was great for business; we had to park on the street because the lot was completely full. JJ knew exactly where we were going and began squeaking with excitement when I opened the car door.

Damian was outside talking to a family at one of the picnic tables. He looked good, I noticed. Island life agreed with him. He wasn't so pale anymore, and his hair had lightened even more with the sun. He was bigger, too—more jacked in the upper body. Hauling boxes of fish could do that, I guessed.

He saw us right away, and once he was done he motioned with a smile for me to follow him. We went in the side door leading into the restaurant area. Everyone was sitting outside since the weather was so beautiful, which gave us some space inside.

"My favorite patron," he proclaimed, reaching down to rub JJ's ears. "I have a whole plate of treats set aside for him. It's nice to see you too, Maddie. Where've you been?"

I had to smile. I was an afterthought to JJ's celebrity around town, but it didn't bother me one bit. JJ's rough start in life made it all the more satisfying to see him living his best life.

"Don't ask. It's been quite a week so far." I slid into a seat at the counter. "Fries?"

"You got it. Anything to go with it?"

I checked my watch and considered. I didn't want to ruin my dinner with Lucas, but we could always get food and eat in the car while trapping, which meant it would be later than usual. "Maybe some fried clams," I said.

"Good choice. Coming right up." He went out back and returned a few minutes later with a steaming hot plate for me, and a loaded plate for JJ with all kinds of fish scraps piled high. He placed mine on the counter and JJ's on the floor. JJ squeaked with delight and attacked the food.

"He was getting pretty mad at me for not taking him over here lately." I popped a clam into my mouth and sighed with pleasure. Damian's clams were perfect—juicy and fresh, with just a light coating of batter so they weren't as awful for you as the extra-crispy fried version sold at most of the other shacks on the island. We'd discussed this early on when he'd asked me for help with marketing and articulating his brand: while he wanted to stay close to the offerings the previous owner had made famous in their seventeen-year run with the restaurant, he also wanted to put his own spin on it. So, we'd decided he would provide a healthier option. So far, it was working wonders.

His fries were delightful too, crispy, no sog. He let me eat a few before he pressed. "So what's been going on?"

"Cat hoarder on Fisherman's Cove." I filled him in on the story. When I got to the part about us going to her house and finding her dead, his eyes widened with interest.

"Dead? How?"

"Accident on the stairs." I shook my head, trying to clear the image of Laurel's body. "Awful. But it accelerated the whole cat thing, since we didn't have to argue with her about taking them. Now we have to get them out of there. We've already pulled out around forty of them."

Damian let out a long, low whistle. "You think the cats killed her?"

"A couple of people have said that. Who knows. It's not

like any of them have fessed up. I'm going back tonight to
trap more. There are a bunch of them living mostly outside, to make things even more difficult. Anyway. What's
been going on around here?" I felt like I hadn't been around
much. I didn't usually spend so much time away from home
and the cafe.

"The usual. Busy here. The ferry dock has been a bit
busier than usual, even, and there have been a lot of cops
around, checking the boats."

I raised my eyebrows at that. "Why?"

He shrugged. "I'm not really sure. I heard something
about how they're checking cars going on and off the island
for stolen goods, but I'm not sure what the whole story is."

"Weird," I said. I'd have to ask Becky what was up. "So,
you know how you were talking about getting a cat?"

Damian adored JJ and I'd been pushing him for a while
to adopt one of the cafe cats. He'd been resisting because
he was working such long hours, but I knew the closer we
got to winter the more I could wear him down. It was a
long, kind of lonely winter around here and since he lived
alone, a cat (or two) would be the perfect companion.

He pushed his glasses up on his nose and nodded warily.
"It was more you talking about how I should get a cat,
but yes."

"Well, I know it's a big commitment. That's why I was
thinking about how it might be cool if you tried it out first.
You know, as a foster home." I beamed at him as I dragged
my last couple of fries through my ketchup and finished
them off.

"Foster, huh?" He leaned against the counter, considering this.

"Yeah. Honestly, we have more cats than we have space
for with this case. Katrina doesn't have room at the shel-

ter, and she hasn't even told her boss yet that she's helping with this. I'm bringing a bunch to our place and the vet is stashing as many as he can, but we're trying to expand our foster network. It would be so amazing and helpful if you took a couple on a short-term basis. We'd cover food and supplies."

As if we'd planned it, JJ wound around Damian's ankles, his tail high, and squeaked.

Damian sighed, then reached down and picked JJ up. "Sure," he said.

I jumped up with a squeal and hugged him. "Thank you! I'll find out which ones tonight. We'll give you easy ones. Not sick ones," I promised. "Oh, thanks so much, Damian. It means a lot."

"It'll be nice to have some friends at home," Damian said, rubbing his cheek against JJ's head. "I just hope I have enough fish scraps left for JJ once I have to give them to my fosters," he teased.

"Don't say that too loud or he'll bite you," I said.

Chapter 20

I got back from Damian's just as Lucas was pulling up. I lifted JJ out of the car as Lucas opened the door to let Ollie hop out. But he wasn't alone. A little black doodle-looking dog popped his head up in the back window, waiting for his turn. Lucas reached in and grabbed the leash before letting the little dog out of the car.

I crouched down to get kisses from Ollie and the other dog, who strained to reach me. His—or her—little stubby tail wagged. JJ stood as far away from the newcomer as possible, glaring. "Who is this?" I asked, laughing as the two of them licked me almost to death. "Hi Ollie. Yes, I see you." I rubbed Ollie's head reassuringly.

"This is Walter. The dog Katrina dropped off last minute. She couldn't get back to pick him up." He hesitated. "Okay if he hangs out tonight?"

"Of course. I guess this means I don't have to ask how your day was." I stood, wiping dog slobber off my cheek and standing up again.

"Busy," Lucas said.

"You look tired." I reached up and touched his cheek.

"You too tired to go trapping tonight? It's totally okay if you are."

"Never. When do you want to go?"

"We can leave around eight? I'll get us dinner and snacks. We can have a picnic."

He grinned. "Sounds good to me."

I hugged him. "You're the best." I was pretty sure Lucas wasn't totally jazzed about the idea, but he was good at pretending. I really had lucked out with him. And at least we got to hang out. We'd both been busy lately, and we hadn't been able to spend a ton of time together.

"Hey, you think Walter will be okay, though?" he asked. "He likes cats?"

"I think so. He seems to like everything." We both observed the little dog, who sat at our feet staring adoringly at both of us. "He's a schnoodle," Lucas said.

"He looks like a stuffed animal. Let's bring him in and get him acquainted."

But Val had already seen him from the window and rushed outside as we came in. "Who is this?" she squealed, dropping down in front of Walter.

I exchanged looks with Lucas. My sister had never been as animal crazy as I was. She loved JJ and she seemed to like the cafe cats, which was helpful since she lived here, but she didn't lose her mind over them. But now she looked downright smitten.

"This is Walter," Lucas told her. "He's visiting tonight."

"And we have to go out," I added. "Can you watch him?"

"I would love to," Val said, scooping up her new friend. "He's the cutest thing I've ever seen!" She rushed inside with him.

"Hey! What about JJ and Ollie?" I called after her, but she already wasn't listening.

Ollie let out a woof of disapproval and looked at me imploringly. "I know," I said, rubbing his ears. "You're the cutest. Along with JJ. Let's go get a snack."

Once we'd sorted out the animals and the food situation, I packed us some snacks, waters, and cans of cat food for the traps, put JJ's harness back on—he hated to be left behind—and called in an order of sushi. Then Lucas helped me load the traps into the car before we picked up our food and headed out to Laurel's.

The sky was streaked with pinks and oranges as the sun finished going down over the ocean. It would be just getting dark when we arrived, which was safer for the real scaredy cats—that would be when they felt more comfortable venturing out. I planned on setting traps in Laurel's yard and down at the notorious playground, then we'd wait in the car until someone, or multiple someones, wandered into them. I also needed to go inside and put some food out for the remaining cats.

"You're quiet," Lucas said after a while. He had offered to drive, and we were on the coastal road leading to Fisherman's Cove. I had the windows rolled down to enjoy the scent of the ocean. It always cleared my head.

I glanced over at him. "Sorry. Just thinking about the cats. And the crazy neighbors." And the sushi, but I didn't need to admit that.

"How many did you say she had?"

"Cats, or crazy neighbors?"

He laughed. "Both, I guess."

"For crazy neighbors, I'm not sure. I mean, they all seem a little crazy. I met one hippie chick who hates the cats and an older lady who was friends with Laurel, but even *she* didn't seem to love the cats. It sounds like there were perhaps multiple others who had issues with her. At least one who called the cops on her. For cats, we're still doing the math. More than sixty."

"That's insane," Lucas said. "How can someone live that way? Was the house disgusting?"

"Oddly enough, the living space wasn't as bad as I expected. The basement, though . . ." I made a face. "Gross." I glanced at him. "Hopefully you don't think we're that crazy at the cafe." I was kind of kidding, but I wanted to be sure. Especially since we'd already gone way beyond my original intention of ten. It was inevitable, I supposed. Once the word got out that you were a safe haven for animals, they tended to show up from all different places.

"Not like that," he said. "We're a place of business. And we have the means to care for them."

I loved that he used *we*. "I know. I'm just really sensitive about how people look at cat caretakers. Not that Laurel was what I would call a caretaker, but you know what I mean. Anything over two usually gets you labeled with something derogatory."

"And since when do you care what people think?" Lucas asked.

He had a point. "You're right. I don't."

I scanned the road as we approached Laurel's. Something told me not to park in her driveway, although I wasn't sure why. Instead, I had Lucas pull up to the curb opposite her house.

As he turned the car off, he glanced at me. "I'm sorry about the dog."

"Why are you sorry? He's adorable!"

"I know, but your house is crowded, and I shouldn't have

just brought him over like that. I could've brought him to my place, but then I couldn't have come with you tonight."

"Lucas. Are you kidding? I'm more than happy to have Walter stay with us. Val is clearly more than happy to have him. Besides, I would've been bummed if you couldn't come with me."

Relief washed over his face. "I was worried you'd be mad. I know you've taken in a lot more lately."

I waved him off. "Never. There's always room for one more. Just don't tell Katrina I said that. Now. Let's set some traps before we eat. I'm going to set most of them up in her yard, and a couple in the park down the street. I heard they like to hang out there and that was one of the problems."

"Problems?" Lucas got out and hefted a few of the traps from the back seat.

"Yeah." I dropped my voice and looked around to make sure Delaney wasn't eavesdropping from her front porch. No one seemed to be around. The neighborhood was quiet. Lights were on in most houses. Delaney's, though, was dark. Bea's too. I filled him in on Delaney's complaints. "I think she thought I was going to give her sympathy."

"I'm sure she figured out she came to the wrong person." Lucas chuckled and followed me into the yard.

I set up three traps in various spots around the yard, including one on the back porch. I tried the back door to make sure it was still unlocked. It was. Once we'd set the traps up in the park, I'd go in and put food out.

I opened cans of food, slid them into the traps, and tested the springs to make sure they worked. Havaharts simply closed the door behind the cat when they walked over the tripping mechanism. They hated being confined like that, but it didn't hurt them in any way.

Once we were done, we headed back to the SUV. There

were two traps left, and I figured I could set them in the bushes around the park. We drove over there to scope it out. It was getting dark, so there were no kids or families playing, which was good. I didn't want to call attention to myself or what we were doing. The people around here seemed like they were good at kicking up a stink about things, and I didn't want to do anything else that could hurt the cats.

We got out and walked around. The playground was fairly small, but it had a decent slide and a little jungle-gym setup. A lot nicer than the ones I remembered from when I was a kid, which had been metal and made your hands all rusty and calloused if you used them too much. I used to love the monkey bars, though—I'd always make a run for the middle bar in the playground. It was the one physical activity I actually cared about enough to fight for.

Just then, a sound caught my attention. I stopped and listened next to a small grouping of shrubs. It was faint, but I could hear it if I was super quiet. A tiny rustling noise.

I turned to Lucas. "We'll put one here, and one over there." I pointed to a darker area of the park, away from the playground equipment. "Do you have the food?"

Lucas handed me a can of food. I took the trap and set it up under the shrubs so it was as secluded as possible. I didn't see any cats running out of the bushes, so I hoped that meant they were hungry and would go into the trap for the food as soon as we left.

Lucas set up the other trap and we went back to his car. "Want to wait here, or go back to the house?"

"Let's go back to the house. I need to leave food inside for those guys, and we can check those traps," I said. "Then we can eat, and we'll wrap it up by midnight at the latest, unless we fill the traps before then. That work?"

Lucas nodded. "You're the boss."

I laughed. "Love it. Usually cats are the only ones I can boss around, and they don't even listen to me."

As we drove back down the street toward Laurel's, I saw a car coming the other way. Headlights off. Frowning, I slowed down to see where it was going. And watched it turn into Laurel's driveway.

Lucas saw it too and glanced at me. "Who's that?"

"I don't know." I pulled to the curb a couple houses down and killed my own lights. Which didn't help me see the person who stepped out of the car. But then those motion lights that Delaney hated so much saved the day. As the person rounded the side of the house, apparently heading to the back door, the light switched on, illuminating Bill the boyfriend's face. He cringed a little when the light came on and looked around, then bolted toward the back of Laurel's house. To the back door that I had left unlocked.

Chapter 21

I wasn't sure what to make of this. What was Bill doing creeping around here at night with the lights off?

"Do you know who that is?" Lucas asked.

"Yeah. It's the hoarder's boyfriend. I'm not sure what he's doing, though. Especially in the dark. He never went in her house, he said." I turned off the car engine and looked at Lucas. "Are you coming in?"

He stared at me. "In the house? Now?"

"Yeah. I need to feed the cats and I want to know what he's doing."

"Maddie. I don't know if that's the best idea. Do you know anything about this guy? What will he say about you being inside?"

I shrugged. "He told me I could get the cats. I'm sure it's fine."

"I don't know, Maddie—" Lucas began, but I was already out of the car, decision made.

He jumped out and followed me. "You're just going to walk in?"

"Why not? I'm the one who left the door open for everyone." I headed around to the back door, noticing on the way that one of my traps had a cat in it. Sweet. "Look. We got one. Want to put the cat in the car?" I asked Lucas.

"After. I'm going in with you first," he said through gritted teeth.

I stifled a smile. Lucas still wasn't quite used to my headstrong tendencies.

The back door was closed, but thankfully not locked. I pushed it open, rapping my knuckles on it at the same time. "Hello?"

No answer. I shrugged and felt around for the light in the kitchen. When I turned it on, I heard little pattering feet running for a hiding place. *Still more cats to go,* I thought, resigned. "Hello?" I called again, louder this time. I could feel Lucas behind me, his body tense.

Footsteps sounded on the living room stairs, then Bill appeared in the doorway. "Who—oh. Maddie. Here for cats?" He held a black briefcase-like bag against his chest, a little too tightly, his gaze going to Lucas, who'd stepped up protectively next to me.

"Yes. I figured I'd try our luck at trapping some of the outdoor ones now that it's dark out." I glanced curiously at the bag, wondering if I could push my luck and ask him what was in it.

He looked behind me to where Lucas had appeared. "Good. And your friends, they're okay? After the run-in with the police today?"

I nodded. "They're fine. They're tough ladies."

"Good," he said again, but I didn't think he was really listening. "Well, I hope you get them all." Still holding the bag tight against him, he started to go around me to get out the door.

"Still no keys?" I asked casually, shifting my weight so that I was kind of blocking the door.

Bill paused, and I could tell he was impatient to leave. "No. I mean, not that I found. I wasn't looking for those. I'd lent Laurel a spare computer and I figured I'd come grab it. I knew you had left the door unlocked so you could get the cats. I really have to go," he said. "Good luck." And he slipped around me and out the door.

Lucas and I watched him go, then he glanced at me. "Weird."

"Yeah," I said. "It seemed like kind of a weird relationship."

"I guess so, if he didn't know she had all these cats." Lucas shook his head. Then he pulled me close and hugged me. "I'd want you to know if I was a crazy cat guy," he said into my hair.

I laughed. "Are you hiding cats somewhere and haven't told me?"

"No. I just mean . . ." He sighed. "I want you to know everything about me. And I want to know everything about you."

My heart felt so full I thought I might cry. Instead, I kissed him. "Well, you definitely know how many cats I have. And you've stuck around this long."

"Try and get rid of me," he said.

While I put food and water out for the cats upstairs and down in the basement of horrors, Lucas loaded the first trap and its resident into the car, then we settled in to eat our sushi. When I reached into my bag hoping to find some napkins I'd forgotten to ask for at the restaurant, I realized Laurel's paperwork was stuffed in there. Maybe that would be a good way to pass the time, as long as we didn't dump soy sauce all over them.

I pulled the stack out of my bag, along with a couple of

crumpled napkins I'd found, and gave Lucas my best winning smile. "Since we're here, want to help me look for vet paperwork?"

He popped a dynamite roll into his mouth and chewed before answering. "I knew I shouldn't have believed your promises about a make-out session." He held out a hand. "Sure. What am I looking for?"

"You'll get your make-out session later. It will be even better if you can find me information we can match up with any cats." I handed over the bottom half of the stack. "Just anything from a vet hospital."

"Okay, but I get the last spring roll."

"It's yours." I handed him the container and started flipping through the papers in front of me. The first folder contained paperwork for some work Laurel had done on her house—floor repair. There was an estimate in there for a sunroom too, but since she didn't have one I figured it had been too expensive. At twenty thousand, I could see why. She didn't look like she had a lot of cash lying around. Then again, not all rich people looked rich.

I closed that file and put it aside in the "return to her house" pile, then opened the next one. It had some doctor records. I felt nosy looking through them, but I wanted to see if perhaps there was some clue about why she'd fallen down the stairs. Did she have multiple sclerosis? Parkinson's? Or had it really just been as simple as slipping and falling? For someone as clumsy as I was, that was scary.

But the doctor visits were related to a sinus infection and to results from a mammogram from three years ago. No problems. I put that file aside too. I went through similar exercises with a few more folders. Some stuff looked to be work related. Lots of meeting minutes and town correspondence.

"Here's some," Lucas said, waving a few papers at me.

"Thank goodness," I said. "I feel kind of like a Peeping Tom going through the minutia of this woman's life. We need at least some return on investment." I scanned the receipts he handed me. Sadly, the cat information was sparse. A cat named Toby had gone in for an upper respiratory illness. It seemed to be chronic because he'd been back twice. I wondered if he was one of the poor guys in the basement snotting all over the wall. Another cat, known only as "calico female," had been spayed. I tried to remember if I'd seen a calico in the cats we'd already sprung, but they were all blending together. Maybe if I found her, Mrs. Hennessy could take her. And finally, a batch of four black kittens had been treated for parasites.

"Six out of sixty or so isn't such a great number," I said.

"Hey, it's something. She kept really old receipts, though," Lucas said.

"I'm sure her hoarder tendencies spill over into other things. It's just not as apparent." I went back to my paperwork and found the credit card statements that had been stuffed in the shredder. I flipped through them. No vet charges. No charges at all, but there were two cash advances on her Citibank card from last month, one for two thousand dollars and one for four. I took a closer look at the scribbles. Notes that I could barely decipher, phone numbers, names of customer-service representatives, by the looks of it, along with account numbers. And some nonpayment notices from Chase and Citi. Dated recently. All within the last four weeks.

I flipped open the next manila folder. More credit card statements. They had scribbles on them too, and some charges were circled. More cash advances, going back three months, ranging from one thousand all the way up to six thousand. The statements all had notations on them—names and numbers circled with an angry red pen. Question marks next to the cash advances. There were also late fees and interest charges.

"Hmmm," I said out loud.

Lucas glanced up. "What?"

"Looks like she was having some financial issues." I showed him the papers.

Lucas studied them. "Questioning charges or something. Maybe her card got stolen?"

"Yeah. Before May, everything looks fine." No scribbles, no phone numbers. Then I noticed something else. A couple of copies of checks stuffed in the middle of the papers. Big checks. Three for twenty thousand dollars each, to be exact. I sucked in a breath and checked the payees. Cavanaugh's Boat Repair. All three checks. I remembered the pickup truck with that name plastered on the door that had showed up earlier today. Laurel's boyfriend's business.

Where had Laurel gotten sixty grand? All the credit card advances? Then why was she questioning them—if that's what all this meant?

I sat back, the wheels in my brain starting to turn. Why was a woman who lived in a tired old house with way too many cats who clearly weren't getting much-needed medical care writing out checks for sixty thousand dollars to her boyfriend? I pulled out my phone and opened the calculator, tallying up the amounts that were circled on her card. They only totaled thirty-two thousand, roughly half the amount of the checks. Unless there were other statements that weren't in this pile.

Sixty thousand dollars was a lot of money. Was she paying it back from a loan he had made for her? If she was paying back a loan, why would he make her take out cash advances on her credit card? Was he that desperate for money that he didn't care about the effects it would have on her? Had she owed him more than this—or promised him more than this? Where on earth was she supposed to be getting it? Unless she was secretly wealthy or at least had a stash of money somewhere. But then why was she using her credit cards?

Lucas had noticed the change in my concentration. "I think your pile is more interesting than mine," he said. "What else did you find?"

I handed him the checks wordlessly. He let out a low whistle. "That seems out of character," he said. "I mean, not that I knew her, but if this is any indication . . ." He waved at the house, the street.

"Yeah." It didn't sit right with me either. I picked up my phone and googled the business. Cavanaugh's looked to be a small shop—and kind of run down, if the pictures were recent—and Bill Cavanaugh was listed as the proprietor. I browsed the website, but it was pretty basic. A list of services, a map to their location, a resource link to local activities, weather, tide reports. There was a sales link, but the page it took me to gave me an error message. Apparently, Bill had no boats to sell at the moment.

I went back to the search-results page to see if I could find anything else on Bill's business, but there wasn't much. A few testimonials that were overall positive, a link to a Facebook page that hadn't had any activity since last summer.

"Hey, look," Lucas said, poking me. I peered past him out the open window at a cat cautiously making its way to one of the traps. We both held our breath as it paused outside, sniffing. That's why I liked to use the smelliest cat food I could find, or even tuna fish if I had it on hand. The cats couldn't resist.

This one was no different. As we watched, he crept into

the trap. I felt a surge of victory as the door clicked shut behind him.

Lucas high-fived me. "I'll grab him," he said, and got out of the car. I watched him head over to the trap, but my attention drifted back to Laurel's finances, sitting right in my lap. There was a small alarm bell that had dinged in my head a couple times since we'd found her yesterday, but the dinging was getting louder the more I learned. Any one thing could possibly be chalked up to me overreacting: Laurel's two open doors, the missing purse and cell phone, the recent robberies. But now there was weird financial stuff on top of it? Not to mention the neighbors who clearly had issues with her and her cats? Something was starting to smell fishy, and I was sure it wasn't only the cat food.

Lucas came back to the car, triumphant, and loaded the cat in next to his friend. "The others are still empty, though," he said.

I smiled, trying to show him I was paying attention. Whatever he said next was drowned out by the sudden, harsh shrill of sirens disturbing the silence of the evening. I waited until the noise had passed before I spoke. "It's almost eleven. I think we can call it a night."

He nodded. "I closed the other traps and left the food out in front."

"Thanks. We'll have to run over to the park and get those traps too."

As we headed down the street, I could hear more sirens in the distance. Probably a fire or something. I sent some good vibes to whoever was having a tough night. I figured if it was a big story I'd hear about it tomorrow when we were back in town.

Chapter 22

When I woke the next morning, I was surprised to find it was nearly seven. That was late for me, but we'd gotten back late and had to get the two cats we'd trapped settled in Grandpa Leo's basement room. They both immediately bolted for hiding places under the couch and a table. I was hoping they'd get used to us like the others had and come out eventually, but I had to give it time. The others had adjusted really well, mostly not running for cover when people came downstairs anymore. They were all very sweet, and I knew once they were medically cleared they'd be easy to adopt. I'd sat with the cats in the basement for a few more minutes, trying to empty my mind of thoughts and get in a short meditation.

It hadn't worked. I'd been so revved up from everything that it wasn't surprising, so I'd given up and gone to bed wondering if I'd be able to sleep at all. But the stress and adrenaline of the past few days, and the corresponding lack of sleep, had clearly exhausted me. I hadn't even heard Lucas get up, but he and the dogs must've headed out to the salon because JJ and I were alone in bed. JJ was wrapped around my head like a furry hat. Some people complained that their cats woke them up early to eat in the mornings, but JJ was happy to snuggle and sleep until I got up. Which I thought was the sweetest thing ever.

Since I didn't want to disturb him, I thought it would be a good time to sneak in a short meditation practice. I'd been highly unsuccessful to date at my ten minutes daily, although one could hardly blame me given the circumstances. Still, if I didn't get better at this fast, the retreat would be unbearable. Especially with Val hovering around, probably laughing at my attempts to act like I belonged.

I reached for my phone on the nightstand without disturbing JJ. As I scrolled to the downloaded meditations, I saw a text from my mother.

Madalyn. Are you ever going to call me back???

I groaned. "Yes, Mom, I promise. Right after I meditate," I said out loud, then turned on one of the meditations Cass had sent me. I settled in and closed my eyes. The man's voice for this one was soothing and after a minute or two I felt my mind settle, focusing on the sounds of the morning outside my window. I let the mantra the voice repeated set the pace of my breathing, and felt it relax into a steady rhythm. I was starting to like it in my little cocoon.

Then JJ stretched, his paw coming to rest on my cheek. Then I felt him tense up. Then he vaulted off the bed, using my cheek as a springboard, sending what felt like the pricks of ten needles into my face.

Letting out a screech, I sat up, holding my palm to my cheek. When I removed it, I saw blood. Plus, his other paw had landed right on my eyeball. No claws were involved and my eye had been closed, but still. I could feel my eye watering uncontrollably, water running down my cheek and dripping into my lap.

"Are you kidding me?" I said to him, grabbing a tissue

for my bleeding cheek and pressing my other fist to my closed, throbbing eye.

He sat at the closed door and squeaked. I assumed it wasn't an apology.

"That was so rude." I jabbed at the phone to shut the soothing voice off and got up, opening the door for him. When he raced out, I closed it behind him. That would serve him right.

I laid back down, pressing one tissue to my cheek and the other to my eye. I should start again. But a million reasons why I couldn't right now shouted loudly at me—*I was injured, blinded; I have to check on the new cats; I wonder if there's coffee; who's on the schedule for the cafe today; we need to get the rest of the cats at Laurel's; what the heck is up with the sixty thousand dollars; what really happened at Laurel's house that night; what does my mother WANT, already?*

With a groan, I dropped my tissues and pulled the pillow over my head. Cass would say that these are the things I had to work through to get to that right state of mind that would let me meditate. Truth was, I was weak. So instead of trying again, I got up and went into the bathroom where I splashed cold water into my eye, washed the blood off my face, brushed my teeth, and pulled my long hair into a messy bun, resigning myself to a marathon meditation session later, promising my reflection that I would get my brain in gear. The thought that had come racing into my mind—*What really happened at Laurel's that night?*— seemed to have jostled loose at some point during the night, or maybe during my abbreviated meditation. And I couldn't shake it. I needed to think that through more. Maybe coffee would help.

I headed into the kitchen where Ethan, Val, and Grandpa

all congregated, which was lovely after a couple days of me being so absent. As cranky as my failed meditation session and subsequent injury had made me, I did love the familiar sight of them: Grandpa at the table with coffee and one of Ethan's freshly baked muffins; Val on her iPad with a notebook open next to her, working on an event; and Ethan at the counter working on some new culinary creation. I loved my family. I even loved living with them, which had surprised me when I realized it. After a decade of living mostly alone, I'd worried about feeling crowded and like I had no privacy in this situation. Instead, I realized that it was comforting to constantly be surrounded by people I loved, and who loved me back.

They all turned to look at me.

"What the heck happened to your face?" Val asked.

Leave it to Val to bring things back to reality. My hand defensively went to cover the gash on my cheek. "Nothing. I was meditating."

Val and Ethan looked quizzically at each other. "In that case, Mads, I think you might have been doing it wrong," Ethan said, sounding apologetic at having to tell me this.

I gave him a look. "JJ jumped on my face while I was meditating."

"Well, he was pretty hungry." Grandpa indicated the floor where JJ licked one of his bowls clean. "You probably took too long."

"Of course. It's all my fault. So much for family loyalty. Is it that bad?" I pressed my fingertips to my cheek to see if it was still bleeding.

"It gives you character," Ethan said, sliding a mug full of steaming black coffee across the table.

"Great. Just what I need. Thank you." I took the mug and sat down. "Are you working on Cass's event?" I asked

Val. "What kind of food will there be? And can you smuggle in some coffee?"

"Nope. Cass said no coffee. I'm actually working on one of my other events today though. A high school reunion. And I just got a wedding for next summer." She grinned. "Who knew I'd get to be a wedding planner too?"

I had no idea why that was a good thing, but to each her own, I guess. Big weddings weren't my thing. "That's great. Whose wedding?"

"One of Mom's friends' kids."

"Really? Who?"

"Nicole Jennings. Remember her? I think she's Sam's age." Our youngest sister was twenty-seven.

"She's getting married? Yikes." I tried to picture Sam married and fell miserably short. Our sister was a free spirit, floating around the spiritual world trying to find her calling. She'd explored it all: Reiki, sound healing, chakra balancing, tarot, Lord only knew what else. Right now, she was teaching yoga at a new studio downtown while living with our parents.

Val shrugged. "Sometimes it works. I certainly wasn't a good example, but still."

"Yeah." An image of me and Lucas on a beach in wedding gear flashed into my head. Mortified, I shoved it out, feeling red splotches rise on my cheeks. I'd never really let myself think about that. Usually my relationships crashed and burned, so I didn't allow it. Things were going so well with us, and I didn't want to ruin it by bringing those crazy thoughts into the picture. Bad enough I was thinking about broaching the living-together subject. "You got Ethan catering for you yet?"

"I might contract him for the wedding cake." She smiled sweetly at him when he turned. "Forgot to tell you."

"You might need to hire a bakery assistant," I said to him.

Ethan grinned. "I could do a lot with an assistant. Speaking of which, I did hire someone. He starts today. We might need to expand the cafe, though, if we're going to cater. There's room to build out the garage—"

I held up a hand to cut him off. I'd had enough of contractors and expansions for a couple of years, at least. "I'm going to go check on the cats downstairs," I said, and hurried out with my coffee.

My first thought as I stepped into the basement was, *I'm glad Grandpa didn't come down here first!* Clearly the cats were settling in well to their new surroundings. The cats from the first batch were no longer hiding at all. In fact, they looked like they'd been having a raucous party to celebrate their liberation from their former situation. Litter was scattered from one end of the room to the other. The half-black, half-white one lounged on Grandpa's pool table. I prayed he hadn't scratched it up. Two were snuggled up on the couch, and the other seemed to be pretty comfortable on Grandpa's minibar, his long body entwined around the whiskey decanter. I could see one of the new ones from last night poking its little face out from under the couch, peering uncertainly at me.

"Well then," I said to the newly brazen ones, crossing my arms and surveying the scene in front of me. "I take it you like it here? You should tell the newbies to come out and join you."

None of them even reacted. Which was a good sign. Before, whenever anyone came into the room they'd bolt and hide. Now they gave me the JJ response—one eye open, a judgment about how I'd woken them up, then back to sleep.

I put out food and water and left them to it. I picked up my coffee—it needed a refill—and turned to go back upstairs, pulling my phone out of my pocket. I'd been so distracted by my face that I hadn't noticed the little red circle indicating I had a voice mail hovering at the top right of my phone icon. The missed call indicated it was from Cass. I played it, half listening as I thought about topping off my coffee and what I needed to do first this morning.

Then I snapped to attention, almost dropping the mug. I jabbed viciously at my phone to play it again, which was hard to do with only one hand—the same hand holding the phone.

Then ran up the rest of the stairs, shouting for Grandpa.

Chapter 23

"Madalyn, you need to take a breath and let me get some information."

Grandpa was at his desk in his basement office. We'd come back down after listening to Cass's voice mail, which informed me that he'd spent the night at the police station in Fisherman's Cove after Jonathan Arquette, the assistant town administrator and applicant for the permanent job, was found dead. Murdered, apparently, and Cass had come across his body in the parking lot of the town hall when he'd gone there for their rendezvous last night after the town meeting. Now I couldn't get a hold of Cass, even though he said they'd let him come home.

I thought of the sirens Lucas and I had heard as we were leaving Laurel's and felt a pit in my stomach.

After I'd gone screaming to Grandpa, he had started making phone calls. He didn't tell me to whom, but I supposed that was the key to the *private* part of "private investigator." Still, I didn't have a lot of grace to give in times like these.

After three calls, two of which he couldn't reach the person, he put the phone down and thought for a moment. "He definitely said they let him go home?"

I nodded. Cass's message had left me unnerved. His voice had risen and fallen like waves in a rough sea, and I hadn't caught every word. Even worse, it had resonated with fear, which I'd never heard before from Cass. Cass wasn't afraid of anything. And if he was scared, well, that didn't bode well.

"What was he doing there again?" Grandpa asked. "At the scene?"

"Meeting Jonathan." I thought of Jonathan's eager, fresh-faced demeanor yesterday on Laurel's porch. Even in the face of tragedy, he'd still looked optimistic and hopeful. And now he was dead. Even worse, Cass had distinctly said "murdered." That particular word had come through loud and clear. "I heard him confirm that Cass would meet him after the town meeting."

"You know why?"

I shook my head. "Cass thought he wanted to talk about more programming, but he wasn't sure. They were kind of buds. Jonathan is the one who got him involved in the Fisherman's Cove community in the first place." I picked up my cell phone and called Cass again. Voice mail. Again. I tossed the phone on the desk with a cry of frustration.

Grandpa's phone rang. He picked it up and said tersely, "Mancini." He paused. "Mick. What's going on?"

Sergeant Mick Ellory was Katrina's boyfriend and one of the cops on the Daybreak Harbor force. Mick had come to the force after Grandpa retired, but they had gotten acquainted fairly quickly given Grandpa's continued involvement in all things crime on Daybreak Island. Also because I had been under suspicion of murder last summer, and Mick had been the one investigating the case. Mick and I had a very shaky relationship for a while, but once he'd started dating Katrina and she'd become, well, happy, I'd grudgingly conceded that it was time to let our past go and embrace him as a good guy.

Grandpa was still listening. As usual, his face gave nothing away. After five minutes of near silence I was ready to jump out of my skin. "So they're loaning you out," he said. More silence. "Okay. Thanks for letting me know."

He hung up and looked at me. I willed myself not to shout at him to tell me whatever it was. Grandpa hated being rushed.

"That was Mick."

"I gathered," I said through gritted teeth.

"He got a call this morning from McAuliffe." The new chief, and Grandpa's replacement. None of us were fans. Including, I think, Mick. "He's getting loaned out."

I frowned. "To where?" I hoped it wasn't off-island. Katrina would be crushed if it was a long assignment. He helped her out with the animal stuff sometimes now. Not that he really had a choice. She kind of demanded it.

"Fisherman's Cove."

I let that sink in. "For this murder?"

Grandpa nodded. "They don't have detectives up there. Too small, not enough major crime."

He said it so seriously it made me smile a little. Major crime here on the island was a lot different than major crime in, say, Boston, or even one of its suburbs. There wasn't really major crime out here to speak of. Notwithstanding the few murders that had occurred over the past year.

"Daybreak Harbor has the biggest force, the most detectives. And Mick has been making a name for himself. And he said he's taking Craig to work it with him."

"Wow. That's big." Craig was certainly on his way to a detective shield himself soon. He'd become Ellory's right hand of late, working the high-profile cases. "So that's good, right? Did he call you just to tell you that?"

"No. He heard about Cass and wanted to make sure you and I knew, since he knew you were involved with the other situation up there."

Laurel. I'd nearly forgotten about her since I heard Cass's voice mail. But a horrifying *what if* was starting to race around in my mind.

"Grandpa," I said. "I mentioned the other day how I was concerned about Laurel's death maybe not being an accident. After yesterday, I'm starting to feel like I'm not just imagining things." I filled him in on the burglaries Delaney Mathews had told me about, the credit card statements and apparent nonpayment problems Laurel was having, and the sixty grand worth of checks she'd written to her boyfriend. "And now Jonathan . . ."

Grandpa nodded slowly. "They worked together."

"Yes. She was on the budget committee for the town. Word on the street was she didn't like him much. Actively tried to stop him from getting the job."

This caught Grandpa's interest. "Where did you hear that?"

"From Arquette himself. He showed up at her house yesterday morning when we were there clearing cats out." I cocked my head at Grandpa. "You think these deaths could be connected?" I couldn't imagine how, but with my head spinning the way it was, it was no wonder.

Grandpa made a note on a small pad of paper in front of him. "Too soon to tell. If they'd been on the same side of some hot-button issue it would make for a more compelling connection, but maybe there's something under the surface. But the financial component is certainly interesting." He thought for a moment then looked up, tapping the pen against his desktop. "Let's talk to Mick. Meantime, you said you have all that paperwork?"

I nodded. "Upstairs in my bag."

"Then let's go take a look, shall we?"

Chapter 24

Grandpa followed me upstairs. I ran up to my bedroom and retrieved my bag from where I'd dropped it on the floor the night before and rushed back down, pulling out the stack of papers as I did. I handed them to Grandpa as the doorbell rang.

"You read. I'll get that." I headed to the front door and yanked it open.

Katrina waited impatiently on the porch, her finger poised to ring the bell again until she saw me. "Kittens," she said, thrusting a carrier full of squirming, squealing babies at me.

I peered inside. There were four babies, grayish-white tiger cats with black stripes, medium-haired, and adorable as heck.

But I didn't remember kittens this small at Laurel's. And they seemed awfully healthy. Unless Adele had found them. I glanced at Katrina. "Laurel had kittens too? When did we get these guys?"

She had the grace to blush. "I swapped out some planned Laurel cats for them. I figured these little cuties will get adopted faster." When I opened my mouth to protest, she said, "And I'm saving you from having to do a lot of meds.

The ones I was going to bring over have some problems. Minor ones, but will still need special care."

"Katrina." I sighed. "That's all well and good, but why do I have the feeling you're still going to bring more of Laurel's cats over?"

"Because I am," Katrina said, flashing me her most angelic smile.

"Well, I brought two more cats back last night from trapping who moved in downstairs already. How many are we talking?" I asked.

She blew me a noncommittal kiss. "Not sure yet. I'll let you know later. I'm going by Dr. Kelly's now to check on his progress." And with that, she turned to leave.

"Hey," I called. "I met the dog you dropped off at Lucas's place." I raised an eyebrow at her, letting her know that I knew what she was up to.

Katrina turned back, shading her eyes from the sun. "You did? Isn't he cute?" She blinked innocently at me. "Picked him up on the side of Atlantic Highway. I'm trying to find an owner, but he looked pretty rough. Matted, dirty, like he's been on his own for a while. Thanks so much for doing this, by the way. He really needed a foster. He's too timid to be in the kennel."

Before I could register what she was actually saying, she waved and trotted down the front steps and back to the van.

I opened my mouth to call after her, then closed it again. Apparently, she'd had no intention of taking Walter back after his grooming appointment. Her asking Lucas to look after him last night was just a way to open the door. I couldn't help but laugh. She was good.

As if on cue, my cell vibrated in my back pocket. Lucas. *Hey babe. Hope you're having a good morning. Didn't want to wake you—you were exhausted. I have something to run by you when you have a minute.*

I think I already know, I texted back, adding a smiley emoji so he wouldn't worry. *I'll call you soon. In the middle of something.*

I headed into the cafe with the carrier full of mewling babies. They were adorable, I had to admit. I was sure they wouldn't last a week in the cafe before being snapped up. Harry was working. Well, at the moment he was drinking coffee and eating one of Ethan's cheese Danishes. When he saw me, he dropped a napkin over the plate as if he was doing something bad.

I laughed. "You're welcome to eat whatever you want, Harry."

He grinned. "Well, in that case." He popped the rest of the pastry into his mouth and brushed crumbs off his shirt and tie. Harry always wore a dress shirt and tie to the cafe. With jeans, but still. I think part of it was because dressing up to go to work was bred in him, and part of it was to impress Adele.

"We have new residents. Can you help me get them set up?" I placed the carrier down on the counter.

"New residents?" Harry turned the carrier so he could see inside and bent over, wiggling his fingers through the open spaces in the metal door of the carrier. Kittens tumbled over each other, batting playfully at these new toys. Harry laughed. "Delightful. In the stand-alone condo? I think the others can be out and about now. They're big enough."

I looked around the cafe, feeling like I hadn't been around much all week. Things looked different already. Harry and Adele were always moving and rearranging things, partly when they cleaned, and partly, I suspected, just for the fun of it. There was even a new batch of throw pillows on the floor, likely to create an additional seating area for patrons. The colors matched perfectly—it all looked so cozy and the kittens were so cuddly. I'd missed being here.

"I brought those over," Harry said, following my gaze. "People like to sit on the floor and play, you know?"

"They're perfect," I assured him. "Yes, let's move those kittens out of the condo." Harry was right. They were big enough to roam free, especially since we kept the cafe doors closed so the cats couldn't roam the house itself freely. That would give them way too many hiding places.

"Got it. I'll get right on it." Harry picked up the carrier.

As if he'd sensed there were new babies in the house, JJ wandered in to see what was going on.

"Their babysitter has arrived," I said dryly. "He'll supervise. Good luck."

I left Harry to it and hurried back to the kitchen. Cass still hadn't called me back and I was about to get in the car and drive over there to make sure he was okay, but first I wanted to see if Grandpa had any thoughts on Laurel's paperwork.

Chapter 25

When I burst into the kitchen I found Grandpa at the table, poring over the papers I'd left. "You look very engrossed. What do you think? Anything of interest?"

"Still looking," he said without glancing up.

I bit back a sigh. When Grandpa was really focusing, he got like this. Uncommunicative. I appreciated the methodical way he approached these kinds of things, but it was hard for an impatient person like me. But, it was why he'd been so successful in his career. While he trusted his own intuition, he didn't go off half-cocked when an idea or a theory took hold. Instead he balanced between his gut and the facts. "Want some coffee?" I asked.

"Have some, thanks."

I glanced at the mug on the table. It was still full and by the looks of it, cold. "That looks gross."

He didn't answer.

I reached into the cabinet for a mug and poured a cup. The pot was almost empty. I should make more, but it would be just as easy to run out to the cafe if I needed to and grab some from Ethan's domain. I sipped, trying not to stare over Grandpa's shoulder to see what he was reading. Had he found something beyond what had aroused my suspicions? I was dying to know. I realized I was hungry and poked around in the nearest cabinet, where I found a biscotti that was probably Val's, judging from the way it was partially hidden. I took it anyway and brought it to the table, trying not to stare at Grandpa as he continued perusing.

I wasn't very good at this.

As if sensing my efforts, he peered at me over the top of his glasses. "Madalyn. I'm doing what you asked. Let me be for a minute, would you?"

"Fine," I grumbled and dunked my biscotti in my coffee, swirling it around to soften it. Cass would echo Grandpa's sentiments right now if he were here.

Maybe Cass was home meditating and that's why he hadn't called me back.

It seemed like hours passed before Grandpa finally took off his reading glasses and placed them on top of the pile. He picked up his mug, sipped, made a face, then got up to put it in the microwave. He heated it for a minute, took it out, blew on it, then sat down again and focused on me. "Tell me about this Jacobsen."

I made a face. "The weenie."

"Weenie?" he repeated, his lips tipping up in a smile. "Haven't heard that in a while."

"It's true. He was trying to be all *Miami Vice* or something. And he fawned all over the boyfriend. I get the sense they were friends, or at least he knew him well enough to give him special treatment." I frowned at that thought. "Why would the cop be so blasé about this if there were burglaries happening in the neighborhood?"

"Good question," Grandpa said. "Back to the boyfriend. Does he have some kind of standing in the community that would make him somewhat immune?"

"He owns a business. Some boat repair. He was there last night. At her house." I told Grandpa about seeing Bill acting all sketchy driving up with no lights on, going into the house, and leaving with a bag. "He told me he'd lent her a computer and wanted to get it back. It seemed weird that he was going at night, kind of sneaking around."

"It certainly does," Grandpa said. "Especially if he didn't go in her house regularly."

"So you're suspicious too?"

"Let's just say that if it was my force, I'd want to be looking into this."

My stomach flipped. I wasn't sure I wanted to be right. "So, it's possible she was murdered," I said slowly. "Just like Jonathan. You think it was the same killer? The timing is so suspicious. Two people dead in a week, both of unnatural causes, seems . . . highly coincidental."

"No way to tell, yet. We'll have to see if there's anything truly connecting the two of them."

"What about the boyfriend?"

"Surely he'll be a person of interest," Grandpa said. "The checks are curious, certainly, but if she was giving this guy money, why would he kill her?"

"Maybe she loaned it to him and she wanted it back?" But where had she gotten that kind of money in the first place?

Grandpa sipped his coffee before he answered. "Possibly. But also, she'd filed a police report." He flipped the folder open again and pulled out a piece of notebook paper that looked like it had been hastily torn from a spiral-bound notebook. There were a couple of series of numbers on it. I'd seen it, but it hadn't meant anything to me. "This?" He tapped the numbers with his middle finger. "These are police report numbers. One for theft. And this one? Burglary."

I'd totally missed that. I pulled the paper closer and studied it, then looked up at Grandpa. "She reported a computer and a toaster oven stolen." I thought about that. If her computer had been stolen, then borrowing one from Bill wasn't a stretch. But if a burglar had already targeted her house and taken what he thought was valuable, why would he come back and try again? It didn't make sense. And a toaster oven? Really? You could buy those things for thirty bucks on Amazon.

"So what's next?" I asked Grandpa. "I still haven't reached Cass. Should we talk to Mick? He'll need to know this. And what about the sister? Did you track her down? Can we get Mick to talk to her? She might know something too."

"Whoa, slow down," Grandpa said. "He's tied up with last night's events right now. He's going to call me back when things quiet down a bit. Meantime, let's take a ride to Cass's place."

I was grateful Grandpa was thinking along the same lines I was, because I was starting to get worried. "Hey," I said suddenly. "You never told me how Arquette died."

"Not for public consumption, but blunt force trauma," he said. "They think the weapon was a brick they found nearby."

Chapter 26

A brick. I vaguely remembered Jonathan telling me that they were unveiling the bricks from the playground fundraiser at the town meeting last night. Had he been killed with his own fundraising prop? It seemed so ironic. And awful.

I hurried upstairs to get dressed. Val was coming down, texting as she did so. "Don't fall," I said, wincing as she nearly missed a step.

She glanced up, then gauged the rest of the steps. "I'm fine. What are you up to?"

"I just . . . have to go see Cass." I didn't think Val had overheard any of my conversation with Grandpa and I didn't want to offer up anything. She was still a bit traumatized by the murder that had occurred earlier in the summer, where she'd actually been the one to stumble upon a body. I didn't want to bring the *M* word up to her again. "What are *you* up to?"

"Meetings, planning, the usual," she said with a grin. "Gotta go!" She headed for the door with a wave.

I let out a breath and headed upstairs, where I showered quickly and threw on some clothes. I grabbed some flip-flops and ran back downstairs. Grandpa had gone up to change too and wasn't back yet. I thought about grabbing more coffee, then decided I would be way too wired, so instead I poked my head into the cafe. Adele and Clarissa had joined Harry. Adele was at the counter, muttering at the schedule. Clarissa was busy snapping photos of the cats in between cleaning. I could see Adele giving her the stink eye, which I made a mental note to tell her to stop doing. I needed Clarissa doing marketing and social. Which reminded me, I needed to talk to her about the marketing plans. And JJ, who I'd been looking for, sat sentry in front of the new kittens' condo.

Adele glanced up when she saw me come in. "We need more volunteers with more cats coming in," she said without preamble.

I'd hoped to sneak by her and go talk to Clarissa, but I resigned myself to this conversation. "Good morning to you too."

"Morning," she said. "Are we going back today to get more cats? Do you have any updates from Katrina?" Adele was definitely all business. Cat business, at least.

"She just dropped off those kittens," I said, nodding at the condo where Harry was busy hanging feather toys from the top for the kittens to play with. "She was going to see Dr. Kelly this morning to get a handle on things. I know she found some foster homes. We're getting there."

"Okay. So what's the plan for today?" Adele thrust her hands onto her hips and looked at me expectantly.

I willed myself to have more patience than I actually did at this moment. My nerves were already frayed. "Are you feeling okay about going back? After yesterday?"

She snorted. "You mean with those joker cops? 'Course I am. Bring it on. Let them arrest an old lady and see how fast I sue their sorry behinds."

Harry glanced over, nodding approvingly. "You tell 'em, honey!"

Oh, boy. "I don't think we'll get to that point, but I wanted to make sure you and Dinah were okay."

"Dinah was being a baby about it but I got her to shake it off. So, what's the plan?"

"I don't have one yet, but if you want to go ahead that's fine. Grandpa and I have to run an errand this morning." I didn't elaborate.

Adele frowned. "Fine, I'll go soon. Harry is staying to work the cafe. Mish is coming later too, so we have plenty of staff to cover appointments." Mish was another one of our regular volunteers.

I hesitated. I didn't want to say anything that would make Adele suspicious, but I also wasn't sure going over there alone was a great idea given recent developments. "Are you taking someone with you?"

"I have Dinah on standby. I'll call her."

"Great. I'll see you later on." I grabbed JJ and about-faced, heading back into the main house while Adele watched disapprovingly. Now I knew how Grandpa felt when I rushed him. Which I was definitely about to do because I did want to get moving, although for different reasons than Adele. I was confident the cats were handled. Cass, I wasn't so sure.

Luckily, I didn't have to rush Grandpa Leo. He was already in the kitchen, pouring some coffee into a travel mug. He was dressed all in black, his usual private-eye outfit, and he looked serious. Ready to roll. He glanced up at me. "Your mother called. She hasn't heard from you all week, she says."

I groaned. "I've been meaning to call her back. I will today. Promise." I'd thought when I moved back to the island, a stone's throw away from my parents, that I wouldn't have that knee-jerk guilt reaction anymore to not calling.

After all, when I was clear across the country and didn't call, that was different. Nowadays, she could literally drive a few minutes over to Grandpa's and find me anytime she wanted. But the guilt tripping was still real. "I've been kind of busy this week. Did you tell her that?"

Grandpa smiled a little. "I told her you were dealing with a cat hoarder. I left out the other details. But call her today, you hear?"

"I hear," I grumbled, grabbing my bag and JJ's harness from the hook on the door. "Let's go. After we see Cass, I thought we could take a trip to Fisherman's Cove. I need to check in on the cat progress, and then I thought we could go see Bill, maybe. And that way, we'll be close by when Mick calls you with news. I'll call her from the car."

Grandpa gave me a gentle shove toward the door. "One step at a time. You're bringing JJ?"

"Of course," I said. "He's a great way to knock people's defenses down."

We took Grandma's car instead of Grandpa's truck. Grandpa drove while I sat with JJ on my lap. We got to Cass's, but he wasn't in the main shop. I headed to the back room, but it was locked. Weird. JJ let out a squeak of disappointment too. He'd been looking forward to visiting his fishpond out back. I went to the counter and waited for Michael, Cass's store manager, to finish ringing up a woman's purchases.

He turned to me when he was done. "Hey Maddie. You looking for the man?"

I nodded. "He isn't here?"

"Nope. He went down to the park. Said he needed to clear his head, do some tai chi out there. Should be back in a bit." Then he leaned forward, lowering his voice. "Hey, two cops came in looking for him a few minutes ago. Not from here."

"Two cops?" I could feel my heart rate accelerate. "Who?"

"Didn't get their names. They asked for him. I told them where he was. Didn't really want to, but it sounded important."

"Okay. Thanks." I went over to where Grandpa browsed a table with featured books. He was reading the back of Gabby Bernstein's *Super Attractor*. I raised my eyebrows.

Grandpa returned the book to the table, unfazed by my amusement. "What? It's all about feeling good. A concept I happen to agree with."

"Great. I'll get it for you for Christmas." I took his hand and led him outside. "Cass is at the park. And two cops came looking for him. Let's go there."

"Cops?" Grandpa asked.

I nodded. "He said they weren't from here. Meaning Daybreak, I guess."

"Which park?" Grandpa asked, getting into the car.

"He likes to do tai chi at Bluff Point Park," I said. Bluff Point was a mile or so down the coastal road. It was an open green space, often used for music festivals and other outdoor events that drew big crowds. Cass liked to do tai chi there because it overlooked the ocean. He taught some classes there, as did the local yoga studio. It was a gorgeous location.

While Grandpa drove, I rolled the window down so JJ could poke his head out. He loved to sniff the salt air. And people driving past on the other side of the road always honked at him, which made me laugh.

When we pulled into the parking lot, I could see Cass's little VW Bug parked down in the last spot near the fence.

No cop car. I couldn't get eyes on Cass anywhere. There weren't a ton of people out, just a few families so far sitting on the grass, watching kids play or eating their takeout breakfasts. It was still fairly early on a Thursday morning, which worked in our favor. Also, Cass was kind of hard to miss. Yet I still wasn't seeing him.

Grandpa rolled slowly down to Cass's car. Empty. I got out and checked the doors. Unlocked, since Cass was way too trusting. His cell phone sat in the center console. No keys though. I wasn't liking this at all.

I grabbed the phone and went back to our car. "His phone is here."

Grandpa thought about this. "Restroom?" he suggested, pointing to the public bathroom on the outskirts of the park. "I can go check."

While he did, I turned Cass's phone over in my hand. It was locked, unlike his car. There were no text previews showing on the screen, which meant either he didn't get alerts or he'd seen my messages. The screen told me he had three missed calls, which were all mine. I stared at the phone, willing it to give me some clue as to where Cass was, but it sat silent in my hand.

Grandpa came back a few minutes later. "Men's room is empty," he said. "Maybe he walked somewhere to get coffee."

"Cass doesn't drink coffee," I reminded him automatically. "And why would he leave his phone?"

Grandpa gave me a look. "Because not everyone is as glued to those things as you are?"

I ignored that. "Can you call Mick and ask him why cops were looking for Cass?" I asked Grandpa.

He obliged, but shook his head a minute later. "Not picking up."

I felt a growing sense of dread. I couldn't help but feel like Cass was in trouble. But I had no idea what kind, or where he could be. My phone rang again. Craig.

I answered, trying to ignore the growing pit in my stomach. "Hey. What's up?"

"Mick and I are on our way to the PD up here in FC," he said without preamble. "The idiots up here went and brought Cass back in. They arrested him."

Chapter 27

I nearly fumbled the phone trying to get it on Speaker so Grandpa could hear. "What do you mean, arrested him?" I demanded. "For what?"

Next to me, Grandpa snapped to attention. "Who?" he mouthed.

"Cass," I told him. "I'm with Grandpa," I said to Craig. "We're on our way up there right now. I was looking for Cass. His car is at Bluff Point Park. And his phone."

"Yeah. Those mopes went down there and staked out his shop." I could hear the eye roll in Craig's voice. "Said they had reason to want to speak to him based on 'a concerned citizen' who claims to have seen him in the area a lot recently acting suspicious. Followed him to the park where there was no one around and put him in handcuffs on some bogus vandalism charge. Which was a blatant disregard of Mick's authority in this case. Patrol guys out arresting people like they're on freaking *Bosch* or something."

Normally I would laugh at the reference to one of my favorite shows, but right now I felt like I was about to throw up. "A concerned citizen? Really? He was working up there. Can you get them to let him go?"

"Mick's on it now. He's going in to ream them out but he has to get the full story first. Anyway. We were out talking to people from last night, so we just got back. Wanted to let you know."

"We'll meet you at the police station," I said, but he'd already hung up. I turned to Grandpa, who was already speeding out of the lot. "Can you believe this?"

Grandpa's lips had thinned so much they had nearly vanished. "Mick will handle it," he said. "Don't worry." But I could see this was bothering him too. I knew Grandpa liked Cass a lot even if he didn't really understand him or what he did. He just liked his tea. And he knew Cass was a positive influence on me and the island as a whole, and that was good enough for him.

I sat back in my seat, willing the ride to go fast. JJ of course sensed my distress and nuzzled his head against my chin before he turned back to sniff at the salt air rushing in the window.

We pulled into the Fisherman's Cove police station almost twenty minutes later. I had to rush to keep up with Grandpa when he got out of the car and headed to the door. When we burst inside, the cop at the desk looked up, startled. I had to bite back a hysterical giggle at what we must've looked like—the bushy-haired retiree dressed all in black and the crazy girl with the cat on a leash.

"Help you?" the cop asked, his expression settling back into disinterest.

"I'm looking for Sergeant Mick Ellory," Grandpa said, unsmiling.

"He's tied up right now." The cop went back to whatever was on his desk, dismissive.

Grandpa remained standing there until he looked back up. "Officer Craig Tomlin, then."

The cop regarded him for a second, then picked up the phone and said something into it. "He'll be out."

"What's wrong with this department?" I muttered to Grandpa as we moved away from the desk.

He didn't answer.

I sat back in my seat, fuming. My phone rang. I glanced down at it. Katrina's face appeared holding a possum she'd rescued—her profile picture. I picked it up to take my mind off everything else. "Hey."

"We're backed up at the vet's," she said without preamble. "Dr. Vance had an emergency outside of the clinic and had to go off-island. So, Dr. Kelly isn't going to be able to get to the whole crew. Some of the vetted ones will need to go to your place to wait for their spays and neuters. He's out of room."

"Sure, whatever you need," I said, snapping to attention as Craig came out of the inner sanctum. "Drop them off whenever. I have to go." In the silence of Katrina's stunned surprise, I hung up and stood.

He held up a hand to ward off my questions and ushered us outside.

"Where is he?" I burst out once the door had shut.

Grandpa put a hand on my shoulder, a silent rebuke, but I couldn't stop myself from asking, "What's happening?"

"Mick is trying to sort it out. Unfortunately it's not that easy to just undo. The chief is pushing back."

"You guys didn't even get to investigate anything yet!" I exploded. "How is this even possible?"

"Hold on," Craig said. "They didn't arrest him for Arquette. Yet. Said they went to question him about vandalizing a cop car, but my gut says they're pushing to add the murder charges." Craig sounded matter-of-fact, but I could see the smoke smoldering in his eyes. You had to really look for it in those sandy eyes, but if you knew him well, it was easy to spot.

Here's the thing—Craig had been my high school boyfriend, so it was fair to say I knew him well. We'd even considered rekindling our romance when I first came back last year, but that had been more of a knee-jerk reaction than a real consideration. Craig had really grown up since I'd last seen him, biceps and all, but then Lucas came into my life, and Craig ended up with Jade. At first I'd thought they were an odd couple, but the more I saw them together the more I thought they were perfect for each other.

I still probably knew him better, though, and right now he was upset even though he was trying hard to be a stone-cold cop.

"Cass would never!" I exclaimed. "How could they even—"

"He was there at the murder scene. He's not from this town. He's easy to blame."

"Did Mick talk to him yet?" Grandpa asked Craig. "Or has he been talking to the chain of command?"

"Chain of command. Trying to convince them he's got other avenues to pursue and it's way too soon to make an arrest. And he's pointed out that these guys had no business doing detective work when clearly the department had brought him in to do just that."

"Does he?" I asked. "Have other avenues to pursue?"

"Yeah. Of course. Like you said, we've barely gotten started. And right off the bat, there was a whole group of politicians at the town hall that night who—from what we've gathered—didn't love the guy. Professionally, anyway."

"What do you mean? I heard he was super popular in town."

"Maybe with the masses, but not with the town elders.

His application for the town administrator job had been rejected that night. They announced their new hire, and it wasn't him."

Before I could process that, the front door opened again. Mick came out and closed it behind him. "Leo," he said. "Chief Winslow agreed to see you."

I looked at Grandpa. "That's good, right?"

"Depends," Grandpa said, with a sideways glance at Mick. "I didn't know I was seeing her."

"But you have to," I said. "Cass needs you."

Grandpa nodded. "I will. I suppose it's an opportunity to bring up that other thing." He looked meaningfully at me. I caught his drift immediately.

"Laurel?"

He nodded. "Tell the fellas," he said, and went inside.

Chapter 28

Thursday, 11 a.m.

"Wait till I get back," Mick ordered, then followed Grandpa in, ostensibly to shepherd him past the clown at the desk.

I was not impressed with this police department in the least. I told Craig as much.

"That makes two of us," he said. "I mean, it's embarrassing."

"Was the chief in on this?"

He shook his head. "Doesn't sound like it, but now she's probably trying to figure out how to address it so that she'll have the least amount of egg on her face."

We both turned as Mick came out. "I'd say we should get coffee, but the options are limited here," he said. "There's a deli down the street, though." He checked his watch. "I need to talk to Cass, but Leo said I should hear what you have to say first." He sent me a sidelong glance. "It better be good."

"Hey. It usually is with me." We all got into Mick's unmarked and drove a few blocks down the street to Shorty's Deli, a dubious-looking establishment. Or maybe I was just a snob. I texted the name to Grandpa in case he got done before us, and we went inside. Everyone turned to stare as we came in. I guessed there were a couple reasons for that.

One, word was probably getting around that the local cops had been effectively sidelined in investigating this murder and these were the outsiders. And two, I had a cat on a leash.

"You can't bring an animal in here," the woman behind the counter called over. She was about thirty pounds overweight and her face had that greasy look of someone who spent way too much time in or near a hot kitchen. Her dark blond hair was pulled back into a ponytail so tight it was no wonder she was cranky.

Before I could say anything, Ellory flashed his badge. "Service animal," he said.

The woman frowned. "I've never heard of a service cat," she muttered.

He just stared at her. She didn't argue further.

Grateful, I slipped into the restaurant and grabbed a table in the back. I wasn't hungry, but Mick and Craig both ordered sandwiches when our waitress, a younger woman who clearly felt bad about her coworker's attitude toward JJ, came to the table. I couldn't believe it was already past lunchtime. This whole day so far just felt surreal.

"Nothing for you?" she asked me. Her name tag read Lola and she wore bright red lipstick.

"Water, please," I said.

Lola glanced behind her to see if counter chick was looking, then bent down to scratch behind JJ's ears. "He's cute," she whispered. "I'll try to grab him a treat."

I smiled. "Thank you."

"So what do you have?" Mick asked when she'd walked away.

"Grandpa and I wanted to talk to you about Laurel McKenna. I'm concerned that her death might not be just an accident."

Mick and Craig glanced at each other. Mick motioned for me to continue.

I gave them the highlights of the story, trying to make sure I hit every detail that might catch their attention or help in some way, pausing only when Lola brought back their sandwiches, a small scoop of tuna for JJ, and my water. She held her finger to her lips when she slid JJ's bowl in front of me, winking before she walked away.

I put the bowl on the seat next to me and let JJ eat, hopefully keeping him out of sight of his nemesis, while I finished the story. "In light of everything—like this guy getting murdered—it seems suspicious. Grandpa agreed."

Craig put his sandwich down when I got to the part about Bill going in and taking the laptop back last night. Mick kept eating, but I could tell by the intent way he was listening that he was intrigued.

"What time was this?"

"Around nine. We left about half an hour, forty-five minutes later, and we heard sirens when we were leaving."

"Yeah. Cass called in the body around nine thirty. Who was the responding at the McKenna death?"

"Jacobsen." I saw him and Craig exchange glances. "What?"

"That's one of the guys who arrested Cass," Mick said. "It was his patrol car that got smashed up."

"You're kidding." I tried to process that. On the one hand, it was a small department. There probably weren't a lot of options. Still, it seemed odd that the same cop who'd showed up for Laurel's death was also involved in the Arquette investigation, and trying to pin it on Cass. I knew I hadn't gotten a good vibe from that guy.

"Wish I was," Mick said. "At the very least, he should

get suspended. I know the biggest crime in this town is usually someone swiping a box of fish off a dock, but still. Their police force shouldn't be this incompetent."

"I kind of had a weird feeling that day. About Laurel. The alarm sounded a little louder when I found the paperwork. But with the robberies, then Arquette ending up dead, it seemed too much to ignore. Have they brought you in on the robberies yet?"

"I've heard bits and pieces," Mick said. "Unless they're connected to Arquette, they're not really our problem. And so far we can't confirm it was a robbery. He had a couple hundred bucks in his wallet, phone was still on him. We're looking into whether he had a computer bag on him. If he did and it was taken, could be a different story."

I thought about that. "If it wasn't a robbery, why would someone walk up to a town official in the town offices parking lot and bash his head in? If you were going to murder someone, wouldn't you try to do it in a more private place?"

"Unless it was a heat of the moment thing," Craig said. "Which is what I think they'll try to say about Cass, if that's the route they're going. They met, had a disagreement, Cass bashed him over the head. Then pretended to find him there, bleeding."

The whole concept was so far beyond possible to me that I couldn't even listen to it. This was *Cass*. The guy who held meditations on the town green for world peace and ran fundraisers for his native Haiti, then doubled all the proceeds for our island's own needy population. "Aren't there cameras in the parking lot?" I asked.

Mick shook his head. "I'm telling you. This place is low-tech."

"So are you going to look into Laurel?"

"I don't think we can ignore it," Mick said. "This town

doesn't usually see much action. And if there are as many questions as you suggest there are, well, we'd be remiss if we didn't consider it. And there's enough they've been remiss about already, in my opinion."

That was certainly true. "Hey, one more thing. Who was the *concerned citizen* who pointed the finger at Cass?"

Mick pulled his notebook out and opened it. "Patricia Slattery," he said.

"Slattery," I repeated. "You don't say."

"You know her?"

"No. But I'm thinking I know someone who does." Nora Slattery had told me her stepmother lived near Laurel Mc-Kenna, close enough to know about the cats. I wondered how many Slatterys lived in Fisherman's Cove, or if this was the same woman.

Chapter 29

Mick had to go see to Cass, and Craig was going to wait with me until Grandpa returned. Grandpa's timing was always impeccable, though. He walked into the diner just as Mick was getting up to leave. I could see the locals watching the lot of us curiously, as if we were some new species that had just been introduced to their land and they were trying to determine if we were friends or foes.

Mick and Grandpa conferred briefly in low tones, then clapped each other on the back. Mick motioned to Craig to join him. I reached for Craig's arm as he got up. "Please keep me posted."

"Of course." He squeezed my hand, then headed out.

Grandpa joined me at the table. "You hungry?" I asked.

He nodded. "I might get a sandwich."

I motioned to the waitress, who returned with a smile for Grandpa. "What can I get you, hon?"

He looked at me. "Want something?"

"No. I'm not hungry at all."

He ordered a Reuben sandwich, a plate of French fries, and two waters.

"So what happened?" I asked.

"I met with Chief Winslow."

"How well do you know her?"

He tilted his hand from side to side. "A bit. Enough that she'd take my call when I was trying to stop Adele from getting arrested," he said with a wink. "She filled in for Captain Ross over in Duck Cove during his leave about eleven years ago. Then she went off-island, climbing the ranks in Falmouth. She took this job when the former chief retired to get the bars at a young age. She's not even fifty yet. It's not real challenging out here, but it'll still hold water when she goes for the next position. She's got a rep for being smart and fair. I think she knows that if she drops the ball on something that might have big consequences, she'll be stuck in this town forever. And she's an up-and-comer for sure. It's quite an accomplishment to get to a chief position before fifty, even in a tiny town like this."

I nodded. Being a cop's granddaughter, I knew what that meant. If she played her cards right, she'd be running a big department at some point in the not-so-far future.

"And right now I think she's either regretting her decision to come here or planning to clean house with the bozos Gruber kept on staff." Grandpa smiled a little. "First off, she agreed that her bonehead patrol cops had no right to be in Daybreak Harbor questioning a suspect without the investigating detective's knowledge. She has to stand by the vandalism charge until she investigates that. Car was smashed up pretty good, somewhere around the time of Arquette's murder. Time isn't exact because Jacobsen was out in his civilian car."

"Oh, that's crap!" I said, incensed. "Cass would never—"

"I know," Grandpa interrupted me. "But she's got to look

into it now that it happened. She's also going to talk to the officer. See what other alleged evidence he has that it was Cass. I'm guessing there isn't any."

The waitress returned with the food. Grandpa pushed the plate of fries over to me. "For you."

"I told you I'm not hungry." But despite myself, I sniffed at the fries. They smelled delicious. Fries were my favorite, and I hadn't had anything but black coffee so far today.

"Eat," Grandpa ordered.

I picked up a fry and popped it into my mouth. It was surprisingly delicious—hot and crispy on the outside, tender on the inside. I ate another, then another. Surprisingly good—and I had been prepared to be unimpressed. There I was being a snob again.

Grandpa nodded, satisfied, and dug into his sandwich. "So Mick is going to do the follow-up with Cass, since he hadn't had a chance to talk to him yet anyway, and by then she should have an answer from the officer," he said, once he'd chewed and swallowed.

"And you told her Cass isn't the vandalism type?"

He nodded slowly. "I did. She did ask me why he was at the scene of the Arquette murder."

"Arquette asked him to meet him. I heard them. I can go tell her." I was halfway out of my chair before Grandpa put his hand on my forearm.

"If she needs you, she'll call me," he said.

I reluctantly lowered myself back into the chair. He pushed the bowl of fries closer, a reminder to eat. I picked one up and chewed sullenly.

"Now. What did Mick say about the Laurel situation?"

"He agreed it was too big of a coincidence," I said.

"Good. I told her the same."

My eyes widened. "You did?"

"Of course. I think any cop worth his or her salt would be asking these questions. Especially since she'd been robbed previously, and people are still reporting robberies." Grandpa polished off his sandwich, wiped his mouth, then set the napkin down. "So you want to go shake a few trees while we wait for Cass?"

I grinned. "Absolutely. I have a list of trees."

I directed Grandpa to Laurel's house first, partly because I wanted to check on Adele, and partly because I wanted to see if Bea was around. While she had been Laurel's friend, she also clearly seemed to adore Jonathan Arquette, and I wondered how she was taking the news. I also wanted to know if she'd been robbed too.

On the way, I called Dr. Kelly's office. Nora answered, sounding chipper.

"It's Maddie. Is your stepmother Patricia Slattery?"

"Oh, boy. What did she do?" Nora asked immediately.

"Um. Nothing," I said. "I just wondered if I might be able to talk to her. About the Laurel situation."

"Oh, dear." Nora sounded worried. "Is this about the police?"

"What do you mean?"

"The police went to her house. They were knocking on doors yesterday, asking if the neighbors had seen a man in the area. I guess he's a suspect in something. I know she talked to them. She couldn't wait to call and tell me all about it."

"What's her address?" I asked. I typed it into my phone as Nora recited it. "Thank you. Appreciate it."

I hung up as we pulled into Laurel's driveway. The white van was there, doors open, and Adele waved gaily at me from the front steps. She had just emerged from the house with a cat carrier.

"You made it!" she called. "Hey, Leo. Grab a cat or two!" She winked at him.

Grandpa laughed. "I'll leave the cat capers to you. How's things here? Any problems?"

"Other than sick cats hiding in walls? Nah. Clear sailing." Her tone dripped with sarcasm.

Grandpa flashed her a thumbs-up and walked around the house. I gathered he wanted to get a sense of the set-up, based on what I'd told him.

"How many today?" I asked.

"We got a bunch more sickies. Eight more. The basement is starting to look emptier, but I'm afraid there are still some hiding in the walls. We're going to have to start leaving traps down here. Anyway, I'm probably going to grab another six or seven this morning before we head out. There's a few upstairs who came out when I put food down. They're seeming friendlier. Dr. Kelly will see as many as he can today, but none of them can stay. The ones from yesterday weren't able to go to any fosters. Too sick." She shook her head. "But the miracle is, we haven't lost any yet. And the sick ones, he's confident will be okay. Just a lot of upper respiratory stuff going on."

I nodded. "Good. I already told Katrina to bring what you need to back to the house."

"Can you say that again?" Adele asked.

"Why?"

"Because I want to record it."

"Oh, be quiet." I turned to survey the street, unsure where to go first. According to my GPS, Patricia Slattery lived about forty feet away. Before I headed over there, I figured I would start with Bea.

I hurried over to her little house. It was closed up tight, though, and there was no car around. I tried the doorbell anyway. No one answered. I checked my watch. Nearly one. It was during the week, I reminded myself. She said she worked. At the senior center, if memory served me. I didn't see Delaney either, and her house looked just as quiet.

Maybe by the time I was done with Patricia, one of them would show up. I headed around the back of the house, meeting Grandpa coming back around. "Come on," I said. "Let's go talk to the concerned citizen."

Chapter 30

As I crossed the grass, I realized Patricia Slattery's yard was the one in which I'd seen the older woman walking around outside with a notebook taking inventory of the people she saw going in and out of Laurel's house yesterday. Terrific.

Her yard was much more well-tended than Laurel's, which made sense if Patricia was part of the gardening club as Nora had said. The grass was green and lush, as opposed to Laurel's slightly dry, yellowish grass. Apparently, the cats knew better than to pee on this lawn.

Today, she wasn't gardening. Instead, she sat on the swing on her back porch, one eye on the novel in her lap and the other on me and Grandpa. A little gray schnauzer whose face reminded me a bit of Walter sat at her feet, stubby tail wagging as we got closer. Patricia watched us curiously as we approached, laying the book aside.

I paused at the foot of the stairs and waved, hoping she was friendly. "Hi," I called out, maybe a bit louder than necessary. "Are you Patricia Slattery?"

She kept swinging. "Why, did I win a prize?" There was a teasing lilt to her voice.

I smiled. "I'm Maddie James. This is my grandfather,

Leo Mancini. We're helping out with Laurel's cats. With Nora," I added, so she wouldn't worry that we were scammers of some sort. "We were hoping to talk to you if you have a moment?"

Patricia Slattery smiled. "It's Patty. And you don't have to shout, dear. I'm old, not deaf."

I blushed. "Sorry."

She waved it off. "Come on up. It's nice to meet you both. I saw you outside here yesterday," she said to me.

"Nice to meet you as well," Grandpa said, nudging me forward.

I climbed the few steps to the little deck, turning to glance behind me at Laurel's. Patty had a pretty clear view of any goings-on in Laurel's backyard. And even inside the house, if the lights were on. "Yes, that was me," I said.

"Thank you for entertaining us," Grandpa said. "We won't take much of your time."

"Of course," Patty said. "You're a cutie." She winked at him, sending his entire face into a crimson blush. I was glad he hadn't noticed the title of the book she was reading: *Fifty Shades of Grey*. Nora's description of her as a spitfire seemed pretty accurate so far. "Please, sit." She motioned to the little bistro table. "This is Angus." She motioned to her dog, who still wagged his stubby little tail. I reached down to pet him. He licked my fingers. JJ flicked his tail at him. I noticed Patty wore glittery Converse sneakers, and smiled.

"So. You're collecting cats, are ya?" Patty asked. "That one of them?" She motioned to JJ.

"No. This is my cat. His name is JJ. But yes, we're helping get Laurel's cats new homes."

"Good. I told my stepdaughter she should help that poor woman out." Patty shook her head, lips thinning. "That girl has no spine. I was about to take matters into my own hands when all this happened." She waved a hand toward the house. "Shame what was going on there. Cats running all over. Got the neighbors all riled up too. I mean, doesn't take much around here, it's true. This street . . . bunch a busybodies. It's worth it to get the popcorn and come out here to watch. Better than TV."

Yikes. That didn't sound good. "Were there any particular neighbors who were upset?" I asked.

Patty considered this. "I guess that young one over there." She pointed at Delaney's house. "The one with the little boy. Angry at the world, that one. But she took it to a whole new level with the rat poison."

My mouth dropped open. "The . . . rat poison?"

Patty nodded. "She bought rat poison. Went marching over to Laurel's to tell her about it. Threatened to use it on the cats if she didn't keep them inside."

"*What?*" I couldn't help the horrified outburst.

"Yep. She's not all there, in my opinion." She tapped a finger to her temple. "Maybe because that husband of hers is meaner than a junkyard dog. Anyways, don't look so distraught, honey. I think she did it for the shock factor. She didn't actually do it. That I know of, anyway. Maybe because Laurel got so violently angry. They had a terrible fight. I saw the whole thing. Thought Laurel was going to rip that pretty braid right out of her head. Then Laurel made the posters."

"Posters?" I glanced at Grandpa, who still had his impassive cop face on. No wonder he'd been so good at his job. I was miserable at a poker face.

Patty cackled. "It was pretty creative of Laurel, have to give her that. She snapped a photo of Delaney when she was yelling. Good shot, too. Looks like she's off her rocker. Then she made posters. Stuck them all along the neighborhood with the picture, a stock photo of rat poison, and a caption that read Cat Murderer. Had the number to the police on the bottom."

I knew I shouldn't think that was funny, but I kind of did. Served Delaney right. "How did Delaney react to the posters?"

"She tore them down. Called the police, made a big scene and threatened to sue Laurel for slander. Telling you. Better than reality shows. Not that I watch that trash anyway." She made a face.

"But you don't think she actually hurt any cats," I confirmed.

"Can't be sure, but don't think so. Anyway, that's when I told Nora again that someone needs to help. I woulda taken some in myself if I thought Laurel wouldn't come marching over to take them back."

"When was this incident?" Grandpa asked.

Patty reached into her pants pocket and pulled out a small notebook, flipped pages. "August third."

I calculated in my head—roughly two weeks ago. So before their last altercation about the cat scratching the kid. Laurel must've been angry to see Delaney heading her way again.

"Did the police do anything?" Grandpa asked.

"They threatened Laurel with a fine this time. Before, they just came over I think 'cause they had to, told her to keep the cats inside, same old thing. But this time they told her they'd fine her if they got another call about the cats or anything related."

"So you keep track of things like that in your notebook?" Grandpa asked.

Patty smiled proudly and patted the notebook. "Next to

Angus, my notebooks are my best friends. I like to make sure I'm precise about things. Helps if the old memory starts to fade at all. And this way I never forget anything."

Good to know it wasn't just me she was tracking.

"The man you spoke to the police about. That you saw in the neighborhood acting suspiciously. Do you have the details on that?" Grandpa asked.

She frowned. "I spoke to the police this morning after I heard about Jonathan's death. Our town administrator. He just died, you know."

Grandpa nodded solemnly. "Yes. We heard. It's very sad."

"It sure is. I wanted to help in any way I could, but it wasn't just one man I told them about. There were lots of men in the neighborhood. Namely, over at Laurel's, and specifically the night before she died."

"Were the police looking for information on Laurel?" he asked.

"Just wanted to know if I'd seen anything or anyone unusual recently. So I told them about the traffic at Laurel's house that evenin'."

"You mean Monday night," Grandpa confirmed.

"You betcha." As if to prove it, she flipped pages in her little notebook and held it up. It kind of reminded me of Becky, who also never went anywhere without a pad and pencil. "Also Monday is barbecue night. So I remember it very clearly."

"Barbecue night?" Grandpa asked.

"The senior center has a program to deliver themed meals twice a week. Jonathan and I designed it, actually. The volunteers eat with us. We get two meals per week, the nights the center is closed early. Monday and Wednesday. During the summer, Monday is barbecue night. We eat outside," she added. "Like a real barbecue."

"That sounds fun," I said. Also, something about that niggled at the back of my mind, though I couldn't put my finger on why.

Grandpa ignored me. "So you saw traffic at Laurel's. What kind of traffic?"

"Men. Three of them, right in a row. I never pegged straightlaced Laurel as a cougar." She smiled a little at the thought of that. "I'm joking, of course. That would *never* happen. Jonathan was here first." At his name, she sighed and shook her head. "It really is a terrible tragedy that he's gone. He made the senior center a place people actually wanted to go to. Everything was better thanks to him, after that old fuddy-duddy Lucy croaked. She would've been happy if we all sat in our rocking chairs in the dining room once a week, eating slimy mashed potatoes. He actually cared about us. I knew he and Laurel weren't friendly—she was very vocal about her concerns with him—which was why I was surprised to see him here. I think she was too. Unhappily so."

"How do you mean?" I asked.

"Well, they were shouting at each other right back there," Patty said matter-of-factly. "And that was right before Bill came over. Laurel threw him right out." She cackled a little at that. "I always thought he was a blowhard."

"Bill Cavanaugh?" I asked.

"That's right. Laurel's boyfriend." She made a face.

"Who did she throw out? Jonathan or Bill?" I asked.

"Bill, of course." Patty gave me a look as if to say, *Keep up, dear.* "She should've thrown him out permanently, if you know what I mean."

"Jonathan left on his own, then?" I asked.

She shrugged. "Yes. They were finished with their argument."

"What were they arguing about?" Grandpa asked.

"I couldn't really hear. Not for lack of trying, either," she added. "I just heard raised voices."

"Did Bill and Jonathan bump into each other?" I asked.

"No. Jonathan had gone a little bit before Bill came."

"You know Bill?" I asked.

"Of course I know Bill." She gave me a brilliant side-eye. "Honey. Everyone in this town knows everyone in this town. That's the first thing you gotta know. Then there are some who know each other better than others, and that's the case with Bill and me."

"How do you know him?"

"Bill used to fix our boat. My husband had a sailboat. His pride and joy. Bill still comes over sometimes to mooch a beer off me even though my husband and my boat are both gone," Patty said. "He only buys cheap beer, but he'll drink my Sam Adams." She made a face. "He's an opportunist, that one."

"Did Bill go into the house? Or was he just picking up Laurel?" I asked.

Patty frowned. "He'd have to be inside for her to throw him out, dear." She shook her head, clearly thinking I was not very bright.

"And the third man?" Grandpa asked.

"The handsome one. At first I wondered if Laurel threw Bill out because he was coming. He's much better looking than Bill. Tall fella. Black man with very long hair. Teaches some slow dance class or something. If I was younger . . ." She sighed. "But she didn't even answer the door for him, so that couldn't be it. Anyway, that's the one the police were interested in. They had his picture. Asked me if he was the one I'd seen. But I certainly didn't say there was anything suspicious about him. In fact, I told Jonathan to get him to come here more often. If those police are twisting my words, I'll march down there right now and tell them what's what." She looked like she was about to get up and do just that.

"Do you know the officers' names?" Grandpa asked.

"Jacobsen and Blondin," Patty said immediately. "I know Jacobsen because he once had to come out and pick up his own kid. Little punk was vandalizing cars in the neighborhood."

Grandpa and I glanced at each other. Vandalizing cars?

"Thought he could get away with it because of Daddy's job," Patty continued. "These kids, you know? Don't want to do an honest day's work." She sighed and leaned back in her swing. "I hope that nice man doesn't get in trouble for anything. He seems like an honest, God-fearing man. You ask me, we need more of his kind round here."

I agreed with her, and was glad to know that Patty—who I was really starting to like—hadn't thrown poor Cass under the bus. "One more thing," I said. "Did you see Delaney around Laurel's house, by chance? Either that night or any other?"

Patty shook her head. "She stays in her own yard most of the time. Not very sociable. Though maybe she has friends outside of here. Saw her get in a car and take off with her kid and suitcase yesterday afternoon. Maybe spending some time away from that husband of hers will improve her mood."

"Yesterday?" I asked, glancing at Grandpa.

"Yes, ma'am. I saw her from my window. Car pulled up, she rushed out, got in with the kid, and they took off."

"Like an Uber?" I asked.

"Don't think so. She got in the front seat. Put the kid on

her lap too, which is dangerous. But I didn't have time to go out and mind her business about that. They took off too fast."

We thanked Patty for her insights. Grandpa started down the stairs, but I turned back, suddenly realizing what had been bothering me. "You say the senior center is closed Monday nights?"

"That's right. Closes up at two on Mondays."

"So where else would there be a bingo game in town?"

Patty looked surprised. "There wouldn't be, honey. That's the only place we do anything like that. It's why it's so important to keep it going."

"I see. Is Bea involved in any of the town stuff?"

Patty nodded. "She works at the senior center. Helps organize a lot of the trips. I know she was part of the earth group for a while, not sure if she still is. Seems like she's mostly been fixated on these trips. I guess it's good for her. She doesn't have much in her life either."

Chapter 31

Thursday, 2 p.m.

Grandpa and I headed back across the yard. I was deep in thought. Bea had told me she was at a bingo game the night Laurel died. Yet there was no bingo here in town. Although she could have gone out of town for it. I made a note in my phone to check. If she'd lied . . . well, that meant she was unaccounted for on Monday evening.

The other thing on my mind was Delaney. I'd spoken to her yesterday morning. Then she'd taken off in a rush later that day. So much so that she didn't even put her kid in his car seat. Something to do with Laurel? Also, Cass had never mentioned being at Laurel's again on Monday night—just earlier that day, when he'd seen her fighting with Delaney. I wondered if he'd just forgotten in all the excitement.

The only thing for certain was that Patty Slattery was a wealth of information.

When we reached Laurel's driveway, I glanced over at the neighbors' homes. Delaney's was still shut tight, as was Bea's. We got back into Grandpa's car and looked at each other. "What do you think?" I asked. "I mean, Jacobsen's kid getting in trouble for vandalizing cars?"

"Yeah. I heard that too. Sounds to me like they're trying to make a case against Cass based on, well, not very much," Grandpa said. "Of course he's been seen around the neighborhood. He taught right down the street, yes?" He waved in the direction of the park.

"Yes, that's right. Do you think they're trying to make a case about the robberies? Or Arquette? Or both?"

"I don't know, Doll. Mick is going to have to go through the reports and notes and figure that out."

It seemed really unfair to me and I wanted to fix it. Now. But I had to try that patience thing. I fidgeted in my seat.

"Who's next?" he asked.

I was torn between Bill and Bea. In the end, I decided on Bea first. Maybe she could give me a little more of an idea about the town dynamics, especially as it related to Jonathan and Laurel. "Let's hit the senior center first," I said. "Laurel's friend Bea works there." I googled the address and set the phone in the cupholder so the app could direct him. I would call Mick later and tell him about Delaney.

Grandpa grinned as he pulled out of Laurel's driveway and headed toward the center of town. "Great. Maybe there's some dance lessons I can take while we're there. Or I can sit in on a bingo game."

I snorted. "That, I'd love to see." Grandpa Leo didn't consider himself a senior, and as such, he had never set foot in a senior center unless it was related to a case. Instead, he played cutthroat poker games in our basement with his group of friends, none of whom considered themselves seniors either. I knew they played for money—and not just tens and twenties. His comment reminded me of my question, and I wondered if now was the time to ask Bea about her own bingo proclivities.

He turned into the parking lot in front of the small building that housed the senior center. It was only half a mile or so away from Laurel and Bea's neighborhood, and next to the town hall. There were a lot of cars here, so it must be a popular hangout. The building looked a lot newer than the other town buildings, and it was near the ocean. I mean, it was hard to not be near the ocean on an island like this, but this building actually had an ocean view. I got out of the car and took a moment to stop and appreciate the smell of the salt water. I was convinced that the ocean smelled differently depending on where you were on the island.

When we walked into the reception area, the first person I saw was Bea. She sat at the front desk, a cowboy hat nearly covering her face. I only recognized her because of those giant glasses. She was crying into a tissue. But it was the person comforting her who made me stop in my tracks.

The guy bending over the counter with a box of tissues was gorgeous. He'd grown out his hair since I'd last seen him earlier this summer, enough that it was pulled back into a short ponytail, streaked platinum blond. His biceps were still enormous, bulging out from under the short-sleeved scrub top he wore. I could see the snake's tail sneaking out from under the fabric.

"Adam?" I said, stepping into the room.

Adam DeSantis glanced up, then burst into a brilliant smile. Dropping the box of tissues, he took two giant steps toward me and scooped me up in a huge hug, spinning me around in a circle until I was dizzy.

"Maddie James!" Adam deposited me back on the ground, still grinning like I was his long-lost best friend. "What the heck are you doing here?"

Adam was a nurse at Daybreak Hospital, so technically he worked for my dad, who was the CEO. I'd met Adam earlier this summer during our brush with celebrity, during the Peyton Chandler fundraiser-turned-murder incident.

Adam was the real-life love interest of another famous actor, who had allegedly given up the Hollywood hustle for the simple life out here on the island.

"I'm here to talk to Bea," I said, gesturing at the counter where Bea still sat with her tissues. "It's a long story," I added, seeing the questions forming in his eyes. "I'll explain later. This is my grandpa, Leo."

"Adam DeSantis." Adam shook Grandpa's hand. "I owe your granddaughter a lot."

I could feel my face getting red. "You do not."

"I do! Marco wouldn't be here without everything you did." Marco Moore was Adam's boyfriend.

I brushed him off. "So he's good? I haven't seen him around at all!"

Adam laughed. "That's on purpose. He's keeping a low profile. For now. He'll emerge when the tourists go home and things slow down. He wants to come see you at the cafe soon. We both do."

"I can't wait to see him. Tell him I said hi. But what are *you* doing here? Did you quit the hospital? My dad not treating you right?"

"Not at all. This is an extra program I signed on for. I help out with activities up here a few times a month. They need nurses on site for the events. The hospital sponsors it. Helping out the smaller towns that don't have access to extra staff. Although, that might go away now." His face clouded over. "We lost our advocate."

"Jonathan," I said, as it dawned on me.

"Exactly. Jonathan was the one who pushed to get Fisherman's Cove added to the program. How'd you know?" He cocked his head, curious.

"Long story," I said. "So you know—knew—Jonathan well?"

"Yeah, he was a great guy. I've been working with him since last fall on this program. Got to know him pretty well. What happened is terrible. And scary. This is such a small, close-knit town. Everyone is really broken up about it," he said with a nod to where Bea sat, still crying, at the desk. "Jonathan was popular among our crowd here. And now people are afraid."

"I don't blame them," Grandpa said. "It's very scary when something like this happens. Especially to someone so beloved."

It was true. It certainly seemed like Jonathan had been doing a lot for the community. So who wanted him dead? And who would actually follow through with it?

Adam still watched Bea, clearly concerned. "Excuse me one second," he said to us, and went over to Bea. "I think you may need to go home for the rest of the day," he told her in a low voice. "Really, you shouldn't be here."

She waved him off. "What am I going to do at home aside from stare at my other dead friend's house?" she said morosely.

Adam winced, but he had no response to that. "Then I'm going to get us a late lunch before the line-dancing program," he said. "I know you've been dying for some fried scallops from Bogie's."

She shook her head. "I don't want anything."

"You need to eat. And I'm going, so if you want something else tell me now or forever hold your peace."

She relented. "Fine. I want French fries on the side."

"A double batch," he promised. "And a milk shake."

Finally Bea offered up a smile. "That sounds good."

"Get you anything?" Adam asked me and Grandpa.

We both declined.

"Let's catch up later?" he said, touching my shoulder.

"Yeah, definitely." I really wanted to talk to him more about Jonathan, but he didn't seem to have time right now.

After he left, I headed over to Bea. "Hi," I said, approaching the counter. "Remember me?"

Bea picked up her oversized glasses from the desk and put them on, peering at me through red, swollen eyes. "Of course I remember you," she said. "You're taking Laurel's cats. But what are you doing here?" Before I could answer, her eyes filled with tears again. "Everyone's dead," she wailed, loudly enough that a couple of seniors walking slowly through the room turned to stare at her in alarm.

Grandpa, who had wandered over to look at the board with today's schedule on it printed out from the computer in giant text, glanced back at me, eyebrows raised.

I turned back to Bea. "I'm so sorry for this additional loss. I know you were close to Jonathan."

His name set off a fresh set of wails. "He was such a good man." She sobbed into her tissue, which was falling apart in her hands. Awkwardly, I handed her the box so she could grab another. "I just can't believe he's gone. This whole town is going to fall apart now."

I let her sobs subside before I spoke again. "Were you at the town meeting last night?"

Bea shook her head. "No. I don't always go to the meetings. There was nothing on last night's agenda that interested me."

I was surprised by that. "But they announced the hire for the town administrator position."

She stared at me. "That wasn't on the agenda."

"Oh. Well, maybe it fell into the news portion of the meeting." Was there one of those? I hadn't been to a small-town governance meeting since . . . well, honestly, I never had.

"So he got the job and then he was killed." She slumped back into her seat, looking even more crushed than ever.

"Actually," I said slowly, "he didn't get the job."

She sat up straight. "What? What do you mean?"

"I—that's what I heard, anyway. They hired the other candidate, I was told." I didn't tell her the police had told me that.

"Billy didn't tell me that," she said slowly.

"Billy? Like, Laurel's Bill?"

"Yes. He goes to all the meetings. He called me first thing today to tell me about . . ." She broke off.

"So Bill was there," I said slowly.

She nodded. "He always goes to the meetings." The phone rang and she leaned forward to pick it up. "Fisherman's Cove Senior Center," she said.

While she was on the phone, I thought about what that meant. Bill had been at Laurel's taking his computer the night Jonathan was killed. I wondered what time the meeting had let out. Bill had been at Laurel's around nine, which was right around the corner from the town hall. I had no idea why Bill might want to kill Jonathan Arquette, other than that it must somehow be linked to Laurel. What if he'd gone to the meeting, waited outside for Jonathan to leave, then killed him? Then gone to Laurel's to get the computer?

Bea was off the phone now, looking at me expectantly.

"Do you have any idea who would've wanted to hurt him?" I asked.

She plucked at her wet tissue, tearing it into pieces. "He was a saint and everyone loved him," she said. "I have no idea who would've done this. Must've been some kid hyped up on drugs or something."

I wasn't sure that was it, but didn't say so. "Bea, did you know Laurel was robbed?"

She frowned. "Robbed?"

"Yes. Delaney Mathews mentioned a rash of robberies, and Laurel had reported a robbery at her home. Some items were stolen."

"I didn't know."

"Did *you* have a break-in?"

"No. But I have an alarm system."

"Anyone else on the street that you know of?"

"I really don't know," she said. "What does this have to do with anything? Was Jonathan robbed? Oh my God." That sent her into a fresh burst of tears. "Is that why he was killed?"

"Bea. We don't know yet. But I did want to ask you about Laurel. Aside from the . . . cat-related problems, did she have any other problems? Anyone giving her trouble?"

"What do you mean?" She reached up and took her glasses off, wiping her eyes. "What kind of trouble?"

"I don't know. Just curious."

The phone rang again. I bit back my frustration as I looked around for Grandpa but he was nowhere in sight. Adam returned with lunch before Bea got off the phone, and a few people came in and clustered around the front desk. I saw our chance to talk more slipping away. Adam deposited her food on the desk, waved to me, then hurried down the hall. A minute later Grandpa emerged from the same direction, his face red.

"Let's go," he said, grabbing my arm and pulling me toward the door.

"What's wrong?" I asked.

"I got invited to line dance," he said with a grimace.

I burst out laughing. Grandpa line dancing was a sight I desperately wanted to see, but we were already in the parking lot and I could see I had no chance of convincing him to turn back.

He gave me a dirty look. "Anything?" he asked as we got into the car.

"Laurel's boyfriend was at the meeting last night. He called Bea to tell her about Jonathan this morning. Which gives him opportunity. I still have no idea about motive, though. Where did you disappear to, aside from line dancing?"

"I talked to some of the people here. A lot of them come regularly. Most of them are upset about Jonathan. Said he really did a lot to help them. A few people said they only came here because of him. I wished I'd had more time to talk to them but their dance was starting."

"We can come back," I said. "Meantime, what do you think of Bill being around both people right before they died? One could argue Cass wasn't the only one in both vicinities."

"I think we need to go talk to Bill," Grandpa said.

Chapter 32

I checked my phone as we drove over to Bill's boat repair shop. Nothing from Mick or Craig. "You hear from anyone?" I asked Grandpa. "He's been there all day."

He shook his head. "Not yet. Patience, Madalyn."

I hated to admit it, even to myself, but this quest for patience I was on was starting to feel fruitless. My mother had been telling me since I was a little girl that I needed to learn to hold my horses. *Shoot.* I sat up straight. My mother. I still hadn't called her. I debated trying her now, but since everything on Fisherman's Cove was pretty close to each other, I figured I didn't have much time.

I was right. The GPS announced a moment later that our destination was point-five miles away. Cavanaugh's Boat Repair was on the water at the very tip of the island. But unlike the marina and boat center on Daybreak Harbor, this was not a big fancy place. The little building out front appeared to be a pretty dilapidated office. The pickup truck Bill had driven to Laurel's was parked out front, but there were no other cars. I couldn't see from here if there were a lot of boats waiting for repair, but it was so quiet I somehow doubted it.

JJ and I followed Grandpa to the office door, JJ trotting along like we were on a fun outing. He knew we were near the ocean, which meant fish, and his nose was in the air the whole time trying to settle on the scent of what would hopefully be his next meal. Grandpa knocked once, then tried the door. Locked. He motioned for me to follow, and we went around back. There was one small sailboat parked at the dock. I could see a man doing something to one of the joists—at least I thought that's what they were called—and could tell even from here that it was Bill. Same build, same beard.

"That's him," I told Grandpa.

We headed to the edge of the dock. Bill saw us coming and finished what he was doing, then hopped off the boat and headed over to us.

"Mornin'," he said, his curious gaze moving from me to Grandpa. "Hi, Maddie."

"Good morning. Mr. Cavanaugh?" Grandpa asked.

"Yeah. What can I do for you?"

"I'm Leo Mancini. A private investigator. And you know my granddaughter, Maddie."

Bill nodded at me, then pointed at JJ. "Is that . . . one of her cats? Laurel's?"

I shook my head. "This is my cat."

Bill chuckled a little. "I never seen a cat on a leash before."

"JJ's definitely unique."

He watched JJ sniff the dock for a minute, then looked back at Grandpa. "A PI? What's this about? Tell me this isn't about the cats again."

"No sir. Not about the cats. My granddaughter has that pretty much under control. You've heard what happened to Mr. Arquette?"

Bill paled under that rugged, sunburned skin. "I did. Shame what's happening to this town. People are going to be afraid to go out anymore, pretty soon."

"Mr. Cavanaugh—"

"Call me Bill."

"Bill. You were at the town meeting last night?"

He nodded, warily. "I go to all the town meetings."

"Anything unusual happen?"

"No. All pretty standard stuff."

"Except that Mr. Arquette was denied the town administrator job."

"Yeah. That," Bill said. "Not sure he was expecting that."

"Was anyone else?" Grandpa asked.

A shrug now. "Some. There were people other than Laurel who thought he wasn't the best thing for the town," he said, a tad defensively, I thought.

"Does that include you?" Grandpa asked.

"What's this about?" Bill asked.

"Trying to get a handle on who might've wanted to harm Mr. Arquette," Grandpa said.

Bill's eyebrows shot up. "Well, why would you be asking me? I have no idea. Where are the police?"

"I'm consulting with the Daybreak Harbor officers on the case," Grandpa said smoothly. It was semi true, but Bill didn't need to know the details.

Bill snorted. "Bringing out-of-towners in. What a crock. Let this community handle it."

"Tell me about your girlfriend's working relationship with Mr. Arquette. Laurel McKenna was your girlfriend, right?"

Bill's eyes moved from me to Grandpa and back constantly, like he was preparing to ward off an attack. "Yeah. They worked together some. On town stuff. She thought he was too free with the money. I kind of agreed with her, you know? I mean"—he gestured around him at the empty docks—"they wanna throw money around, they should throw it at the local businesses that need a boost. But he wanted to spend it on crap."

"Your business needs a boost?" Grandpa asked.

Bill flushed a little. "I run a good business. I've just hit a downturn, is all. I'll be alright. Always am. But it woulda been nice to get some help from the people who claim to care."

"Did you spend a lot of time with Mr. Arquette?"

"Nah. Didn't know him that well. Just from the meetings and such."

"So you had no personal experience with him?" Grandpa asked.

Bill sighed. "Look. The guy was kind of a do-gooder. Always butting into things. Other people's business, you know? I tried to stay away. Too much drama for me."

"He ever *butt into* your business?" Grandpa asked.

Bill's eyes narrowed. "Not sure what you're driving at, but unless you have a boat for me to fix, I think we're done here. I have work to get back to." His eyes darted between us once more, then he turned and walked back to the dock, climbing onto the sailboat in one graceful move.

Grandpa and I looked at each other. "I think Mick will want to talk to this guy."

Chapter 33

We left Cavanaugh's and got back into Grandpa's car. Grandpa took his phone out of his pocket and texted someone. Mick, I assumed. We still hadn't heard from him. What was taking so long? I needed to call Becky too. I hadn't caught wind that any reporters had been in town, and that was odd. If there was a murder, Becky would normally be all over it—and if there were two, she'd be having a field day. I wondered if word hadn't gotten to her yet. I knew the reporters didn't get out here much, so it was entirely possible she didn't know. Which would make her lose her mind.

"What now?" I asked Grandpa, fidgeting in my seat a bit.

"Patience," he said. "I want to see if he does anything."

We'd parked across the street and down from the building a bit, which I now realized that Grandpa had done on purpose and not just because it was easier when we'd driven up. He wanted to be able to watch the building without Bill realizing we were doing just that. We sat in silence for another ten minutes. I was just about to ask Grandpa if we could go when Bill came out the front door of the boat repair shop, talking on his phone. He got into his shabby pickup truck and drove slowly down the street.

Grandpa put the car in Drive, let him turn the corner, then followed.

"Ooh, a tail." I grinned at Grandpa. At least we were doing something. Sitting there quietly wasn't really my thing. I guess I wouldn't have been a good cop after all, at least if I had to do stakeouts.

Grandpa was being very serious, though, as he always was during an investigation. He was in the zone, and didn't join in my glee at this next adventure. He followed the pickup from a decent distance as it drove at a respectable pace toward the coastal highway and out of Fisherman's Cove.

I glanced at Grandpa. "Shouldn't we be sticking close? We'll need to pick up Cass soon, right?"

"I just want to see where he's headed," Grandpa said. "Mick will call me."

I concentrated on petting JJ for a moment. He seemed unfazed by all the activity of the day, and had gone back to sleep in my lap. We were just about to reach the Turtle Point town line when I realized where we were headed. "The sister!" I exclaimed, sitting straight up and startling JJ.

Grandpa glanced at me, curious.

"Margery Haberle lives in Turtle Point, remember? The neighbor said that all three of them had grown up together. You haven't mentioned her to Mick yet, then?"

Grandpa shook his head. "I was doing a little research first, then, well, things went a little sideways."

We followed Bill through the winding, spacious neighborhoods, a world away from the tiny shacks and small homes that sat right on top of one another in his own town just a few miles away. I tried to put myself in his and Laurel's shoes. It must've irked them to think of someone close to them having all this while they seemed to be barely scraping by.

The houses seemed to get bigger the more we drove until finally Bill slowed and turned right. I craned my neck to see the street sign. Hubbard Street. Grandpa pulled over before making the full turn, watching the truck slow at the third driveway on the left. We waited until he went to the door, where he was hidden by some trees. Grandpa cruised slowly down the street. Bill was still out on the front step, but he didn't turn. "Number forty-three on the mailbox," Grandpa said. "No name."

I pulled out my phone and added the address to my notes app. "Got it."

He nodded and drove by, turning right at the end of the street to head back out of town just as his phone rang. He motioned for me to answer. I put it on Speaker.

"It's me," Mick said. "You can come pick up Cass now. I'd bring him back but I really want to start working some of these leads."

I grinned. "You rock, Mick."

"Yeah, well." He sounded grim despite this good news, which immediately put my antennae up. "I'll explain later. Where are you, by the way?"

"Turtle Point," Grandpa said. "Bill Cavanaugh is at the dead woman's sister's house. Maddie and I just followed him here, despite his previous assertion that he doesn't speak to her, and had no plans to. If you want to run the address, we can confirm. Or at least Maddie can. She knows her name."

I recited the address to Mick. I could hear him typing. A minute later he said, "That address belongs to Stanley and Margery Haberle."

I looked at Grandpa. "Bingo."

"The boyfriend is there now?" Mick asked.

"Yep."

"Interesting," he said. "Guess I'll have something else to ask him when I go for a visit. I'm going to let Cass wait in my temporary office. Call me when you get here."

Chapter 34

When we arrived back at the police department, I called Mick to tell him we were outside. Craig walked Cass out a minute later. The two men shook hands and Cass came over to our car.

I jumped out and gave him a big hug. "Are you okay?"

He hugged me back, tightly. I always forgot how strong he was. But when I pulled back to look at him, his eyes were haunted. "I am fine," he said. "Let's go." He slid into the back seat.

I got back in the passenger seat and handed JJ back to him for company, then fished his phone out of my bag. "I hope you don't mind. I grabbed this out of your car."

He looked up from nuzzling JJ's head, surprised. "At the park?"

I nodded. "We went there looking for you. Michael told us where you'd gone and that he'd sent the police there. I got worried that your car was unlocked and your phone was in it. Then Mick called."

"I see. Thank you," he said, taking the phone.

"You're welcome. Feel free to ignore all the frantic messages from me." I really wanted to ask why he'd been at Laurel's Monday night and hadn't mentioned it, but I also didn't want to jump on him with that question right away, considering the morning he'd had.

Grandpa turned to look at him. "You doing okay?"

Cass nodded. "The whole thing simply feels surreal. One minute I was doing tai chi by myself, the next I was in the back of their police car. They said I'd been seen acting suspicious around town, and that I'd vandalized his police car." He sounded more sad than angry about it, which made my heart hurt.

"Jacobsen, right? The same guy from Laurel's house?" I asked as Grandpa headed toward home.

"Yes."

I could see by the set of Grandpa's jaw that he was just as angry to hear this as I was.

"So what happened when they got there?" he asked.

Cass's gaze drifted out the window. "It happened so fast. They showed up, came walking over to me. They said they wanted to ask me some questions and I should go with them. I asked what it was about and they grabbed me, handcuffed me, and threw me in the car."

I kept my gaze forward so he wouldn't see how mad I was at this. "And then?"

"And then nothing. I did not say a word. They drove back to the police station. When we arrived, they put me in a room and left me there. I was there for a long time, until Sergeant Ellory arrived."

"So they didn't question you at all?" Grandpa asked.

"No. Another officer saw them bring me in and he asked to see them in his office. They never came back."

"And Mick?" I asked. "Did he question you?"

"He was very decent. He told me that they should not have done this, that the officer rescinded the charge that I had vandalized the car, and that I was free to go. He said if I was open to it, it would first be helpful for him to hear my account of . . . last night. In the parking lot. Since he wasn't on the scene when they'd spoken to me initially. I told him everything I knew. Which wasn't much—that I showed up to meet Jonathan as requested, after the meeting. I arrived around nine. I tried to call but got no answer. I assumed his meeting had gone long too. I did notice there weren't many cars, though, but his was still there so I figured he'd been delayed. After a while, I went over to his car to see if maybe he was already waiting in it and just hadn't seen me. And I . . . found him on the ground next to it."

I felt terrible that he'd had to endure that. Cass was a grown man, big and strong and capable, but I felt very protective of him at the moment.

Grandpa glanced in the rearview mirror. "Did he tell you they're looking at Laurel's death as suspicious too?"

Cass nodded grimly. "Yes. It's shocking."

"So what now?" I asked.

Cass's gaze drifted back out the window. "He said they'd be in touch if they have more questions. I told him that was fine. It's not like I'm planning to go anywhere."

"Cass." I turned to look at him. "The cops are questioning people in the neighborhood about you. They have your picture and everything. One lady behind Laurel's house said she saw you back there Monday night. Is that true?"

He winced. "It is. I did go back. Laurel hadn't shown up at either class that day and I was concerned, after her argument. I went back to try one more time to speak to her. She didn't come to the door."

It made sense. I just hated that they were trying to make it seem like he was skulking around Fisherman's Cove waiting to kill people.

JJ did a good job of snuggling with Cass on the way home. I hoped it made him feel better. The silence hung heavy over the car as we drove into Daybreak Harbor. The contrast in the mood from our little bubble in the car to the outside world when we got back to town was apparent— the streets were congested with people, throngs of tourists coming off the ferry and embracing the summer day. The mood was light, happy. Summer sun and fun. No one had any idea of the dramas unfolding around them. It was like Daybreak was an idyllic spot where, to the outside world, nothing could ever go wrong.

If they only knew.

When we pulled into the parking lot at the park, Cass seemed reluctant to give JJ back. I resisted the urge to remind him that he could very easily have his own cat. That was a conversation for a later date.

"Thank you," he said as he got out of the car. "I appreciate everything you did for me today."

"Not at all," Grandpa said. "Keep us posted, okay?"

I got out too and gave him a hug. "Go meditate," I said with a small smile. "I've heard it helps."

He laughed. "I've heard that too. I may try it." With a wave, he got in his car.

Grandpa pulled out first. I watched Cass in the rearview mirror as he started the car and drove slowly behind us toward the exit. "What do you think?" I asked Grandpa.

"I think Mick will do all he can to find the real killer or killers. Don't worry, Doll."

But I was worried. And angry. "Do you think Jacobsen will get fired?" I asked hopefully. I didn't usually wish the loss of a livelihood on anyone, but in this case he seemed completely corrupt and it seemed a fitting punishment.

"I guess we'll see," he said. "I'm sure Mick will keep us informed."

I leaned back against the seat. "What now? Should we go back and see what other help he needs?"

"He said he'd call you. Let him get his feet under him, Maddie. He's getting a lot of things thrown at him right now."

I knew that was true, but my customary impatience reigned and I wanted to bust in there like a bull in a china shop and start figuring things out.

"Give it time," Grandpa repeated as we turned into our driveway. "In the meantime, I think you have plenty to keep you occupied, yes?" He motioned to the van parked in our driveway. Katrina's, not Adele's. An impromptu cat delivery, I guessed.

Resigned, I opened the door and got out, putting JJ down so he could walk inside. "Make sure you call me the minute he calls you," I said to Grandpa. "No going rogue on this one without me."

Grandpa smiled. "I think that warning applies more to you than me, Doll."

Chapter 35

I went inside, let JJ off his harness, and checked the living room and kitchen. No Katrina. I poked my head into the cafe. Harry and Mish were in there with two guests. They both waved at me. I waved back. There was only one other place she could be, so I headed out to the cafe.

The place was packed. There were people at all the little outside tables Ethan liked to set up when the weather was nice, and when I went inside, I saw that all six of our cafe tables were full. Katrina was at one of them, alone, eating a sandwich and scrolling through her phone.

I slid into the seat next to her. "Are you dropping off cats?"

She glanced up. "Who, me? I'm just here for some good food."

I rolled my eyes. "Yeah, right."

"Actually, I only had to bring one. I took the liberty of putting him downstairs with the others. They're looking pretty good. Not really hiding."

I nodded. "The first ones were already being social. The ones I trapped were hiding this morning when I checked on them, but maybe they're coming around."

"For sure. So you want an update?"

"Of course."

Katrina pulled out a small notebook and flipped to a page with bunch of numbers on it. She was nothing if not organized. "So far, I've checked sixty-six cats in with Dr. Kelly. Not counting the two you trapped. None of them were fixed. Four pregnant."

I winced.

"Hey, that's honestly not bad, given the numbers. I mean, I'm sure we'll find more, but I was worried it would be worse," she said. "So, out of that number, he was able to already do thirteen neuters and four spays, between him and Dr. Vance. They worked late last night. Those were on the healthier ones, and now they are all in foster care. The FIV cats are in foster care too, waiting their turn to come in for spay and neuter. The sickies are another story. He's got a bunch on meds and they're providing care there. He sent five to the other vet in Turtle Point. Then we still have whoever is left in Laurel's basement that still need to be seen for the first time. I'm considering seeing if I can get someone in to pull the walls apart as best we can down there and see what's what. Also, Adele told me that Ellen wants to foster a few."

"Ellen?" I grinned. "That's awesome." Ellen was the Daybreak Harbor librarian. She was also, in a twist worthy of a Shakespearean love story—hopefully one with a happy ending—Leopard Man's girlfriend. He was a town curiosity with a heart of gold, who spoke mostly through quotes from the Bard himself. I still thought it was sweet that after so long as a loner, he'd found a kindred spirit. Ellen loved Shakespeare too.

"Yeah. She said she also wants to adopt Jericho."

"Really! I hadn't heard that," I said. Jericho was a

fourteen-year-old kitty who was super shy. I felt sorry for the poor little furball. Her human had died and the woman's son couldn't be bothered to take her in. Katrina saved her and brought her here, but she wasn't happy around all the other cats and activity. "Also, Damian wants to foster. I convinced him. Can you coordinate?"

"Nice. You've been busy." Katrina cocked her head at me. "Speaking of which. What the heck is going on out there? Mick got loaned out to that department? Someone got killed?"

I sighed. It was too long of a story for right now. "I don't have all the details yet," I said evasively. "But yeah, someone got killed. Possibly two someones."

Her eyes popped. "Two?"

I nodded. "The hoarder might not be the accident they thought it was. Don't tell him I told you."

"Interesting. I'm glad that we didn't know about her hoarding before she died. Otherwise there would definitely be a rumor that Adele or I killed her." She checked her watch, then stood up. "Gotta run. I'll be in touch later."

After she left, I went to the counter. Ethan was behind it with his new employee—our second paid employee!—who I'd vaguely remembered was starting today. Their backs were turned, and it looked like he was teaching her how to operate his espresso machine. Oddly enough, from behind she looked a lot like . . .

"Sam?" I asked, astonished.

My youngest sister whirled around, all smiles. "Hey, Maddie!"

"Hi. What are you . . . ." I trailed off, looking at Ethan.

"Well," he said, "you remember I told you our new employee was starting today?"

"I did," I said. "But I could have sworn you told me it was a he. At the very least I don't remember it being, well, Sam." I hadn't been that busy, had I?

Ethan grinned. "No. Actually, his name was George. But George called me this morning and told me he'd gotten his dream job off-island and unfortunately had to back out."

"Really," I said.

"Yup. And luckily, Sam was here at the time. She asked why I looked so bummed. When I told her, she said she was in the market for a job and could help."

"Well, that's . . . amazing," I said. I couldn't help but notice my sister was dressed in one of her yoga outfits—a white jumpsuit complete with a turban.

Sam still beamed at me. "Isn't it? I so need something new in my life. I think I'm going to be great at this!"

As if on cue, the coffee maker started sputtering behind her, then liquid started pouring out and all over the counter and down onto the floor. She still held the carafe in her hand.

"Oh, shoot!" She scrambled to contain the spill.

Ethan smiled weakly at me.

"Can I talk to you?" I asked sweetly.

"Sure thing. Be right back, Sam."

She was too busy throwing an entire roll of paper towels onto the coffee running over the counter to respond.

I grabbed Ethan's arm and dragged him out of earshot. "Seriously?" I asked.

"What? She's your sister."

"Right. That doesn't mean she's a barista. Or a baker. Or even a waitress!" I sighed. "Look. I know this is your domain and I appreciate your judgment, but my sister can be . . . unreliable." I trailed off, trying to find the politically correct description for Sam. She was a sweetheart, for sure, but she was also very flighty. A free spirit, my mother called her. She never really had a goal or direction in life and didn't stick with anything for very long. "I just worry she'll disappoint you. And, oh my God. I just realized why my mother has been calling me like crazy." I shoved my hands on my hips. "Did she put you up to this?"

"What? No!"

"You're sure." I didn't believe him.

"No. I mean, she stopped by a couple times and we got to chatting. She mentioned Sam was looking for something new . . ." He trailed off. "Look. It will be fine. Do I have permission to treat her like any other employee?" he asked.

"Of course, but why set her up to fail?"

"Mads. I'm sure she can run the counter. Maybe I won't have her doing coffee right away," he said, glancing back over at Sam and her puddles of java. "But she'll learn." Then he delivered the final blow. "I'm sure your mother will be grateful."

"Yeah. I'm sure," I said.

"I'm happy to have Sam. Look, I need someone. I can't have the guy I tried to hire, and she's free, so why not?"

I sighed. "Okay, fine. I'll stop being a naysayer. Of course I'm happy to do whatever you want."

He smiled. "Good."

"Can I get some lunch now?" I asked.

He steered me to the premade food in the little fridge. "Might be your best bet while we're getting settled," he said.

"Right," I said.

Chapter 36

I took my salad and went up to my room, plopping down on my bed. I had completely lost track of what time it was, and I was only vaguely confident that it was Thursday. I hadn't talked to Lucas all day. I pulled out my phone and called, but he didn't answer. I was too tired to leave a message. Maybe I'd take a nap after I ate then go see him.

Instead, I called my mother.

"Well. I thought you'd lost my number," she said when I answered.

"So you came and talked to Ethan instead? You're slick, Mom."

She laughed. "Hey, from what I hear, Sam was in the right place at the right time. I think it will be good for her. Don't you? And that's what family is for, right? To help out?"

"Yeah. If she ever learns how to make coffee. So that's why you were calling? To get Sam a job?"

"I wanted to see how you were too, of course," she said defensively.

"Of course."

"Your grandfather said you had a cat-hoarder problem?"

I dropped my fork, a grin spreading over my face. We—

well, Ethan, but still—had done her a favor. Maybe now she'd do one for us. "Yeah. We actually need some fosters. I know you've been wanting a friend for Moonshine and you have so much space. That's what family is for, right?"

"Well, Maddie, I—"

"Awesome, Mom. You rock. I'll have Adele bring some over tomorrow. Thank you!" And I hung up, still smiling. I knew she wouldn't mind. My dad might be less than thrilled, but he'd come around. That had actually worked out quite well.

But foster homes were still the least of my problems. I dug in to my salad, thinking while I ate. This whole thing was so complicated. I had to admit, I couldn't begin to find a connection between Laurel's death and Jonathan Arquette's. Maybe there wasn't one. Maybe two truly awful, random things had just happened to occur in the same week, in a tiny town where nothing ever happened. I knew next to nothing about Arquette. And since I hadn't been able to get Laurel out of my mind, I figured my time was better spent working through my theories about her.

As far as I could tell, there were a few people who would have wanted her dead. Delaney Mathews stood out for me, especially after Patty's assessment. The boyfriend, of course, was always a suspect, and Bill had been acting squirrelly. It was almost cliché. And then there was Jonathan Arquette, the nice guy loved by all—except Laurel, who had gone out of her way to tell people why they shouldn't want him running the town.

I pulled out my iPad. Using one hand while I ate with the other, I pulled up the *Chronicle* website and checked the opinion section. Jonathan Arquette had mentioned that Laurel's op-ed about why he shouldn't be the town administrator would be out "any day now."

Sure enough, there it was. "Fisherman's Cove needs sense, not flash" the headline read. It was relegated to a relatively small space, saving the letters from the bigger towns' residents for the more prominent spaces, but still. I scanned it. The piece was well written and to the point. She had actually done an admirable job of systematically eviscerating Arquette without saying one poor word about him personally. That was a skill many didn't have. She'd clearly been very analytical—it translated into her arguments. In her view, by spending "unlimited funds on frivolity" they were depriving the town of the kind of resources it needs. For instance, she said, what about businesses in town that were suffering? Wouldn't the money be better spent making sure people could stay employed? Same argument Bill had made. I wondered if it held any water. Towns really couldn't be in the business of bailing out private companies. They'd all go bankrupt in that case. But it definitely said a lot about both Laurel's and Bill's mindset.

I felt sorry for Jonathan after reading the article. For all intents and purposes he'd been trying to do something positive. Although none of it mattered now. I googled him and scrolled through the first page of hits. Lots of mentions in town-related news and selectmen meetings. The article of his interim appointment after the town administrator died. Nothing controversial in this quick and dirty search. I did find lots of information about all the good he'd done—both here in Fisherman's Cove in the short time he'd been on the job, and in his prior role heading up some community center in Raleigh, North Carolina. I clicked and read a few of them. He'd been responsible for opening a second homeless shelter in Raleigh when the need became more than the current shelter could manage; he'd personally started a dinner program in one of the local schools for low-income kids, which the school district had adopted for all the area schools; and, like here on the island, he'd created a robust program for seniors. The guy seemed like a regular Boy Scout.

But even Boy Scouts had their limits. I wondered if this whole op-ed thing had been enough to push Jonathan over the edge? Could he have been at Laurel's house that night in one last-ditch effort to get her to rescind this piece and save his job? The timing of the piece was rotten, but that was probably the point. And maybe she had refused, and he got angry. Angry enough to shove her in the heat of the moment?

I called Becky.

She answered her cell right away, sounding distracted. "Hey. What's up? I have a shoplifter on video that I need to post online to see if we can identify her." Becky had literally been born to be a newspaperwoman. She'd wanted to be a journalist since we were kids, even going so far as to set up an interviewing station outside the ferry to get perspectives from tourists coming to visit the island. And nothing got in the way of her job, not even her best friend.

"Sorry to distract you from that, but this could be just as important," I said. "Probably more."

"Whatcha got?"

"Fisherman's Cove," I said.

"What about it? I need someone to try to make this clearer," I heard her say to someone, probably her digital editor. Then back to me, "Sorry. What were you saying?"

"You didn't hear there was a murder out there?"

"What?" I heard something clatter behind her, as if she'd dropped something onto her desk.

"Yeah. Last night." I hesitated. Mick would probably kill me for adding this next part, but so be it. "Possibly two."

"Two?" Now she sounded incensed. "Was my cops reporter asleep on the job? Darren! Get in here!" While the *Chronicle*'s main focus was Daybreak Harbor, since it was the only paper on the island it covered the other towns, though on a more-limited basis. Fisherman's Cove rarely got much coverage about anything—honestly, it was a boring town—but I knew the police logs in every town were something Becky's reporters were tasked with checking on daily, at least for the big towns. Any interesting items were noted by town in the crime section.

"Beck," I interrupted. "Not two last night. The other might be the cat hoarder. The one who died sometime Monday night or Tuesday morning."

"Cat hoarder? I'm so lost. Hold on." She must've put me on Mute while, I assumed, she reamed out her reporter. A minute later, she came back. "Okay. Continue. Murdered cat hoarder. Who was the other vic?"

"*Maybe* murdered cat hoarder," I corrected. "Her name was Laurel McKenna. We're in the process of rescuing all the cats on and around her property. Over sixty and we aren't done."

"Holy crap. Did *you* kill her?"

"Funny. The other person was the assistant town administrator. Jonathan Arquette. He was definitely murdered."

"Yikes. How? Same person?"

"I don't think the cops are releasing the how," I said. "And they just started investigating, so not sure if they're related. Ellory and Craig got loaned to their department to help them solve it."

She whistled. "Really. Guess that says a lot about their department, huh?"

I didn't respond. Figured I'd save that tip for another day.

Becky was excellent at keeping coverage going on stories from all different angles. Once the murders were solved, I could steer her to an exposé on the incompetent cops up there. "Anyway, one of Laurel's neighbors mentioned a rash of robberies, all pretty much in their general neighborhood. Have you been following the robberies?"

"Robberies? Two murders in one week? When did I move to the city? I haven't heard anything about them. Which means our readers are just as in the dark. Or maybe not. Maybe they know more than I do, because I don't know anything. The reason? Apparently Fisherman's Cove is, and I quote, 'too far to drive once a week *when nothing ever happens.*'" She blew out a frustrated breath. "That, and there has been some activity out here he's been busy with. Potential stolen-goods trafficking. It's still not a good excuse."

I felt sorry for Darren. He was sure to be on Becky's bad list now. More than anything, Becky hated to get scooped. "The hoarder wrote an op-ed that you published today. About how the murdered guy shouldn't get the town job he was going for."

"Wait. The hoarder who maybe got murdered wrote an opinion piece about how the guy who definitely got murdered shouldn't get hired?"

"Yup."

"Hold on." Becky put her phone down on her desk without bothering to mute the line. I listened to all the background activity of the busy newsroom until she returned. "You're right. Reading it now. She didn't like the guy, huh?"

"No," I said. "Clearly not."

"So did *he* kill her?"

I sighed. At least she was validating my thought process. "No one knows yet. The cops haven't really gone public

with calling her death a murder yet, though. Just so you
know when you start asking Ellory for a quote."

"I just sent Darren up there, and told him not to come
back without a good story. Now I guess he'll come back
with two. I'll keep you posted. Or maybe I should say, you
keep me posted, in case we miss something else."

Chapter 37

I hung up, feeling better knowing Becky was on the case. She'd keep things honest. I was still thinking about going to see Lucas, but thought I'd try doing a meditation first. My head was pounding and my brain felt too full to make any decisions right now, so I laid down on my bed and turned on one of Cass's meditations.

I must've ended up falling asleep because the next thing I knew, there was a paw on my face. Wary after this morning's episode with JJ, I carefully opened one eye, expecting to see JJ sprawled out on my neck. But this paw was fluffy and black.

I opened my other eye. More fluff in the form of a face, inches from mine, mouth open in a giant smile. For a second I was really confused, then my brain kicked on and I remembered. Walter the schnoodle. I let out a squeal, startling the poor pup, who scrambled away from me and sat at the foot of the bed, regarding me curiously. For the first time I noticed JJ, sitting in a crouch on Lucas's pillow, regarding the intruder with pure disdain.

"Hi! It's nice to see you," I told Walter. He approached again, cautiously, and let me ruffle his ears. Then he got excited and jumped on me again. I looked around, trying to figure out how he'd gotten here.

Lucas popped his head in from the bathroom. "Sorry to wake you, babe. I didn't know you were asleep when I came up."

"I didn't mean to fall asleep," I said, sitting up and shaking my head to clear the grogginess. "I was trying to meditate. I was actually thinking of coming over to see you. What time is it?" I reached for my phone. Blinked. Eight. At least I hadn't been asleep that long.

"Long day, huh?" He came in and sat on the bed next to me. Ollie bounded in, joining the party. JJ hissed.

"Aww, JJ. It's okay," I said, reaching one hand over to stroke his fur. He flicked his tail at me as if to say, *You're encouraging this*. "Very long. But I should be up. I have a ton of things to do."

"Obviously you were exhausted. Resting isn't a bad thing." He took a closer look at me. "What's going on? Did something happen today?"

I couldn't even answer because Walter was still enthusiastically drowning my face in kisses. Ollie, excited at all the activity, hopped on the bed and joined in. They'd both apparently decided they liked each other, although it would be hard not to like Walter. He seemed like the friendliest little dog on earth. He was a puffball of fur, maybe fifteen pounds. He looked like a stuffed toy.

"He's so adorable. How is this dog homeless?" I asked Lucas.

He lifted his shoulders in a shrug. "No idea. So, Katrina asked about him staying here for a bit." He looked at me tentatively. "I think she already decided for us."

I laughed. "She told me. It's fine. I mean, unless he licks me to death and then it won't matter."

"Okay, Walter. Give her a break. Thanks, Mads. I'm glad you aren't mad. Now tell me what's up." Lucas gently pulled the dog off me just as Val bounded into the room, breathlessly calling my name.

"What's wrong?" We both stared at her.

She stopped short when she caught sight of Walter. "There he is. I saw you all get home and I wanted to play with him, but then he was gone."

"Sorry, I didn't know you were looking for him," Lucas said.

We all looked at Walter, who sat there wagging his tail, a big smile on his face.

Val came over and scooped him up. "Anyway. That's not what I wanted to tell you. Did you hear what Ethan did?" Her scowl told me it was not good.

"No. What? Please don't tell me he cheated on you." I held my breath.

Val stared at me. "What? Why would you say that? Do you know something I don't?"

"Of course not! I'm just trying to imagine what he did that's so bad. You sound stressed."

"He hired Sam!"

"Oh, that."

"What do you mean, *oh, that*? You knew about this?"

"I found out today. Why are you so mad?"

"I'm not mad. I just think . . ." She trailed off, letting her breath out in a frustrated whoosh. "He's not setting himself up for success. You know Sam."

I stifled a smile. Same thing I'd said, practically verbatim.

Lucas watched our exchange with interest. "Your sister is working here?"

"It kind of happened by accident." I explained for both

their benefits what Ethan had told me today about his new employee bailing out and Sam being on site to save the day.

"Maybe this will be her thing," Lucas said. "You have to give her a chance, right?"

"That's what Ethan said. I told him it was fine with me, if that's what he wanted. What?" I asked Val, who was still looking at me like I had three heads. "It's his business too. He didn't tell me who *I* could have as a volunteer."

Val still looked like she didn't approve, but she threw her hands up in resignation. "Fine. His problem, right?" She opened the door to go. "Oh, by the way. Mick is here."

"What?" I jumped up. "Why didn't you tell me that sooner?"

"Jeez, relax. That's what I came up here for. Well, that and Ethan. I got sidetracked."

She turned and left the room, taking the dog with her. I went into the bathroom to throw cold water on my face and brush my hair. It was a little wild since I'd slept on it.

"What's going on?" Lucas asked, following me in. "Why is Mick here?"

"Long story. I'll tell you later. Promise." I kissed him and hurried downstairs. I found Mick and Grandpa in Grandpa's basement office. The cats had decided they felt at home enough to come in and investigate the new people. One was actually sitting in Mick's lap.

"Hey," I said. "Sorry, I fell asleep. What's going on?"

Mick looked as tired as I'd felt. "Just wanted to circle back with you both on today's events. I'd like to go to see the sister tomorrow. Wanted you both to join me. Actually, that's why I'm really here. I need your help with this investigation. Since Laurel McKenna is now officially an open case. The chief hasn't gone to homicide yet, but she agreed that it's a suspicious death and wants Craig and me on it."

Chapter 38

Well, good to know my gut worked, even if what it told me was awful. Mick had already pretty much agreed that was possible, but the chief giving them the green light was a whole other story. "Was it a hard sell?" I asked.

"Actually, it wasn't. The whole slate of evidence you came up with was too much to ignore. Especially the missing phone and bag and the open doors, given the robberies. She already called the coroner and asked for the autopsy to be rushed."

Wow. I wanted to ask if she'd fired her incompetent staff, but I'd wait a bit on that. "So you need our help? Like, mine too?" Grandpa was a no-brainer. I knew Mick used him a lot—without telling his chief, of course—because Grandpa was still a crack investigator even in his seventies. But me? Usually he only accepted my help grudgingly. Although he had let me go undercover once.

"I know how that sounds," he said with a small smile. "But yeah, I do. Look, I'm running into some issues with this department. It's tiny to begin with, and it's a tiny town where nothing usually happens. Their investigative skills are . . . let's just say not up to par."

"Gee, you think?" I asked sarcastically.

"Making it worse, Jacobsen is suddenly on a forced vacation. His colleagues aren't real happy about it. We weren't welcomed with open arms before that happened so they're not really offering to work around the clock to help on this one."

"I'm not surprised," Grandpa said. "Departments don't take kindly to outside help, for one thing. And they're going to band together with their brother, so it's a double whammy."

"Wait—the chief made him take time off?" I asked.

He nodded. "Chief Winslow is investigating the Cass arrest. I expect a suspension—or worse—to come down soon, especially if he botched Laurel McKenna too, but for now she put him on paid leave. I guess she's trying to get him out of the way until she figures out how badly he screwed up. She's also interested in how the burglaries tie into Laurel's death."

"And Arquette's?" I asked.

"Not sure. We do think he had a computer on him, so could've been a robbery. One of the selectmen verified that he was using a computer that night at the meeting. We haven't found any computers at his house or office, so it's reasonable to think whoever hit him grabbed it."

"Were they even sorry he died? And that they had basically taken away his dream job right before that?"

Mick nodded. "They were properly horrified about what happened, but he was definitely disrupting the status quo in town. One of them called Arquette "too progressive." At this, Mick rolled his eyes. "I mean, God forbid we take people off-island to play some slot machines."

I thought about that while I absently reached down to pet one of the cats rubbing against my leg. That had been, according to Bea, Laurel's pet peeve too—the bus trips out of town and all the activities that looked like they cost money. "So was he going to get to keep the assistant job?"

Mick nodded. "Far as I know. But under the strict supervision of this new person—someone who they considered more responsible. Or in line with town values, or something like that."

"What *about* the board?" Grandpa asked. "Possible one of them had anything to do with this?"

"Craig and I have spoken with them all and confirmed that they all went out to dinner after the meeting. It finished just at about eight fifteen. They all left together and went to Turtle Point while Jonathan was still in the building. The reservation checked out. Now, could they have gotten someone to do their dirty work if they were mad enough? Anything is possible. But I didn't get that vibe. And they did praise him for his dedication. They unveiled the fundraiser bricks that night. I heard all about that."

"And one of those bricks killed him," I said slowly.

"Remember, that's not for public consumption," Mick said, taking two cookies off the plate. "We're keeping that quiet."

"He have any family?" Grandpa asked.

"Mother lives out of state. Father died. No siblings, wife, or kids. The mother is devastated. According to her, everyone loved him. Couldn't think of one enemy."

We were silent for a moment, thinking of that poor woman. How awful to get such news about your only son. "Did you talk to Adam?" I asked.

"Who?"

"Adam DeSantis. Marco Moore's boyfriend. He's part of a program at the hospital that loans out nurses to the smaller towns for certain programs. We saw him today at the senior center. Arquette pushed for the program. Sounds like they were close."

Mick wrote that down. "Thanks. So I know you've been talking to people who knew Laurel, Maddie. Anyone else with a big enough bone to pick that this could be the end result?"

"Have you talked to her neighbors?" I asked. "Aside from Patty Slattery. The woman across the street, Bea Knightly, was friends with Laurel. And Delaney Mathews, the woman a couple houses down, hated the cats. She seemed like a loose cannon," I said, remembering the way Delaney had barged over full of cat-negative stories. "And Patty says Delaney's husband is . . . what term did she use, Grandpa?"

"I believe it was 'meaner than a junkyard dog,'" Grandpa said.

"And Patty saw her get in a car and take off with her kid yesterday. Like, in a big rush. So what if she was freaking out about the cats—a cat scratched her kid, which was allegedly the reason for the altercation the day Laurel died—and she went over there and had it out with Laurel, got nowhere. Then the crazy husband went back later?" I felt a stab of guilt—I'd never even met this man—but here I was ready to throw him under the bus for murder. What was wrong with me? "And maybe she either didn't know and found out later, so she's trying to distance herself, or trying to get away before they question her. She probably took off on the ferry. She couldn't have killed Arquette based on that timing, but no idea why she would do that anyway."

"We'll check. What's her husband's name?"

"No idea. Also what about Bill? When are you bringing him in?"

"On the list for tomorrow. I did find out an interesting

tidbit, though. Jacobsen's kid worked for Bill Cavanaugh at his boat shop."

My eyes widened. "Officer Jacobsen? Seriously? Patty Slattery said his kid was trouble. Vandalized a bunch of cars in town. Not sure if he has more than one kid. But that's kind of suspicious, right? Considering that Cass was arrested for allegedly vandalizing a patrol car?"

"Very interesting," Mick said thoughtfully. "Apparently Cavanaugh had to let most of his staff go this summer."

"Why?"

"Financial reasons."

I sat back in my seat. "Guess that's why Laurel gave him sixty grand. Now we just need to figure out where she got it. And if that money possibly got her killed."

We were all quiet as we contemplated that.

"You heard that Jonathan was at Laurel's house the night she died, right?" I said. "As was Bill?"

"Yeah. And Cass," Mick said.

I winced. "I know. But that's typical of Cass. He was worried so he went to check on her. I'm more curious about why Jonathan was at her house, if she didn't like him. And Bill, if he never went over there. It seemed like a big co-incidence that they all ended up at her house on such a big night. And that op-ed she wrote about Jonathan was in today's paper."

Mick looked perplexed. "Op-ed?"

I picked up my phone and navigated to the page, then handed it to him.

He read it silently, then handed back the phone. "Well," he said. "That gave him reason to be upset with her."

"Yeah. What if Bill heard that Jonathan went over there to talk to her and got suspicious?"

"And what? Thinks they're having an affair and kills them both?" Mick thought about this. "It's possible."

"I wonder if Cass knew why Jonathan went over there. Did you ask him?" I asked. "Not that I want him pulled back into this."

"I'm not sure he's out of it," Mick said grimly.

"What do you mean?" I looked at Grandpa. "What does he mean? I thought Cass was cleared?"

Mick hesitated. "He's clear in the vandalism charge. The chief threw it out for lack of evidence."

I frowned. "I sense a *but* in there."

"The chief isn't ready to rule anyone out just yet for Arquette. Cass found the body. And"—he glanced at me—"he found the other body too."

"What's that supposed to mean? I was with him!"

Mick held up a hand. "Don't jump down my throat. I'm telling you Winslow's thought process. In fact, I think that was a factor in her decision to pursue Laurel's death as suspicious."

I stared at him. "What was?"

"That the same person was on the scene for both."

"You're kidding," I said. "But Bill—"

"There's more," Mick said. He picked up a file folder from the table, pulled out a piece of paper, and handed it to me.

I took it and glanced at it. There were a bunch of dates and addresses. "What is this?" I asked.

"These are the dates of recent robberies in town. And addresses that were targeted."

"So? What does that have to do with Cass?"

Mick's mouth set in a grim line. "The first report coincides with Cass's classes starting." He jabbed his finger at another set of dates, scribbled in the margin. "The first reported robbery was at Bill Cavanaugh's house." He paused, letting that sink in. "And a lot of the other incidences oc-curred when Cass was in town."

"Oh, come on." I shoved the paper away, disgusted. "That's weak, Mick. Cass isn't a burglar. He was teaching classes!"

"I know. But the chief isn't stupid. I told you. She doesn't want this to reflect badly on her either. It's getting around that they brought him in and we let him go."

"But they brought him in on a bogus charge!" I exclaimed.

"I know that, Maddie," Mick said. "And we dropped it. But you know how the game of telephone works. And you have to admit, for anyone who doesn't know him or know the story, it does seem really . . . odd that an out-of-towner would be present at the scene of two suspicious deaths as well as a bunch of robberies. Listen, I'm going to do every-thing I can to figure this out, okay?"

I felt like crying. I knew Cass hadn't done anything wrong, but I also knew there were plenty of stories of people who hadn't done anything wrong who were still blamed for some terrible crimes. Mick was a good cop and I knew he would give it his all, but what if he still came up short? All these thoughts were spinning around in my head, making it hard to focus on what he was saying. But he was still talking, and through the fog in my brain a phrase made it through and jolted me back to attention.

"I have seventy-two hours to prove he had nothing to do with it, or they want to push forward on charges." His tone was matter-off-fact, but his expression told me everything I needed to know.

"Seventy-two hours?" I could hear the screech in my own voice. Grandpa looked surprised by this too.

"I mean, by Sunday I need to have another viable suspect

or . . . she's going to want me to bring Cass back in. So. That means we"—he indicated all three of us—"have a lot of work to do if we don't want that to happen. Okay?"

Grandpa recovered first. "Let's make our game plan." He squeezed my hand. "We'll figure it out."

I nodded, numb, as he and Mick started sketching out the plan. There were plenty of viable suspects—Bill was at the top of the list—and lots of avenues to take to get this done.

But to explore them all in seventy-two hours seemed like an impossible task, even if we didn't sleep.

Chapter 39

Sleep felt like a luxury none of us had time for, but Grandpa insisted I try to get some after Mick left. I went upstairs feeling like I was heading to the gallows. How were we going to get this sorted out in two days to save Cass when nothing made sense?

I lay awake for a while, tossing and turning and annoying JJ to the point that he got off the bed and went to his window seat. Walter had even shifted to Lucas's side of the bed, where Lucas (as usual) slept like he'd been drugged. Finally at two a.m. I got up again and went downstairs. I peeked into the cafe. Everyone was asleep. I didn't want to wake the high-energy kittens, so I let them be and wandered down to the basement to see the new cats.

They, too, were asleep. They seemed to be doing well, even the more timid ones. They started venturing over to see me, one by one, and I realized in all the chaos I hadn't even named the poor babies yet.

"We should do that now," I told them. "Cool names, too. What do you think?"

After some debate, we all agreed that eighties rock icons would be a good route to explore. As a result, within a few minutes we had Sebastian (Bach), Bret (Michaels), Vince (Neil), Sammy (Hagar), Jani (Lane), which fit one of my females even though its namesake was male, Tramp (Mike Tramp), Lita (Ford), and Stevie (Nicks, of course).

"Well, at least I got something accomplished," I said. I curled up on the couch, pulling the fuzzy throw blanket over me. Tramp came up and curled into the crook of my knees. Jani hopped up and settled near my head, keeping one watchful eye on me. I figured I'd rest for a few minutes with them so they wouldn't be lonely.

I must've fallen asleep, because when I woke up it was morning and Grandpa stood in front of the couch holding a steaming mug of coffee that I sincerely hoped was for me.

"What time is it?" I asked, rubbing at my stiff neck. The cats had moved on at some point and I was alone on the couch, twisted up in a pretzel.

"Almost time to go," he said, handing me the coffee. "You should go get ready."

Go. Yes. Today we were accompanying Mick to see Laurel's sister. I swung my cramped legs over the side of the couch and took a long sip of coffee.

"What were you doing down here?" he asked.

"I came to name the cats." Which reminded me, I needed to start folders on all of them with their info.

Grandpa shook his head. "You can't help Cass if you collapse from exhaustion," he said, patting me on the shoulder. "Mick will be here in an hour. I'm going to do a little research on Arquette." He went into his office and shut the door.

I drained my mug, hoisted myself off the couch, and headed upstairs to find more coffee and get ready.

Lucas was in the kitchen when I dragged myself in. He

observed me with some concern. "Morning, babe. Where were you all night?" He came over and gave me a hug.

"Couldn't sleep. I went down to see the cats and ended up falling asleep on the couch." I poured coffee, sipped. "Mick asked Grandpa and me to help with the Fisherman's Cove case. Cases, actually."

He turned back, still pouring, eyebrows raised. "He did, huh?"

"Yeah." I gave him the elevator speech of everything that was going on. "We're going to see Laurel's sister this morning," I finished.

Lucas sipped his coffee, his face impassive. "Well, at least you have police supervision for this investigation," he said finally. "That means it has to be less dangerous than the other times."

I still had a little time after my shower, so I headed into the cafe to start folders for the kitties downstairs. I had barely gotten through the door when Clarissa ambushed me. "What do you think of this?" She thrust her phone at me. It took me a second to focus, but the Instagram post she held out at me admittedly was super cute. Probably because it featured JJ snuggling with one of the new kittens.

"Nice. What's this?" I pulled the phone closer and studied the photo.

"It's our new campaign. JJ's Promise. You know, the plan you asked for to get attention for the cats." Clarissa grinned at me. "Since everyone loves JJ, we're using him as the voice for the cats. There are a few components: sponsor promise, foster promise, donate promise, and pledge promise. We're asking people for long-term pledges—a year, two years, five years. We're hoping that if JJ asks for help for our new friends, people will come through. We're also doing two versions. One for out-of-towners who want to keep supporting the cafe and potentially adopt one of our babies while they're here, and the other geotargeting residents in the different towns and regions. That way we can get the rich people to give us money and maybe the others will adopt." She waited impatiently. "So, what do you think?"

"Brilliant," I said, feeling my creative juices kicking in despite my worry and exhaustion. Marketing was one of my favorite parts of business life. "I love that we're building on the JJ equity we have. What's the marketing plan?"

"We're flooding social, first of all. Instagram, TikTok—wait until you see the videos we made of our current residents, including the new babies downstairs—Snapchat, and Facebook. Hitting all of our different audiences. We're going to do a few live events too, mostly Insta, to show off the cats. For the older residents, we're going to arrange tours here at the cafe, and also we're going to work on bringing cats to them. The ones who can't get around well, you know? Like senior centers and such? Also going back to the old days and doing some flyers for that demographic. You know how older people like everything on paper. And also, Maddie, I really think it's time you did a YouTube channel. I've been telling you this for ages and you're not listening. It's a missed opportunity." She frowned at me like I was a wayward student who had been told one too many times to do their homework or the result would be an F.

"Okay, okay, fine. We'll do YouTube."

"Great. I ordered the equipment already."

"Equipment?"

She sighed. "Lights, microphones—you don't want this

to look like amateur hour, do you? The videos have to look *professional!*"

"Of course. Yes. Thank you. Whatever we need." Jeez. I felt old around her.

"And you'll need to be the face. You'll do an intro video, and then you can do daily updates on the cat situation. This is the perfect time to launch it!" She clapped her hands. "The equipment will be here today."

"Today?"

She looked sheepish. "Adele said do whatever it took, so I ordered them the other day. She also said I could get reimbursed."

I had to laugh. "Of course, just leave me the receipt. But I don't have to be the only one doing videos, right? You can do some. And Grandpa. And out in the cafe! Ethan is great at that stuff. You can do videos of the coffee making or baking or something."

"Heck yeah. All of the above," she said. "Grandpa Leo is, like, perfect for this. People will eat that up. And JJ has to be in them too. I've already started designing the graphics. I'm not as good at that, but I have a friend helping me who's majoring in graphic design and she's really good. So they will rock."

"Awesome. Anything else?"

"Yes. Media. I'm working on the PR plan now."

"We've only got one newspaper out here. And I'm pretty sure I can get coverage."

"Oh, I don't mean just the *Chronicle*. I'm going for the *Boston Globe*." She winked at me. "Stay tuned, sister. We're going to get people coming over from the city to adopt our cats. Trust me. And events! We are going to have at least two huge adoption events. We'll be looking for cats when we're done emptying this place out! I need to get with Val to talk about that."

I laughed. "It sounds great. We need a lot of homes, so this is awesome. Thank you. Anything else?"

"A few other things, but I can fill you in later," she said. "Right now I'm going to start working on the social content plan and get some things posted. Hey, can you give me your web guy's info? I need to get some work done on the site. This will need its own page. Actually, we might do a homepage takeover. You good with that?"

I assured her I was and texted her Bones's contact info. I'd been working with him since Ethan and I opened our juice bar out in California. He was a genius at all things web, and most likely a hacker in his spare time, but that was none of my business.

"This all sounds great. Carry on," I said. "I gotta run."

Chapter 40

I'd barely slid into the back seat of Mick's car when he tossed today's *Chronicle* into my lap.

"Paper got on this quick enough," he said. "I didn't think they got out to FC that often." His eyes met mine in the rearview. They were more amused than mad, which was a relief.

"Hey, a murder is big news, no matter which town," I said, glancing at the above-the-fold story. It had a double byline—poor Darren, the embattled reporter who'd dropped the ball, and Becky herself. I read the first paragraph, which gave the basic details on Arquette's untimely death. It said only that his body had been discovered in the parking lot of the town hall after a meeting in which he been denied the town administrator's job. So she had confirmed that fact. It was interesting that she had included it, and I wondered if the op-ed had done its intended job. The story did not, as expected, elaborate on the manner of death, only that it was a homicide.

"Interesting that Laurel's name got a mention," Mick went on.

"I didn't get to it yet." I hurried through the rest of the story, which revealed that two Daybreak Harbor cops had been loaned out to the department to handle the case, until my eyes landed on Laurel's name in the last paragraph. The story said only that this was the second unattended death in town this week, that Laurel McKenna had passed away in her home of unnatural causes and new information had led the police to consider her death "suspicious." The story also noted she had left behind an unwieldy number of cats and hinted at her being a hoarder. The sidebar to the article had facts about cat hoarders, told people how they could help, and finished with the cafe's contact information.

I could always count on Becky. And blissfully, the whole debacle with Cass wasn't in here. Guess no one was mentioning that on the record yet, which I hoped was a good sign. "Didn't she talk to you for this?" I asked Mick now.

He shook his head, keeping his eyes on the road. "She didn't. Apparently the dispatcher got so spooked by the newspaper calling that they passed the call right to the chief. To be fair, I don't think this department has a public affairs officer, but still. Interestingly, she didn't pass it off to me as lead investigator and someone accustomed to speaking with the press. She handled it herself."

"And you think she mentioned Laurel?"

"Well. She confirmed what the reporter was asking about. I know this, because I got a call from her this morning asking how on earth they might even know about Laurel in the first place." Those amused eyes again in the rearview. "How do you think, Maddie?"

I flushed and handed the paper to Grandpa, who had been wordlessly listening to the exchange. "I read it," he said with a smile. "Before I took my walk."

"Becky's a top-notch newspaperwoman," I said. "She'll stop at nothing to uncover the truth."

"Mm-hmm," Mick said.

I turned away and smiled a little, grateful for Becky. There was nothing like a little public outrage to get a sense of urgency going.

"Big difference in lifestyle from her sister," Mick observed as we wove through the Turtle Point streets to Margery Haberle's mansion where we'd followed Bill yesterday.

I knew what he meant. Even though I was well acquainted with Turtle Point—my parents lived here, and darn it, I still hadn't called my mother—I saw it now through Laurel's eyes. For someone who apparently had grown up in the lower-middle class and stayed that way, this level of wealth had to seem ostentatious. If Laurel resented this lifestyle in any way, the idea of her sister having it had to have rubbed her wrong.

"So what did you find out about this woman?" I asked.

"She and her husband built the house she lives in. He died three years ago. He was some hedge-fund guy," Mick answered. "Clean, though, as far as I could tell. No Madoff schemes."

"Well, that's a relief," I said dryly. "Kids?"

"No," Grandpa answered. Clearly he'd been looking into her too.

"Did you find out anything about her and Laurel's relationship?"

"No," Grandpa answered again. "I did ask around. There are a few people in that particular neighborhood that I know. Said she's a quiet woman, keeps to herself, husband was a bit more showy and pretentious than she was. No one recalled seeing anyone matching Laurel's description here."

I wondered exactly how long they had been estranged.

"Leopard Man knows her," Grandpa said. "He didn't know Laurel. Or even realize that Margery had a sister on the island."

I stared at him. "Leopard Man?"

Grandpa grinned. "Yes. He had some investments with Stanley Haberle back in the day."

I had to smile at that. Leopard Man was one surprise after another. For as long as I could remember, everyone thought he was a homeless kook. I'd been obsessed with him as a kid—I had a fascination with his tail—and I'd always had the instinct that there was more to him than met the eye. Well, we certainly had learned about that last year. Including the fact that his real name was Carl, which I still didn't think fit him and had vowed to never call him. He had been delighted to hear it.

We pulled into Margery Haberle's driveway and all got out of the car. Mick led the way to the door and rang the bell. A young woman answered the door. I was relieved to see she wasn't wearing a maid's uniform, but rather was dressed in jeans and a tank top.

"Hello," she said, looking curiously at the motley crew in front of her. "Can I help you?"

"Yes. I'm Sergeant Mick Ellory, Daybreak Island PD. I'm looking for Margery Haberle."

The woman frowned at the badge Mick held out for her, then her eyes traveled back to his face before she took in the rest of us. Then she swung the door open wider. "Please come in. I'll get her."

We all filed into a foyer that looked like one of the smaller exhibit rooms at the Museum of Fine Arts. "Aunt Margie," the young woman called. "You have some guests!"

A niece then, not a maid at all—I guessed it was a good

thing Margery would have some family with her for the news. A moment later, a woman appeared from one of the other rooms, a curious smile on her face. She looked way younger than I was expecting—I wasn't sure why, maybe because she was a widow. She couldn't be more than five one but she had a bounce in her step. I had only seen Laurel in grainy pictures, aside from that unfortunate moment on the floor, so I couldn't tell if there was resemblance. Margery was a pretty woman, with skin that looked like she'd taken exceptional care of it over the years. She was impeccably dressed in a pair of linen pants, a short-sleeved silk blouse, and a light scarf knotted around her neck. Her hair fell in loose, gray waves to her shoulders. "Hello there. Can I help you?"

"Mrs. Haberle. Thank you for seeing us." Mick introduced himself, then me and Grandpa.

"Daybreak Harbor PD? And a PI?" She looked from Mick to Grandpa, but I think it was my presence she was most curious about. "What's this about?"

"This is about your sister, Laurel McKenna. Can we come in?" Mick asked.

She studied him. "My sister lives—lived—in Fisherman's Cove. What does Daybreak Harbor police have to do with her?"

"I'll explain, ma'am, but it would be helpful if we could come in," Mick said.

She waited a beat, then nodded. "Of course. Right this way. Trisha, you can go home, hon. I'm good for today," she said to the younger woman.

Trisha looked doubtful. "Are you sure?"

"Positive," she said, patting her on the shoulder. "See you tomorrow." She waited until Trisha slipped out the front door. "My husband's niece," she explained. "Good girl. Come this way."

She led us down the spacious hallway through a formal living room, and out to a sunroom with which, under different circumstances, I would have immediately fallen completely in love. It had two couches that looked like you could sleep on them, a cozy chair, and books lining three of the four walls. An orange and white cat lounged in one of the windows, swishing its tail disinterestedly at us as we came in. It occurred to me that this house was so large, Laurel's cats would barely have been noticeable here. Laurel's entire basement could've fit into the living room, with space left over.

"This is where I like to spend my time," Margery Haberle said. "The rest of the house still feels too big for me, no matter how long I've lived here." She smiled, a little sadly, I thought. "My husband loved it, though, so I could never sell it. Please, sit."

We all did. I sat next to Grandpa on one of the couches. It was as soft as it looked. Mick sat on the other. Margery sat on her cozy chair and spread her hands wide. "So?" She kept rubbing the back of her neck, the only indication that she was nervous.

"We're looking into your sister's death," Mick said. "We have reason to believe it may be suspicious."

Mick's statement was blunt and to the point. I liked it.

But interestingly enough, Margery Haberle didn't have the surprised reaction I expected. She continued rubbing her neck, eyes blinking rapidly. "What exactly does that mean? I thought she . . . had an accident."

"It initially appeared that way, but other evidence has come to light," Mick said. "Why was Bill Cavanaugh at your house yesterday?"

Now her face quite literally paled. "How . . ."

"Just answer the questions, please, ma'am," Mick said, his tone still pleasant, but with a hint of steel.

I could see her weighing her options (Lie? Come clean? Give a version of the truth?) while rethinking her decision to send Trisha away. The cat, sensing its owner's angst, hopped off the windowsill and went to rub against her legs. She reached down and scooped the cat up, settling it on her lap. JJ would've liked him (her?). "He came to tell me the same thing you just did. That Laurel's death was suspicious."

Chapter 41

We were all silent for a moment as Margery's words sunk in. I tried to calculate in my head. If Mick had only gotten confirmation from the chief yesterday—likely later in the day, after all the excitement of the Cass arrest—that Laurel's death was suspicious, how would Bill have known that early in the day? And if he didn't know it from official channels, that meant he had information or knowledge that he hadn't previously shared. Grandpa had kept his questions purposely focused on the relationship with Arquette, so he hadn't dropped the clue.

Finally Mick said, "Did he tell you why he thought it was suspicious?"

Margery sighed. "I didn't really give him a chance. I thought he was here for money, so I wasn't interested in speaking to him."

"Money? Why would he be here for money?" Mick asked. "Did you two have some kind of relationship?"

She hesitated. "No. I mean, not in a very long time."

When it became clear she wasn't keen on offering up more, Mick leaned forward. "Listen, Mrs. Haberle. I want to make this as easy as possible for you, but I also need you to be forthcoming with me or we'll have to do this more formally."

Her face had closed up again. "What exactly are you insinuating, Sergeant?"

"I'm insinuating nothing. I'm saying that I need whatever information you have about your sister and Bill Cavanaugh."

"We were not in touch," she said coldly. "But I knew him. We all had history, way beyond his present relationship status with Laurel. Billy and I . . . we dated when we were kids."

Billy. So much for Bea being the only one to call him that.

"It was a high school thing," she was quick to add. "Meant nothing to me except passing time, having some fun. I love this island, but I never wanted to stay in that crappy little town where we grew up. I was focused on getting out. Sorry," she added.

Mick shrugged as if to say, *You're not offending me.*

She pulled the cat closer, burying her fingers in its fur. "Laurel, meanwhile, never left. Never changed much at all. She and I . . . we always had a contentious relationship. Complete opposites. But still, we were sisters. I always tried to do what I could, but she was hell bent on staying in that town. I could never understand it. And him . . . he was always a poor choice, but she didn't listen. They've dated on and off all their lives. Maybe it's one of the reasons she never wanted to leave, now that I think about it. Longest they were together was ten years, about twenty years ago. Then Billy dumped her and married someone else, just like that. Didn't last long. She left the island and Billy took back up with Laurel. She never could see she was better than him." Margery shook her head in disgust.

"So how do we get from that to him asking you for money now?" Mick asked.

"Bill's a shyster," Margery said flatly. "Always was. He came into some money after his divorce. The woman he married had money, you see, and had to pay him off. He invested it with Stanley."

"Your husband," Mick confirmed.

"Yes. He didn't let Stanley advise him, though. Told him where he wanted the money. He had a specific fund—or funds, I don't know the details—in mind. Stanley advised against putting it all in one fund. 'Diversify,' he always said. Anyway, Bill lost the money. All of it."

"How much we talking?"

"A couple hundred grand," Margery said with a shrug. I could almost hear her adding, *Not that much*. To her, anyway. I guessed to Bill it was a heck of a lot. "Maybe a little more. There were some returns. But of course, he blamed us when it all went away. Made it a point to harass us as often as he could. He seemed to get worse as the years went on, not better. He never really made any money in his business, although he was sure good at spending it. Things would quiet down for a while, enough that we thought he'd finally stopped, then it would kick up again. He would send letters demanding money, pretending they were from an attorney. It got worse over the last year or two."

Whoa. So Bill had flat out lied to me about, well, probably everything, but at least everything relating to Margery. I wasn't terribly surprised.

"When did this all start?" Mick asked.

Margery thought for a moment. "The investment itself had to be about seven years ago. Stanley had pretty much retired but still handled a few special clients. Bill must have thought the family ties were good security. I told him not to get involved, but Stanley was a good man. He genuinely wanted to help my sister."

"Did you call the police?" Grandpa asked. "About his harassment over the years?"

Margery shook her head slowly. "Stanley never wanted to. He knew Bill was an old friend as well as Laurel's current boyfriend. He was much more concerned about my family and its ties than I was. But I wish we had. Bill has caused me so much angst over the years."

"Did Laurel know about this?" Mick asked.

"I didn't tell her," Margery said quietly. "I don't know if Bill did, or if he told her his version, or nothing at all. He knew we weren't close so he probably figured he could get away with it. Although I did think he was behind her sudden ask for money, but that didn't become clear to me until after the fact."

"She asked you for money? Recently?" Grandpa this time.

Margery nodded. "We had been in one of our silent periods when Laurel and her friend showed up at my door one day about three months ago."

"Bill?" Mick asked.

"No. Beatrice. Beatrice Knightly," she answered the question on Mick's face. "Another childhood friend of ours. She and Laurel had remained close. She drove Laurel because her car was in the shop, and she apparently couldn't pay to fix it. I felt sorry for her, so I gave her some money to just get a new car."

I thought about what it would be like to just spur of the moment buy my sister a new car. It probably felt good. And then I felt kind of bad for thinking that just giving Sam a job was a poor choice.

"How much money?" Mick asked.

"Twenty thousand," Margery said.

She sounded like she was talking about twenty dollars, not twenty thousand. It had to be wild to know that your sister, who'd grown up in the same crappy life as you, suddenly had pocket change that was probably closer to Laurel's annual salary.

"At first she wouldn't take it," Margery said. "But I insisted. Told her to stop being stubborn and enjoy something for once. She felt awkward, I could tell, but she did take it."

"And she bought a car?" I asked. Mick and Grandpa both looked at me. I guessed I wasn't really supposed to talk, but I was curious. There had been no car at Laurel's house the day Cass and I found her.

"Not exactly," she said. "A few days later Bea called me. Said she felt she had to tell me what was really going on about the problems Laurel was having. Too many cats, how she'd become more reclusive. How angry she got when people tried to help, or give advice. She said Laurel actually needed a lot more help but was too proud to ask."

"So what did you do?" Mick asked.

"I drove over there myself to see what was going on."

"You went to her house? Did she know you were coming?"

"No. She was not pleased to see me, although it wasn't as bad as I expected. There was no car, first of all. But I certainly didn't see fifty cats as her friend had suggested. There were a bunch of them, but not that many. The place wasn't disgusting or anything. It just . . . looked like my sister. Sparse. Plain. Run down. So I thought she had started cleaning things up."

I was guessing Laurel hadn't given her the grand tour with a trip to the basement.

"I suggested she get the remainder of the cats placed," Margery continued. "I told her I'd heard of a new cat rescue that opened here on the island that might be able to help. Some cafe?"

Holy moly. She'd referred Laurel to me, but Laurel had

never called. I opened my mouth to say something, but Mick sent me a look, so I closed it.

"I gave her another twenty," Margery said. "And a credit card to help with any vet expenses or money she would need to give the rescue place to take the cats."

"A credit card. Did it have a limit?" Mick asked.

"Probably in the fifty-thousand range. I'm not exactly sure."

"Did the card get used?"

Margery nodded. "One cash advance."

"Do you know the date?" I asked.

"I can find out. One moment. I have the statements set aside." She got up and left the room.

"Good question, Doll," Grandpa said.

"Thank you."

We waited in silence until she returned with the statement. "July fourteen. For five thousand."

I wrote down the date and amount.

"Any conditions on the money or the credit card?" Mick asked.

"No. I have plenty of money, Sergeant." She didn't say it in a smug, *I'm so important* way, just as a fact. "I trusted my sister to be an adult and use the resources she'd been given to get her life together. I did call Bea a couple times after that to get some updates. That's when I learned that Laurel hadn't done anything with the cats, and that she gave Bill a lot of the money." Her lips pursed and she shook her head.

"So Beatrice gave you this information?" Mick asked. "How did she know?"

"They were friends, like I said. Bea actually offered to take charge of helping Laurel. Managing the money and placing the cats. Said she was concerned for her mental health. But I was hesitant to do that, so I never followed through."

Bea wanted to help manage Laurel's money? I wondered how Laurel would have felt about that. Since according to Bea, she didn't even want to give anyone a key to her house.

I cleared my throat. "I'm the cat cafe owner," I said. "I'm helping remove and place all the cats now."

Margery's eyes widened. "Oh. Thank you. I really don't know what to say. I wish I could have been more helpful." She pointed to the orange-and-white cat. "I took him. The day I went over there. When I left, he was sitting at my car. Almost like he was asking me to take him. I felt sorry for him. I know it wasn't much, but I hope it made his life better, at least. His name is Tweety."

"Let's get back to Bill," Mick said. "Tell me about his visit."

Margery focused on stroking the cat. When she spoke, she didn't look up. "He came to the door. I told him he wasn't getting any money from me and to leave or I was going to call the police. He said he wasn't here for money, that he needed to talk to me about Laurel's death."

"What about it?"

"He said he didn't think it was an accident. Her death." She looked straight at Mick. "Said he thought someone was trying to get at my money and she got in the way. Which seemed ironic, coming from him. I told him to leave. He finally did. I thought it was another attempt at scamming me."

"He didn't say who may have been trying to get at her money?" Grandpa asked.

Margery shook her head.

"Did you know she had passed away before his visit?" Mick asked.

"Yes. Bea called to tell me the day . . . she was found." She looked up at Mick. "Is it true? Someone may have killed her?"

"We're investigating," he said. "We do have some concerns about your sister's death. That's why we're here. We're trying to get a sense of her life and what was going on with her when she died. Do you know a man named Jonathan Arquette?" Mick asked, ignoring her question.

She shook her head.

"Delaney Mathews?" I chimed in.

Another head shake.

"Mrs. Haberle. Is there anyone you can think of who could've hurt your sister? Any other problems she was having?" Mick asked.

"Bill was her biggest problem," she said flatly. "Maybe you should go speak to him." She stood up abruptly, causing Tweety to jump off her lap. He flicked his tail much like JJ did, then stalked away.

Taking the cue, we all got up to leave. Before we walked out of the room, Mick paused. "One more thing," he said. "Where were you on Monday night?"

She blinked. "Here, of course. I don't drive at night. I have some problems with my night vision." A pause, then it seemed to dawn on her. "Monday night is when she died. You think *I* hurt my sister?"

"Just trying to get a sense of who was around that night," Mick said. "You've been very helpful, Ms. Haberle. Thank you for your time."

We were barely all the way out before the door slammed shut behind us. I heard the unmistakable, finals sound of locks clicking into place.

Chapter 42

We were all silent as we left Margery's big, empty house and piled back into Mick's car. I was trying to sort through all of this in my head. Warning bells about Bill were going off left and right. But if he'd killed Laurel, why had he gone to her sister's, whom he'd allegedly despised, and voiced his suspicions that someone had? That made no sense.

And why was Bea so involved? What on earth would make her think that Laurel would hand over control of her finances? Unless she was aiming to work with Margery to get Laurel declared incompetent. But if she was so concerned with Laurel's well-being, why hadn't she reported the cats to someone who could truly help?

Then I had another thought. What if Bea and *Billy* were somehow in cahoots with each other to get at Margery's money—through Laurel? They'd been friends all their lives, after all. It wasn't so far-fetched. And if Laurel didn't want to take advantage of her rich sister when she was offering funding, maybe they thought taking matters into their own hands was the prudent thing to do. And maybe Bill was trying to cover his own involvement by bringing the idea to Margery.

I sat up straight, my heart starting to pound like it did when I was on to something. Maybe this whole thing about Bill not knowing about the cats was just a story they had concocted together to keep up appearances.

"Do you think they were in on this together?" I asked, completely interrupting the conversation going on in the front of the car.

Grandpa turned and looked at me. "Who?"

"Bill and Bea," I said. "Maybe they saw a quick payday here with Laurel's sister, and Laurel wasn't interested. They go way back too. Bea, Bill, Laurel, and her sister all grew up in Fisherman's Cove. Bea told me all about how she's the only one who can still call him *Billy*, that not even Laurel can. Although I guess her sister can too." I was getting sidetracked. "Anyway, maybe they saw an opportunity. Maybe Bill was only seeing Laurel to see if he could get close to her sister, maybe get his hands on that money. We know she gave him a bunch of it already, or her husband did anyway. But then when he died she put a stop to it and maybe he got frustrated. And Bea saw a way for her to get in on it with the cats and Laurel's mental state."

Mick's eyes met mine in the rearview mirror. "It's not a bad theory."

"Not at all," Grandpa agreed. "We need to get an idea of how tight the two of them really were. Any sense at all that they were planning something."

"I'll have Craig start looking at phone records," Mick said, reaching for his phone with one hand. It rang just as he was about to dial. "And here he is. Hey. Was just about to call you," he said, putting the phone on Speaker. "I'm with Leo and Maddie."

"That neighbor who left in a hurry? Delaney Mathews? She left the island on the five-o'clock ferry Wednesday.

Has not returned. I got the license plate of the car that picked her up," Craig said, not even bothering with a hello.

"That was fast," Mick said. "How'd you find it?"

"I went over to talk to Mr. Mathews. See if he could tell me where his wife had gone in such a rush. Wasn't home, or didn't answer the door. But on the way in, I noticed their house has a security camera on the garage. I called the company, went through the usual hoops, but ended up getting access to view them. Found the pickup at four-oh-four p.m. Car registered to Kathleen Vance."

It took a second for the synapse in my brain to wire, but when it did, I sat forward with a jolt. "Dr. Vance? The one who works at Dr. Kelly's office? How does she know her?"

"Good question," Craig said. "She went off-island too on the same ferry. I can't reach her by cell or home phone. Got the numbers from Dr. Kelly's office."

"Friend of hers?" Mick asked, looking at me in the rearview again.

"I have no idea," I said slowly. There was a thought vying for attention in my mind, but I couldn't quite reach it.

"Keep looking," Mick said to Craig. "Also, I need you on phone records for Cavanaugh. Need to see if he's been communicating with a Beatrice Knightly. I don't have her numbers."

"Got it," Craig said. "I'll be in touch."

Mick pulled up in front of our house. "I'm going to go talk to Bill," he said. "And you two?"

I glanced at Grandpa. "We should go talk to Bea."

"That's my girl," Grandpa said.

I ran inside to drop off JJ, then went out to the cafe and got a coffee. My sister Sam made it. And she actually got it right, probably because Ethan had a watchful eye on her.

It took longer than I wanted, but that also could've been because I was in a rush. I grabbed sandwiches for both me and Grandpa, then we got into Grandma's car and took off for Fisherman's Cove at a speed slightly under what Mick would be driving with lights and sirens.

"Easy, Doll. The cops who can fix your tickets are out of town this week," Grandpa said dryly as he unwrapped our food and handed me one of the sandwiches.

"Thanks." I took a bite. "I'm going to stop by Bea's house first, before the senior center," I said around a mouthful of tuna as my phone rang. Grandpa came to the rescue and answered it, putting the call on Speaker. It was Lucas.

"Hey," he said. "I'm doing a gig at Jade's bar tomorrow night. Last-minute ask and the band was free. They're coming over for the day. Wanted to make sure you could make it."

"That's great," I said. "Wouldn't miss it." Lucas's band, the Scurvy Elephants, hadn't played much lately. His bandmates lived on the mainland, and one of them had been away for most of the summer. Also, we hadn't been to Jade's bar, Jade Moon, in a few weeks.

Jade. I let out a gasp, startling both Lucas and Grandpa. "What's wrong?" Lucas asked.

"Nothing. Thanks for telling me. Putting it on the calendar now. I have to call you back, babe." Without waiting for an answer, I disconnected and told Siri to call Craig. "I just thought of something," I explained to Grandpa.

When Craig answered, I said, "Ask your girlfriend about Dr. Vance and Delaney Mathews."

"What?" He sounded perplexed.

"Jade works with the women's shelter, right?"

"She does, but—how did you know? She doesn't usually talk about it much."

"Kate Vance told me. Said it's why she moved out here.

Anyway, check with Jade on whether Vance was helping Delaney get off the island and why. I'll wait." I hung up.

"I'm impressed," Grandpa said.

"Well, I have no idea if I'm right, but it would make sense, right? Patty said the husband was mean. Delaney seems to be permanently stressed out. Why else would Kate Vance be picking her up? Other than that connection, those two women seem to be on a completely different wavelength."

I turned onto Laurel's street, still trying to eat my sandwich, and almost collided with the recycling truck, which was stopped haphazardly at the top of the street. The man emptying bins waved at me in apology, then hurried to the driver's side and jumped in to move the truck farther down the street. He was partnerless today, so doing both jobs, it seemed.

I drove slowly past the recycle guy as he pulled over, and parked at the curb in front of Laurel's house. While I waited for Becky to finish her call, I watched the guy methodically empty bins. He had a system, even without his partner. Go down one side of the street, probably come back up the other. He took the bin from the person next to Bea's house, emptied it in the back of his truck into a big bin. Next, he moved on to Bea's house, grabbed her bin, fished the papers out, and tossed them into a smaller bin before emptying the rest into the main bin. Next house—emptied everything into the big bin.

Curious now, I got out of the car and hurried over to him. "Hey," I said.

He paused, still grasping a bin with a big glove, and looked at me warily, pushing his hoodie off. "Hi. Sorry about parking the truck in the road like that. You're not gonna tell my boss, are you?" He was young, probably in his twenties, and kind of a bigger guy. Not fat, but husky. His embroidered name tag read Jack.

"No," I said. "Not at all."

Jack visibly relaxed. "Good. 'Cause the new boss isn't as nice as my last boss."

"You mean Mr. Arquette," I said.

He nodded. "You knew him? Good guy. Shame what happened to him, right?"

"Terrible shame," I said. "Hey, Jack, can I ask you a question?"

Jack's face crinkled with confusion. "Do I know you?" he asked.

"Name tag," I said, pointing at his chest.

"Ohhh. Right. Sure, ask away," he said. "Did I, uh, miss your house or something? I'm sorry. Dennis called out sick today and we don't have enough people to partner up."

"No. I just noticed that you have two bins in the truck," I said. "And you put just the papers from this house into a separate bin. Just wondering why?"

"Oh, that. Yeah, Mr. A asked me to do that a few weeks ago for this particular house. Said he was keeping an eye out for anyone taking advantage of our town's elderly, or something. That was Mr. A. Good guy. Guess he was looking out for Miss Knightly. Although I guess I don't have to do it anymore." He eyed the small bin. "I don't even think this new guy knows anything about what Mr. A was doing."

"And there was no one else's house he had you do it for?" I asked.

"No, ma'am. Just here."

"What did you do with the paper?"

"Brought it to Mr. A. At the senior center. Why, she find out and complain or something?"

This poor guy was a nervous wreck. I assured him that

no one was complaining and he was doing an awesome job before I let him get back to work and went to the door. No answer. I hurried back to the car. I was having serious second thoughts about sweet, innocent, neighborly Beatrice. There had to be some reason her name kept popping up in all this.

"We need to go to the senior center," I said to Grandpa. "And I need you to keep Bea busy for a bit."

Chapter 43

"So, the recycling guy has a strange system for separating Bea's recycling," I told Grandpa. "I saw him do it the other day and didn't think anything of it. Then when I saw him do it today, it got me thinking. I asked him, and he told me that Jonathan had asked him to sort out any papers from Bea's recycling and drop it off for him." I'd almost forgotten about Jonathan today in all the revelations that could be meaningful in Laurel's case. But there were still two murders to solve. "Can you call the senior center and ask for Adam?"

"Sure." Grandpa googled the number and called. "Any idea why he would ask for some of her recycling?" he asked while he waited.

"None," I admitted. "I know Bea adored him. I think they were tight. Oh God." I turned to Grandpa. "What if she had confided in Jonathan or told him something about their plan and Bill found out and killed him?"

He held up a finger to me. "Yes, hello. I'm looking for Adam DeSantis," he said into the phone. "I see. Okay, then. I'll call back at five forty-five." He hung up.

I groaned in frustration. "Seriously?"

"What do you need him for?"

"I need to know if Jonathan kept an office there. And if he did, I need him to get me into it."

"Well, we have some time to kill before Adam shows up to chaperone fifties night."

It seemed like a lifetime. "You can do me a favor and go inside to look at the schedule of events," I said. "That will kill some time. And no one will give you a second look. You look like you belong." I winked at him to show him I was kidding.

"You know you're the only one who can talk to me like that," he said as he got out of the car. I watched him make his way inside, then leaned back and closed my eyes. Cass would be proud if I snuck a quick meditation in even during this stressful, adrenalized time.

I settled in and focused on breathing, feeling my brain start to quiet. And then the phone rang. Muttering a curse, I answered. Craig. "Yeah."

"You were right," he said. "Delaney Mathews reached out to the domestic violence center about getting away from her husband. Kate Vance escorted her off the island on Wednesday. And this is extremely confidential. Jade will kill me if this gets out."

"Oh, wow," I said. I didn't like being right about stuff like that.

"Yeah. Jade didn't even want to tell *me*, so make sure you don't let on that I told you."

"Did you flash your badge at her?" I teased.

He grunted. "Something like that."

"So that crosses her off for Arquette, but still leaves her in the running for Laurel," I said. "Not to mention her husband."

"The husband was away on Monday night. A fishing

trip. Kate had Delaney and her son stay at her house that night so they could make a plan. She was going to leave Tuesday, because he wasn't back until Tuesday evening, but with all the drama on her street about Laurel it got sidelined. On Wednesday night, during the town meeting, the husband was at a bar. Passed out around nine and the owner let him crash on the couch. I confirmed it and there are cameras in the bar to verify he stayed there. So he didn't kill Arquette either. Look, I gotta go. We're talking to Bill Cavanaugh. I had to step out to talk to Jade and figured I'd let you know."

"Thanks." I hung up. Once again, my meditation had been foiled, but at least I'd gotten some information out of it. Grandpa came out the front door, holding it for a little old lady using a walker. I watched her pause and turn a big smile on Grandpa, putting her hand on his arm to say something. By the time he got back to the car, his face was bright red.

"Made a new friend?" I asked innocently.

"She wants me to dance with her tonight. Hopes I'll be back for fifties night." He shook his head and handed me a sheet of paper. "I'm not going in there again."

"You have to." I took it and scanned the list of events for the week. There were activities all day long—book clubs, cooking classes, gardening club—which I knew Patty had been part of. I was more interested in the nighttime events. As Patty had mentioned, Monday and Wednesday nights the center was closed and there was a meal delivery service beginning at five thirty. As she had also mentioned, Mondays were barbecue night. Wednesday nights were Italian. Prince spaghetti day, I guessed. Tuesday night was knitting club. Thursday was a bowling trip. Tonight was the big fifties dance, and tomorrow was another trip to

Foxwoods. The bus left promptly at seven a.m. from the parking lot.

I looked at Grandpa. "You're sure this is everything?"

"Confirmed it with the lady at the desk," he said.

"Was it Bea?"

"You mean the lady from the other day? Yes."

"She recognize you?"

He shook his head. "Don't think so." His phone pinged a text message. "Mick just got done with the Bill interview. Says he has some things to follow up on, then he and Craig are going to come by the house later so we can all regroup. Hey, isn't that your friend?" he pointed.

I followed his finger and watched Adam climb off the sleek, black Harley that had just zoomed into the parking lot, removing his helmet as he did so. "Yep." I jumped out of the car and waved at him. "Adam!"

He turned at the sound of his name. "Maddie?"

"You're early," I said, hurrying over to him. "Was it my telepathic talents that summoned you?"

Now he looked at me like I had five heads. "Uh, no. I have an earlier shift on Fridays, so instead of going home in between I figured I'd come up here and help set things up for tonight and our bus trip tomorrow."

"I was kidding about the telepathy. I'm glad you're here. Look, I need your help. And it's going to sound crazy, but you have to trust me."

"Anything," he said.

"Did Jonathan have an office here?"

He nodded. "Yeah. I think he liked it better here than in town hall. And since he oversaw the place, it made sense."

Bingo. "And it was locked, yes?"

Another nod. "Yes, always. He was extra strict about that lately. I was the only one who had a key. Not sure why me—I didn't even work here full time—but he said he trusted me and needed a spare handy. And made me swear to never let anyone in."

I couldn't believe my luck. "I need to get into it."

Adam hesitated. "You . . . why?"

"It's kind of a long story. But you promised to trust me, yes?" I gave him my best *I'm trustworthy* smile. Lots of teeth.

He regarded me for a long moment. "You were really good to me when all that stuff happened with Marco, and so was your dad. Marco trusts you. So yeah, I can let you in. It's not like he's still around to know I broke my promise. And I have a feeling he'd want me to break it in this case, anyway."

I wanted to hug him. "Thank you. So much. This could help us figure out who killed him. And hey," I said. "I don't really want Beatrice to know. Can you sneak me in? Grandpa said he'd distract her, but a bunch of women are hitting on him and he's being shy."

He looked around the parking lot, as if hoping someone would pop out from behind the trees and tell him what to do. When no one did, he sighed. "Okay. Come this way." He started leading me to a side door. Before we reached it, the recycling truck pulled in and my friend Jack hopped out.

When he saw me, he waved. "You work for the town now?"

"I don't," I assured him.

He went around the back of the truck and pulled out the small bin into which he'd put Bea's paperwork, and started toward the front door.

"Shoot. Stop him," I hissed at Adam. "Get that bin from him. It's for Jonathan."

I could tell Adam thought I'd completely lost it, but luckily I had enough cred with him that he did as I asked.

"Hey man," he called, jogging over to Jack. "I'll take that in for you. I'm actually heading in to organize Mr. Arquette's files. This is very helpful." He reached for the bin.

Jack handed it over. "Sure thing. Happy to help. You still want me to sort this stuff like he had me do?"

"Absolutely," Adam assured him. "You're doing great." He headed back over to me as Jack got back in his truck and drove away. "You're really going to have to bring me up to speed here."

"Later," I said, and pushed him toward the door.

Chapter 44

I followed Adam inside to a small hallway with two rooms on each side. One door was closed, three were open. One was an office that appeared currently unoccupied. One looked like a conference room, and the third was a supply room. Beyond the rooms was a door that likely led out to the main lobby. Adam stopped at the closed door, pulled a ring of keys out of his pocket and unlocked it.

I stepped inside and paused, taking it in. The room was small, and it felt like it had never been personalized. A desk with some papers, some pamphlets for various activities, and a phone. A separate table with a printer. No photos or any of the personal memorabilia you sometimes find on people's desks. A couple of event flyers were stuck on the wall—some events had already passed. It made sense, since Jonathan only spent some of his time here. There was one chair for visitors. I went behind the desk. On the floor half shoved underneath was a stack of small recycling bins the same size as the one Adam carried. The top one had papers in it.

Adam placed the bin on the lone visitor chair. "I'm going to go start setting up. Let me know if you need my help with anything."

"I will. . . . Hey, Adam. When did Jonathan set up shop here, out of curiosity?"

Adam thought about that. "Pretty recently. I would say like two months ago?"

"Thanks. Can you give me your cell number? In case I need you while I'm in here."

He recited it and I saved it in my phone. "Thanks again. Remember, don't mention I'm here."

"Who are you again?" He winked at me and left, closing the door behind him. Just to be safe, I got up and locked it.

I went back behind the desk and sifted through the papers in the top bin. I figured if I could get a sense of what I was looking at, it might help me with the most recent pickup from today. But all that was in there were old magazines, receipts, junk mail about insurance, pieces from AARP. I sat back, perplexed. What was so interesting about this stuff?

I got up and went to the bin from today. More of the same, and hardly anything in it since this seemed to be the second pickup of the week. I pulled out my phone and googled the recycling schedule for Fisherman's Cove. Weekly on Tuesdays. So why was the recycling truck making the rounds again? Patty had mentioned there was a Save the Earth club in town. I guessed they talked about new ways to help the environment. Maybe they had pushed for more pickups to encourage more engagement? I made a note in my phone to ask someone about that and went back to my bin. A menu from a Chinese food restaurant. A flyer about a book sale. An empty envelope from the cable company. A torn-up electric bill. And another envelope from . . . I paused and looked again. It was a credit card offer envelope from Citibank. But the name on the envelope was Martha Flynn. Same street.

I frowned. Maybe the mailman had screwed up and delivered the envelope to Laurel by accident. But why was the envelope empty?

I brought it over to the desk. There were two drawers on one side and one larger one on the other side. The top drawer was full of pens, notepads, paper clips, the usual desk drawer clutter. The bottom drawer had a couple of old psychology books in it. I pulled them out and flipped through. Nothing interesting, no pages marked, no notes. I dropped them back in with a sigh, then pulled at the one large drawer.

It didn't open.

Frowning, I tugged again. Nothing. Locked.

I examined the lock. Pretty flimsy. I fished out a paper clip, bent it out of shape and slipped it into the lock, jiggling it around. It didn't work.

I texted Grandpa. *Can you help me pick a lock?*

He texted back: *Be right there.* No questions asked. I had to laugh.

Come to the side door, I texted back.

I went out to meet him. He followed me inside. I gave him a quick rundown of the recycling guy and Jonathan's odd request while he worked on the lock with a little tool he pulled from his jacket pocket. Seconds later, he pulled the drawer open.

I clapped him on the back. "You rock."

We both peered inside. There was one manila folder, nothing else. I reached in and pulled it out. But when I went to shut the drawer, it sounded like something was clunking around inside. I felt around but found nothing.

"Let me see." Grandpa ran his hands along the bottom of the drawer, then probed gently with his fingers. The bottom piece lifted and he pulled it the rest of the way off. "Old desks have a lot of these secret compartments," he said. "I had one myself. Hid my gun in it every night so your mother couldn't get her hands on it as a kid." He reached inside and pulled out a small drawstring bag. He opened it and pulled out a small stack of credit cards. I flipped through. I didn't recognize any of the names—until I got to one with Laurel McKenna.

I showed it to Grandpa, who was perusing the contents of the folder. "He had one of Laurel's credit cards."

"And he was tracking something that her name was on." Grandpa showed me the spreadsheet on the top of the file. There was a list of names, with Ys and Ns in a column that indicated whether they were senior center patrons. Laurel's name was highlighted with a question mark next to it.

"What does this mean?" I wondered aloud.

Grandpa flipped through the rest of the papers. There was a printout of an email chain in which Jonathan wrote to one of the town selectmen, asking for permission to increase recycling to twice a week for two months at the behest of the Save the Earth committee. The email had been forwarded to a bunch of people, and finally permission was granted—if they could raise the funds to run the truck for the extra shifts. Jonathan had sent the thread to a woman named Betty Madeiras with a short note that read *As discussed. Thanks for backing this.—J.*

So he had asked for the extra pickup. There was also a list of dates and times, with checkmarks and the name "Jack" written next to them. My recycling friend. I saw that the last one was this past Tuesday, when Jonathan had received the bin at "2:10 p.m." Under all of that was a large manila envelope taped shut. I pulled the tape off and looked inside.

And pulled out a stack of envelopes, some opened and repackaged, others empty—all from credit card companies.

I picked up the empty envelope addressed to Martha Flynn and added it to the pile. "Something tells me this would've gone in here."

"Agree," Grandpa said.

"So what do you think was happening? I don't think Jonathan was doing anything wrong."

Grandpa nodded. "But perhaps he discovered that someone else was."

"Bea said she went to bingo Monday night. But Patty said there was no bingo," I said. "But why would Bea kill Laurel?"

"Maybe Jonathan told her his suspicions."

I stared at Grandpa as the last piece clicked into place. "That's why Jonathan went to her house Monday."

"And maybe she confronted Bea after that. Bea kills her, then realizes that Jonathan is about to spill her secret. So why wait to kill him too?"

"Maybe it was the first opportunity."

"But why didn't he go to the police?" I wondered aloud.

Grandpa shook his head slowly. "Maybe he wanted to be extra certain first. We need to bring all this to Mick."

While he gathered everything up, I did a quick search through the rest of the office. Nothing else of note. When we were ready to go, I opened the door and peered out into the hallway. Coast was still clear. I went into the other office and did a cursory search. Nothing. The layer of dust on the desk was so thick it was hard to imagine the last time anyone had been in there.

On a whim, I detoured into the supply room. And promptly stubbed my toe—actually maybe broke it—on something sitting barely to the left of the doorway. Cursing, I hopped around on one foot for a minute before I could focus on what I'd walked into. A large box that didn't budge when I pushed it. I pulled the flaps back.

And stared at rows of engraved bricks lined up inside—with one gaping hole right in the middle.

The bricks hadn't been delivered to the town hall. They'd been delivered here. Which meant Beatrice had access to them.

Chapter 45

Mick, Craig, Grandpa, and I gathered downstairs in Grandpa's office. The rest of the household, including poor Lucas, had pretended not to be interested in what we were doing down there and gone about their business. The cats, all of whom had decided that they liked it here, were in the office with us—all nine of them. I figured it had something to do with their new names. I'd christened the new one Katrina had brought over Kip (Winger).

We had the goods from Jonathan's office spread out on Grandpa's desk. But Grandpa and I had temporarily lost interest in that, we were so engrossed in the events of the afternoon since their hours-long interview with Bill.

"He wasn't spilling the name of the person he was allegedly working for that night. Said he couldn't. He promised. So I told him I was placing him under arrest for murder. I thought he was going to throw up. Instead he opened his mouth and started talking. Gave us Ava-Rose's name," Mick was saying.

"Ava-Rose Buxton." Grandpa chuckled. "Who woulda thought?"

Ava-Rose Buxton was one of the island's highest society

ladies. Which meant she was also one of the richest. Her hooking up with Bill for, well, anything seemed so . . . random.

"So I thought it was just a scam," Mick said. "Like, he'd set his sights on her because of her money and was working her. I figured he thought I was stupid, so he tried to throw her name at me. So we leave and we're all smug, like hey, we'll be back to out you for the scammer you are shortly. And we go and call Ava-Rose. Had to track her down at some foundation lunch, blah blah, her phone was off and we made them page her. She was mad. But once she stopped lecturing me about my caveman-like behavior"—at this Craig snickered—"she told me that yes, she'd hired Bill to do a special top-secret job for her that she couldn't talk about because she's not supposed to be using outside personnel for any boat docked at the Daybreak Marina. She told me at least three times that she's paying him a lot. He has one week to do the job—this week, because the owner is on vacation. He's been at the Daybreak Marina every night this week. And she has people who can vouch for him. He had a crew working with him."

"So he wasn't the killer," Grandpa said slowly, his eyes meeting mine.

"No," Mick said. "Of either victim." He ran his hand through his hair, leaving it standing up on one side. "I really thought we had him. Especially with the calls from his phone to Gamblers Anonymous. But it's not to say he's not otherwise involved. We did find out the Mathews woman's husband worked for him until he had to let the staff go. Which I thought was interesting. Couldn't have made Laurel too happy to have her boyfriend employing a Mathews."

"He had a gambling problem?" Grandpa asked.

"No, but that's what we deduced," Craig said. "It made sense. Gambling could be the reason his business tanked. We thought maybe he was trying to rip off not only Laurel, but other older people. I would've put money myself on that being his intent with Ava-Rose. But he swears up and down he was calling Gamblers Anonymous for a friend." Craig made a *come on* face. "Wouldn't tell me who. Said what was the point of being anonymous if he was going to throw someone under the bus. Either way, we'll need to put that on the back burner until we figure out the murders, even if he's doing something else sketchy."

"And we're back to square one," Mick said.

"I don't think so," I said. Because the one big outstanding question—the why—had just hit me. "Maybe he *was* calling for a friend. Beatrice."

Grandpa and I took turns filling them in on what we'd discovered today. "Also, I talked to Adam before I left. Out of curiosity I asked him if anything weird had happened lately with Jonathan around the time of the last Foxwoods trip. He remembered that Jonathan had been really preoccupied on the bus ride home. Adam went with them as a nurse—extra insurance for the elderly travelers. Also weird? He said a few days later a guy showed up to install a set of lockers at the senior center."

Mick and Craig looked at each other. "So you think she was stealing from everyone around her because she had a gambling problem, Jonathan found out, and warned Laurel? Bea found out? What does Bill have to do with it?" Mick asked.

"No idea. Maybe she confided in him, or he figured it out. They were friends. Maybe she has a history."

"Pull her financials," Mick said to Craig.

"And you better do it quick. There's a bus trip tomorrow to Foxwoods," I said, handing him one of the flyers I'd grabbed from the senior center.

"Something tells me we're going to want to be at that bus," Mick said.

Chapter 46

"You're sure this is going to work?" Adam asked nervously.

We were locked in Jonathan's office at the senior center on Saturday morning. Grandpa, Mick, and Craig waited outside, hidden from view, of course.

We'd strategized late into the night to come up with a way to know for sure what Beatrice was doing. Heading to the casino today would certainly trigger her to be on her worst behavior—at least we hoped so. Adam, who had reluctantly come over when we called, had agreed to help after his shock at the idea of Beatrice being a potential murderer and thief had worn off. And we outlined a plan.

Adam was going to plant my purse with a couple of credit cards in it in the senior center lobby. When Bea came in early, as she did when there was a trip since she was an organizer, Adam would also be there waiting. He would then "notice" that I must have forgotten my purse when I'd stopped by last night, and ask Bea to get in touch with me to return it.

Hopefully, we'd then catch her on the camera we'd set up stealing my credit cards. Mick was monitoring the camera from his car.

I handed Adam my purse. I left everything in it so it would look authentic, including my phone. "You better plant it now before she comes in," I said. "I'll just hide in here."

He nodded, took a deep breath.

"Be careful," I said. "Remember, we think she killed two people."

"Great," Adam said. "Makes me feel real good." He left with my purse, closing the door behind him. I heard the click of the hallway door shut a moment later.

I paced the room. I was full of nervous energy. I didn't want to be right about this—it was just so hard to imagine that little woman as a stone-cold killer—but I did want to see Cass completely off the hook. But what if she didn't go for the bait?

I went to the little window and peered outside. It was still dusky as the morning started to shine through. I couldn't see where Mick had parked, but that was probably the idea. I checked my watch. She'd have to show up soon. The bus left at seven, and people would start arriving by six forty or so, I imagined.

I heard the door open behind me. "All set?" I asked without turning.

"Why, yes, dear," a pleasant voice said.

My heart stuttered. I turned. Not Adam. I hadn't locked the door. And Bea Knightly was standing in front of me, her eyes cold behind those giant turquoise glasses. But that wasn't what scared me. It was the giant pair of scissors in her hand. "Bea!" I exclaimed, trying to sound normal. "What are you . . ."

"Oh, don't *Bea* me," she said, her voice dripping with disgust. "I know what you're up to."

"What do you mean?" I tried again to sound innocent, but my voice was too high.

She moved into the room and closed the door behind her, turning the lock. "I told you, don't play dumb. I'm certainly not dumb. And I've been watching you all morning. Setting up your little scheme to catch me red-handed." She laughed, a bitter, sharp sound. "I didn't just fall off the turnip truck, honey. I know. Saw you hanging around here yesterday, leaving from the side door. Got me thinking that Jonathan did have something in here I needed to get rid of. I couldn't get in here, so I appreciate you opening the door."

"Too late," I said, abandoning the innocent play. "I took everything out of here yesterday and it's all incriminating for you. So even without you on camera stealing credit cards, they have enough to arrest you."

"I doubt it," Bea said pleasantly. "There's no way to prove it. I've set it up so Billy looks guilty too. Hid Margery's credit card in his house. Guess the cops didn't look too hard. But they will. Once you're killed, it will look very bad for him."

"How do you figure? He's not even here." I tried to listen for Adam's footsteps. He had to come back soon, didn't he?

"Oh, but he will be. And I told him to come early and meet me in the office area. So your dead body will be waiting for him." She smiled at me.

"You're going to stab me with a pair of scissors? Think about it." I tried to sound skeptical, but actually I was starting to get nervous. "And Adam will be back here any minute."

"No he won't. I had to make sure he didn't bother us."

I froze. She'd hurt Adam? What if she'd . . .

"He's not dead," she assured me. "He's a big one, that man. I had to . . . subdue him with what I had handy. So we need to move quickly, like I said." She moved closer to me. I took a step back. I was against the window. Nowhere to go but out, and that was if I could get the window open fast enough.

"Wait," I said, playing for time. "Why was Jonathan meeting Cass that night? Was it about you?"

"Of course it was. Bleeding heart felt sorry for me when he figured it out. Thought the other bleeding heart would help figure out how to *save me*." She used air quotes on the words. "He was going to give him copies of all the stuff you took out of here so he could come to the same conclusion, that I was just a nice old lady gone astray." She rolled her eyes. "Truth is, honey, I just like to gamble. And when I run out of money, I need a little help from my friends. Whether or not they want to help."

"So you took a brick and staked him out?"

She nodded. "Figured it would be poetic justice to kill him with his own brick."

"He told Laurel too." I kept talking. If she'd pulled the camera, Mick would notice. If she hadn't seen it and Adam was down, Mick would notice. They had to be on their way. Didn't they?

"Yes, he told her. Found her card in my wallet on that last trip. Got all pouty. He tried to act like he didn't, putting my wallet back on the ground where he found it, but I could tell. Then I saw him go to her house Monday, and later she called me to come over. Said she needed to talk to me. Asked me if it was true. I told her of course not, he was lying, but she didn't believe me. Said she was going to the police even though he'd asked her not to. I followed her upstairs and, well, things didn't go so well." She clucked sympathetically. "It's too bad. I did love Laurel, even though she got on my nerves. But it would have been easy enough to blame the cats. Until you had to get involved." Now she frowned at me, raising her scissors and advancing. "If it wasn't for those silly cats, no one would have ever known."

Her words reminded me of the old Scooby Doo cartoon— *"And I would have gotten away with it too, if it weren't for you meddling kids!"*—which made hysterical laughter bubble up in my throat. My hands instinctively went up to try to ward off what I could see coming, but then I heard a splintering sound and a few thuds as the door busted open, and Mick and Craig streamed in shouting—Grandpa behind them. Then the scissors flew from Bea's hand and they had her in cuffs—and it was finally over.

Chapter 47

The following weekend

"You want me to try to smuggle you some coffee?" Lucas asked, pulling up in front of the oceanfront home in Duck Cove, where I was about to spend the next thirty-six hours meditating in some form or other. Cass had picked a beautiful place, that was for sure. And I was happy to spend this time with him, even if I did have to meditate, because I realized how easily things could've gone very wrong for him.

"It's okay. I'll survive." I leaned over to kiss him, JJ squirming between us. "And knowing you're officially going to be living at the house makes it even easier to get through." We'd decided that Lucas was going to give up his rental cottage and move in for real. We'd also decided that Walter was going to move in. We weren't his foster home anymore. We were his forever home.

He studied me. "You sure you're good with all these decisions? You've been though a lot lately."

I brushed his comment off. "I'm totally fine! Everything worked out."

He gave me that look. "Babe. You were attacked by a crazy old lady with scissors, who somehow managed to knock out a guy three times my size. That's traumatizing."

"Aww, she didn't even get near me," I said, trying to pretend it was no big deal. The truth was, it had been traumatizing. Adam, luckily, was fine—just a bad headache—but still. Bea apparently hadn't noticed the camera, but she'd hit Adam outside of the frame so at first Mick and team hadn't realized anything was wrong. When they never saw anyone come set up the purse and give the thumbs-up sign we'd agreed on, they luckily came in to investigate. And had heard most of Bea's confession.

"Still," he said. "Use this time to rest. It's going to be bonkers when you get back, with the adoption events coming up and everything else."

I smiled at that. "Val won't be happy you've relegated her engagement to *everything else*." Also official—Val and Ethan were getting married.

There were other happy endings too—Becky ended up getting not only the murder stories, but she broke a huge story about a stolen-goods ring led by Delaney Mathews' abusive husband. Ex-Fisherman's Cove officer Jacobsen's son, the vandal, had been the boots on the ground breaking into houses in town and stealing from them. Mathews was using his contacts to ferry the goods over to the mainland to sell in various cities.

Jacobsen's son had confessed to vandalizing the police car after a fight with his father the same night Jonathan was murdered. Jacobsen, who felt like he couldn't tell his superiors this, got the bright idea to try to frame Cass, since he was under suspicion anyway after the murder was discovered. It was a shoddy attempt at best, but at least it had revealed him for who he was—and he wouldn't be allowed to carry a badge anymore.

And finally, Laurel's house was empty of cats. The final count had been seventy-two, including one poor little guy who had been stuck in a wall in the basement. I'd had a feeling that there was someone about to be left behind, and took JJ back one day last week to investigate. JJ had sniffed him out, and I'd been able to get Adele's nephew, a local contractor, to come help me free him. He'd been rushed to the vet, and was doing fine. All the cats were doing fine, and they were all getting the care they needed. Clarissa's marketing plans were proving wildly successful, too—we'd already had pledges totaling twenty grand over five years, and she'd only been at it for a few days.

And Laurel's sister Margery had come forward and adopted three of the cats. Adele hadn't been impressed, especially once I told her how big the house was, but hey. At least she'd made an effort to honor her sister that way.

There was plenty more to still do, but Lucas was right—it could wait until Monday. Right now, I had some emotional healing to do. I kissed him one more time. "I promise to rest. And if I'm allowed to use the phone, I'll call you." I opened the door and set JJ on the ground. "Don't take in any more animals while I'm gone," I warned, only half kidding.

He held up a hand. "Cross my heart."

I blew him a kiss and headed up to the front door with JJ. I hoped Cass wasn't planning to search our bags. If so, he'd certainly be disappointed to find my French press. But still, I figured he'd forgive me.